THE BODY LIES

JO BAKER

BLACK SWAN

TRANSWORLD PUBLISHERS
61–63 Uxbridge Road, London W5 5SA
www.penguin.co.uk

Transworld is part of the Penguin Random House group of companies
whose addresses can be found at global.penguinrandomhouse.com

Penguin
Random House
UK

First published in Great Britain in 2019 by Doubleday
an imprint of Transworld Publishers
Black Swan edition published 2020

A CIP catalogue record for this book
is available from the British Library.

ISBN
9781784164522

Typeset in 10.5/14pt Scala OT by Jouve (UK), Milton Keynes
Printed and bound in Great Britain by Clays Ltd, Elcograf S.p.A.

Penguin Random House is committed to a sustainable
future for our business, our readers and our planet. This book
is made from Forest Stewardship Council® certified paper.

MIX
Paper from
responsible sources
FSC® C018179

1 3 5 7 9 10 8 6 4 2

THE
BODY
LIES

The beck is frozen into silence. Snow falls. It muffles the roads, bundles up the houses, deepens the meadows, turns the river black by contrast. It settles along the grey-green twigs and branches of the beech wood, sifts like sugar to the hard earth below—and dusts the young woman curled there, her skin blue-white, dark hair tumbled over her face. She doesn't say a word; she doesn't even shiver now. Her breath comes thinly.

A deer, scraping at the snow for roots, stops, and snuffs the air, and scents her, and turns to move silently from the place.

Above the canopy, the sky is clear, the moon stands full. An owl scuds across the meadow, drops to kill a vole. In the shadow of the beech tree, there is stillness, not a breath. The body lies.

It was on the busy, dirty Anerley Road in South London that the man hit me. It was the nineteenth of September, it was around quarter past seven in the evening, and I was walking downhill from the train station to our flat after a shift at the bookshop. The weather had been fine in the morning when I set out for work, but now it was raining, and I wasn't dressed for it.

I had just crossed the railway bridge when I noticed someone running up the hill towards me. He was wearing black trackies and a blue anorak; he had the hood up, toggle pulled tight against the rain, and was running easily, a steady lope. He said something as he went by. I didn't quite catch it.

If I had been at a distance, watching me, rather than being stuck inside my own head, I would have seen the man slow down, come to a halt, and turn, and stare. Then I would have seen him run back down the hill towards me. I'd have seen something like that, anyway.

But as it was, I just saw the streaks of streetlamp on the pavement, and felt the hush of cars passing in the rain, and felt the cold damp seeping through my jacket; my hands, in my pockets, rested against the bulge of my belly. I was thinking that my back ached, and that I really needed new shoes and that tomorrow, on my day off, I'd finally screw up courage to phone Mum; if I left it any later it'd be a whole heap of new offence for her to take. I became aware of the sound of running footsteps behind me, and I moved aside, towards the dark trees, to let what I thought was another runner past.

But it was the same guy. He ducked in front of me, smiling. He spoke again, and this time I caught what he was saying. He was telling me what he'd like to do to me.

I went to dodge past him, but he sidestepped into my path. I backed away, but he came with me; every move was anticipated. And all the time he was talking, his breath on my face. The smell of him. He forced me further back, between the dark trees, up against the wire fence. Then his body was on mine; I could feel his hard-on pushing at my belly. I shoved at him, struggled, but was hamstrung by strangeness: I couldn't process. I thought, I thought, *This is really happening.* I thought, *I should be handling this better.*

"Get off me." I pushed at him.

A hand mauled at my breast.

"Fuck's sake, get off me."

And then a hand clamped over my mouth. He was telling me what he was going to do to my body, and I thought, *There is nothing I can do to stop this.* Cars streamed past behind him in the wet; someone walked by on the far side of the street, umbrella tilted in our direction. I was pinned. I couldn't shout. I could hardly breathe. I twisted my head aside, desperate for breath. His hand slipped, and I got my teeth around it. I bit.

He swore and jerked away. His weight was off me. He looked at me, shaking out his hand. I staggered to go around him, but he caught me by the shoulder and swung me back. I saw it coming; I just stood there. His fist slammed into my jaw. My head whipped back. My teeth clashed together. I fell back into the branches, the wire fence sinking beneath me.

So this is what the world is like. I had no idea.

I have a clear image of him standing there, over me, in the light of the streetlamp and in the rain, his blue hood still pulled tight like some kind of hazard gear, like handling me was somehow contaminating but necessary; there was water beading on his face, and he was smiling like he was smiling for a photograph. And he was, I suppose. He must have known it would be indelible, that image; that I would be stuck with it forever. That I'd remember him forever, and I'd always be afraid.

Because then he just turned and loped away. I watched till he was over the cusp of the hill, to be certain he had gone.

My jaw hurt and when I reached up to touch it there was blood. I straightened out my jacket, smoothed it over my belly. I felt like I'd done something stupid. I made my way back towards the flat.

Two huge men were sitting on the front steps of our building, eating fried chicken under the shelter of the doorway. They glanced up at me, then shunted aside to let me pass.

I told Mark what had happened and he hugged me.

"Oh my God," he said.

He let me go, held me at arm's length and looked long at me. He went pink. "Fuck. Fuck fuck fuck fuck fuck."

I nodded, eyes full.

"What kind of an asshole would do a thing like that?"

I didn't have an answer. He touched my belly, looking me in the eyes.

"I don't think there's anything wrong," I said. "He only hit me in the face."

I went to the bathroom and washed my face and peered down my top at the red marks on my breast. I stuck the split on my chin together with Steri-Strips. Mark brought in a cup of tea and winced again at the sight of my chin.

"I mean, Jesus." And he went silent and shook his head. "I'm going to call the police," he said.

I blew a breath, still staring at the mirror.

He closed the bathroom door; I could hear him in the sitting room, phoning the local station.

Mark held my hand. We sat side by side on the sofa. I told the officers what had happened and it felt like we were playing parts, like Mark and I were story of the week in some TV drama; that the police were the regular actors who were there for whole careers.

The officers said they'd be in touch, and then they went away. Mark fetched me a blanket and lifted my feet up onto the sofa and brought me tea and toast, and then he rang our midwife. She called by late that evening, at the end of her rounds. She took a squint at my Steri-Strips and said I'd done a decent job of it. Then she had me lie down and bare my belly and the three of us listened to the baby's squelch and squish heartbeat on her little monitor. She smiled at me over my bulge and I smiled unevenly back at her.

"What about you, though, hon?" she asked. "How are you?"

"So long as the baby's okay," I said, "I'm okay."

She said, "You know, women say that all the time. But I don't always believe them."

I didn't get around to calling Mum. Not that day, nor the next. Good news is one thing to spread around; bad news, though, I screw the lid down tight and nothing gets out.

Mark was reluctant to go to work, but I said not to worry, I'd be fine. I'd have to be fine eventually and I might as well start now. He said he'd skip out directly after school, get someone else to cover Homework Club; he'd be home by five. It was my day off, which struck me as a bit of a waste, but at least I didn't have to call Sinead and explain why I wasn't coming in.

I tried to fill the time. I tried to write but I couldn't. I tried to read but I couldn't. I wanted an apple, but there were no apples in the flat, so I went out to buy some. I got as far as the front door of the building. Someone skimmed past on a bike; cars hurtled by; a loud tangle of lads came jostling down the pavement. I closed the door and went back up the stairs to our flat and locked the door. I texted Mark.

Mark came home just after five with a bag of Granny Smiths. He also brought a stack of work with him. He said he'd had to tell Amy what had happened; he hoped I didn't mind. He couldn't dump Homework Club on her without some kind of explanation. She sent her love, and hoped I was feeling better soon.

"That's nice," I said. But I didn't like that Amy knew.

It hurt to eat apples: it made the cut on my chin weep.

Over the coming days, the bruise faded, the cut healed, and I managed to leave the flat. I made it into work. I started getting the bus to and from the station, rather than walk.

I was okay, I thought. I was getting over it. It could have been so much worse.

I received a quiet kind letter from Victim Support. They offered emotional and practical help; all I had to do was make myself an appointment. I left the letter on the kitchen counter with the reminder for the gas bill, and the council tax statement, and the club card vouchers.

I met up with Dad. He bought me lunch at Brown & Green. I didn't have to tell him about the baby; I just waddled in and his eyes lit on my belly and then up to meet mine, and then just, *whumpf,* they filled up. He was on his feet and pushing past the table and hugged me. I'd waited till the bruise had faded; he didn't notice the scar. It's on the underside of my chin and you'd have to know it was there to see it. We talked and talked and he promised that he would talk to Mum too; he was sure that she'd come around. Two days later there was a card in the post—*Congratulations!,* a picture of a big-eyed teddy bear in dungarees holding a bunch of balloons—and a cheque for a hundred pounds. *Buy yourself something nice,* he wrote in the card; he'd signed it *from Mum and Dad.* So she hadn't come around after all. I bought groceries.

I made an appointment with the dentist: while I was pregnant treatment was free. I told her I'd chipped my tooth falling off my bike. She wanted to know what I was doing, riding a bike in London, in my condition? Or indeed at all, ever? And more importantly did I carry an organ donor card? Because anything else was a waste of good fresh kidneys. She peered into my mouth and decided there wasn't any point trying to repair the tooth. I'd stop noticing it, she said, in time.

I said to Mark one evening, "I wonder what is going on in someone's life, that they feel the need to do a thing like that."

He looked up from his book. "Is this about that guy?"

"I mean, maybe if I hadn't bitten him. Violence begets violence, doesn't it. Maybe he wouldn't have punched me."

"Don't do that, don't blame yourself. Jesus."

"I'm just trying to understand."

He hesitated, then he said, "You need to let it go, love."

I chewed my lip.

"It's not doing you any good, brooding on it like this." He leaned over to stroke my arm. "You have to let it go. You can't let it change your life."

The following day, I saw Blue Anorak Man in the street. He shot past on a bike while I was waiting for the bus. I think it was him. I managed to get on board and sit down. I couldn't stop shaking. The bus pulled away. We ground our way uphill, in the opposite direction, and I realised that whilst he was fixed like a photograph in my mind, he might not even recognise me.

A few weeks after that, the bus didn't come, and didn't come and I had to walk. Heading downhill towards Thicket Road, someone came running up behind me. I froze, waiting for the crash of him back into me. But nothing happened. A woman ran past in black-and-pink leggings and pink vest top. She jogged on down the street, bouncing ponytail, swinging elbows. I felt a rush of love for her, for her just running by without a backwards glance. But I was still shaking when I got back to the flat.

And then the baby was born. My little boy. Samuel. Sammy. Sam. He was squashed and purple and skinny and his two-weeks-overdue arrival nearly did for both of us. After a shaky start, he just got on with the business of being a baby and became more beautiful and funny every day.

THREE YEARS LATER

The job interview was in August and the university was golden. The bus swept me up past pools and woods and lawns towards the white-walled, terracotta-roofed campus. From the stop in a dank underpass, I climbed with a handful of other passengers up concrete steps into the low late-summer sun of the central square. The clean northern air already had a hint of autumn in it; I took in the terraced stone, the dim glass, the stirring trees, the tubs and baskets spilling out flowers. This was the cool still heart of the place. It felt good, and civilized, and necessary; it felt safe.

On the train back afterwards, I chewed my nails and muttered to myself. I felt that I'd frowned and nodded and equivocated and backtracked, and not been myself or actually said what I thought at all.

Sammy was in the bath when I got back to the flat. Mark called to me from the bathroom. I leaned in to blow a raspberry on Sam's cheek; he touched my cheek with his wet little hand.

"How did it go?" Mark asked.

"I have no idea."

I sat down on the edge of the bath. I rippled the water with my fingertips. Mark didn't ask anything else, and I didn't volunteer anything else; this was the impasse at which we had arrived: we were broke, the three of us were crammed into a one-bedroom flat, I couldn't go back to my job at the bookshop since it paid only one pound fifty an hour more than childcare, and I simply did not feel safe round there. I'd stopped talking about it, but the fear hadn't gone away. So I'd applied over the last year or so for any job that looked remotely like me, anywhere but here.

There weren't many. I'd had three interviews. I'd blown two already.

The following day, Mark had to go in for a subject meeting at school, so I was on my own with Sammy when the call came. It was Professor Scaife, Head of Department. He was offering me, in one long digressive sentence, the lectureship. He drew breath, and I accepted. I thanked him, thanked him again. He seemed a tad taken aback; maybe for form's sake I should have asked for some time to think about it.

I danced Sammy round the tiny living room till we were giddy, then flumped down on the sofa. He lay on top of me, head up, laughing till he dribbled.

When Mark got home, I was waiting with Rightmove open on my mobile phone. "Look, look, a *house,* three bedrooms, and a garden! And look at the rent! You couldn't get a broom-cupboard for that round here. Cos look we can probably even afford to *buy* up there. I'm serious. Look, this one has a tree house. A fucking *tree house.*" I turned my phone to look at the picture. "D'you know what, I think that tree house is bigger than our flat."

"You got the job."

Big grin. "Yup." Then off his careful expression, my smile fading: "Aren't you pleased?"

Kiss on cheek. "Congratulations, love; well done."

He went through to the kitchen. I followed. He filled the kettle.

"There are some great schools up there," I said.

"Yeah?"

"Yeah, there's a half-dozen state schools in the town itself, two of them are grammars so yeah they're out, and fair enough, I'm not suggesting you compromise on that; but the rest are non-selective, and there are more rural schools in the surrounding area, so there will be plenty of jobs coming up. More, if you're prepared to commute."

"You've done your homework."

"Two minutes on Google."

"You know what," he said. And then he didn't say anything else. He clattered around with mugs, stared into a cupboard. I could feel it coming—the impasse was now shifting.

"What?"

"Can we leave it a bit?"

"Leave what?"

"You job hunting for me." He lifted down the tea-tin, rubbed at his nose, didn't look at me. My phone screen dimmed and went black. Goodbye three bedrooms, goodbye tree house.

"You thought I wouldn't get the job."

"No," he said. "You're brilliant, of course you got it."

"So what then?"

"It's just—it's bad timing."

"In what way?"

"Wrong time of year." He looked at me now. "They don't much advertise teaching jobs in the autumn."

"Well then, you take care of Sammy till something good turns up. It can be your turn."

He acknowledged this with a tilt of his head, but: "If I left now, I'd be letting work down."

"They'll reappoint; there are other teachers out there."

"Yeah, but there's my A-level group; I can't abandon them now. Half of them wouldn't still be in school if it weren't for me."

I understood, and I agreed. I'd always loved that sense of commitment in him, and you can't love something about someone when it's convenient, and then just dismiss it out of hand when it isn't.

And yet I said, "They'd manage."

"They shouldn't have to."

I nodded. I squeezed his hand. He was right and I felt sick.

We thrashed out a compromise. I'd start my job and he'd continue his; we'd keep on our flat down here; he'd be up north and we'd come down south as often as possible. We'd see each other every bank holiday, every half-term, every other weekend. No promises, at this stage, either way, that he'd pack in his job and move; or I'd pack in mine and move back.

"Is that okay then? Are we agreed?"

Without hesitation he said, "Yeah, yes; that'll work."

Gill House stood stolid, foursquare, in its garden, like a child's drawing; there were even pink roses round the door. We were renting it furnished, which made things a bit easier. We drove up together the first Friday in September, Mark and Sam and me, the car packed solid. The roses, when we moved in, were unkempt and overblown, and collapsed in showers around us so we trod petals through into the house, mushing them into the hall tiles.

It really was, Mark said, the back of beyond: just past our house, the tarmac cracked and fell away and a gravel track ploughed up the hillside and faded to a footpath on the fell. From the front windows, there was a view of open fields, a derelict barn, pylons, woodland and sky; at night, the barn and the pylons were silhouetted by the orange glow of the town. Our nearest neighbours were down the lane, at a pungent steaming little farm, and a mile or so further down, where the lane met the main road from town, there was a village, with a little shop, and a pub, and a cosy-looking primary school. It was a world away from our old life; it all looked so comfortable, and safe.

Mark stayed Friday and Saturday, and we made a game of it, getting organised and unpacked and exploring and improvising meals. We scattered our toast crumbs on the path, and sat on the doorstep to watch the birds. Then on Sunday morning, Mark drove back down to London. Sam and I stood in the lane to wave goodbye. The car dipped down the hill and round the bend and out of sight. And I felt it then, the first ripple of apprehension. Now it was just me and Sam and the empty countryside and undifferentiated time till Monday morning, and not a soul that I knew, not for hundreds of miles. No sounds but birdsong, and the wind, and cattle; our car engine fading out into the distance.

I buckled Sam into the pushchair and we marched down to the village past the big houses and the nice cars; we found the footpath through the woods, to the river, stood on the bank and threw stones to see who could make the biggest splash. "Oh look, tractor. Can you hear the birdie singing?" He fell asleep in the pushchair on the way home, and I paced around the house, unsettled as a cat.

That evening we did all the normal things, like tea and stories and bath. I told myself that this was what made a home, that doing all the normal everyday things here would make it all, eventually, normal, and everyday.

After Sam was settled in bed, I made myself a cup of tea and sat on the doorstep. The sun was setting across the fields and the sky was silver-grey and pink. I managed to sit there for about a quarter of an hour, telling myself that it was beautiful, and that I could never have done this in London. But behind me swelled the empty spaces of the house, and in front of me loomed the great empty distances of fields and moorland, and I felt it in my marrow then, how isolated I had made us, how alone I was with my responsibilities. A bird cried, and it startled me; my heart hammered. I got up and went inside, and I locked the door behind me.

The body lies. In the morning fingertips of sun find her; her skin is almost blue against the white, her spit is frozen into the snow.

By day, the snow begins to thaw; her curls soften; her eyelashes gather drops of water.

From time to time there are voices, down below, on the footpath. A dog clatters on the shilloe. Traffic passes on a distant road.

The sun slips over the hill, the shadows stretch and the temperature plummets. The half-thawed snow crusts itself over with ice. Ice creeps over cold flesh. The body lies.

MICHAELMAS

I had my own office, with my name on the door. I was official. I didn't quite believe in it myself.

At that first departmental meeting, my legs crossed and hands folded on my knee, I looked round for my colleagues in Creative Writing, both poets, both men, whom I had met at the interview. No sign of them, but the rest of the English Department had turned out in force. I smiled awkwardly as Professor Scaife—a man of luncheon-meat complexion and fine fair hair—introduced me, the new appointment, to the gathering.

". . . wonderful first novel," he was saying, which was a relief because I'd been worried that he might have read it. "We expect great things of her."

I caught eyes with a young Asian woman in a leather skirt and raddled black chenille sweater, and stretched my smile still further; my gaze bumped along and snagged on various other faces, a crumpled-looking chap in jeans and linen shirt who gave me a nod and smile; a ginger-frizzed woman in a green tartan trouser suit; she grimaced at me almost as nervously as I grimaced at her. I realised that Scaife had finished one of those elaborate sentences of his, and was now waiting for me to say something, and so I said, "No pressure then."

Which wasn't particularly funny, but still people laughed, and the meeting moved on, and on. I tried to follow but the discussion was thick with unfamiliar acronyms and references to events and circumstances of which I had no knowledge, and I found myself gazing out at the sunshine, and thinking of Sammy in the nursery, stacking blocks, or running a car along the floor. I hurt with missing him. I hoped he wasn't missing me.

We had to carry spare chairs from our offices because there weren't enough in the meeting room. I ended up wrestling my chair along the corridor with the tartan-trouser-suited woman, who was in the office next to me, and whose name plate revealed her to be Kate Speirs, Professor of Romantic Studies, which sounded pretty racy, I said, and she looked at me blankly and I had to explain what I meant, and she said "Oh, yes, I see. Funny," and then, "You do know that it means the aesthetic movement, don't you?"

I resolved not to try and be funny with her again. "Are the meetings always that long?"

The leather-skirt woman was lugging a chair past by this point, accompanied by the crumpled guy; he'd brought his desk chair, wheeling it casually along with one hand. I liked his thinking.

"Two and a half hours is actually pretty slick," the guy said. "I've known them to go on for four."

"How's anyone got the time for that?"

"Well exactly. I'm Patrick Maloney," he said, offering me his hand, and I shook it. He smiled, which made him look all the more crumpled. "This is Mina."

She put down her chair to shake hands too. Her nails were painted dark iridescent blue, and her eyes were lined with liquid eyeliner. She had a sharp undercut, the razed hair beneath dyed turquoise. She was maybe late twenties, early thirties; he was knocking on forty. I glanced from one to the other, decided that they were a couple, that it was a biggish age gap, but not queasily big, and that it was none of my business anyway, and that I was going to like them.

"You finding your feet okay?" he asked.

"Yeah, I think so."

"Did they stick you with the teacher-training course?" asked Mina.

"My God," I said. "The reading list!"

The reading list ran to twelve pages. That was as far as I'd got—to notice how long the reading list was, and feel a bit sick, and not actually go on to hunt down any books or articles.

"I did the course a coupla years ago," Mina said. "If you want to crib my notes any time, I'm just down the corridor."

"I hope you're not advocating plagiarism, Dr. Banerjee?" Patrick asked.

"Just survival."

And she gave him a look, and hefted up her chair, and he grinned and swung his around on its wheels, and they went on.

It was sunny so I sat down on the steps in the main square to work. Classes started next week; I'd been appointed to teach students how to write novels. It felt rather like asking someone who'd once crash-landed a light aircraft to train people as commercial airline pilots. I didn't feel I could draw on my own scant and shaky experience, so I'd scavenged together a stack of books about writing books, and was chewing my way through them.

There was a steady stream of people through the square. Some stayed to sun themselves, study or stare at smartphones on the steps. I read and made notes. Vape and cigarette smoke spooled up into the air.

Forty or so pages of E. M. Forster in, I took off my glasses and rubbed my eyes. When I glanced round I caught someone looking at me. A young man; a student. I got an impression of a broad, strong-featured face, dark complexion and hair; there was some-thing odd about his eyes. He smiled at me. I raised my eyebrows at him, returned to my book.

I thought he was still looking at me, but with my reading glasses on I couldn't be sure. I felt itchy. I found myself turning pages without taking anything in. I slapped the book shut, yanked my specs off and glowered at him. He seemed to consider this an invitation: he got to his feet and ambled over. He was tall, easy in himself. He was dressed like a homeless guy—wrecked T-shirt, jeans falling off him—but when he hunkered down beside me, I could see none of it had come cheap. His beanie had a little North Face label on the edge, and his battered jacket was from All Saints—I spotted their sinister little logo on the breast pocket. Everything about him had the air of being artfully distressed. His eyes were unusually pale, a silvery greyish blue, and difficult to read.

"Hard at work," he ventured, with a nod to my books. There was a haze of stubble at his jaw. He shifted from his hunkers to sit down.

"Uh. Yeah."

"What you reading?" He touched the book, tilted it upwards, so that it flopped back towards my chest. He took a sidelong look at the spine. "*Aspects of the Novel*. Oh you're doing the MA. Mamet's more my guy."

I could have said, in fact I probably should have said, *I'm not "doing" the MA; I'm teaching it.* But I just watched as he took a cigarette packet out of his jacket pocket, picked out a cigarette for himself then offered the pack to me. It was hard work not to scuttle off. I made myself look at him. He was almost ugly, but not quite, and even if he was it didn't matter. I noticed a scar through one heavy eyebrow; I scuffed at the scarred underside of my chin.

"I don't smoke." My voice was dry. I cleared my throat.

"Wanna start?" He shook the open packet cheekily.

"No." I cleared my throat again. "Just, I've given up once already."

He played with the neat little paper cylinder. The smell of it, dry and papery. I felt a pang of loss, for being twenty-something and still immortal.

"It's tough, I know," he said, "cos actually, funny story, I—"

"I'm sorry," I cut across him. "I've got so much work here."

"Term hasn't even started."

"I—have to get this finished. Sorry."

"Yeah," he said. "Okay. No worries. See you around."

And he got up and walked away. I watched him go, watched him stop to speak to a girl; he waited while she rummaged and fiddled and clicked and offered up a flame and a smile to him. Her long dark hair slid down her back like a piece of brown silk. They sat down together on the steps, she a slip of a thing beside him, the two of them chatting. Which, you know, is something people do. Normal people. And part of the point of university.

He was only being—friendly. Wanting to make a connection. He wasn't to know how easily I bristle.

I had to do better. Be nicer. Didn't I.

"Ah, hello there. Could I possibly have a quick word?"

"No problem." Though Professor Scaife's words were rarely quick.

His most recent book, which I'd scanned in the library, was *Bodies/Politics: Textuality and Sexuality in the 21st Century Novel*. I'd only had time to read the opening essay ("Penetrating the Body Politic: Ian McEwan's *Saturday*"), but it did strike me as odd that someone with such a heightened critical awareness of fictional bodies should seem so blissfully unaware of the actual real-world effects of his own. His presence seemed to tentacle its way into every available space, so that one shrank and sidled and crammed oneself into corners to avoid it.

There was no sidling past today. I tried a step back, but he moved into the space I'd left, so that I was cornered in a doorway and found myself contemplating his pinkish-purple complexion at close range. I turned to look instead at the track-worn carpet.

"In my office?" he said, standing between me and his office.

I peered ineffectually past him, and he moved aside a little, and gestured for me to pass, so I did, getting a whiff of coffee and last night's wine. He followed me down the corridor, reached past me to open the office door and then, rather than going in, stood there, splayed like a starfish, holding it open.

"Do have a seat."

I had to slide past him again. He sat in at his desk, picked at the computer keys with his long fingers. I perched on one of his seminar chairs. His office was twice the size of mine. He had space for a coffee table, with his own kettle and mugs, as well as a reformed smoker's ashtray filled with paper clips, drawing pins and treasury tags. He didn't offer me a coffee.

"You know we're very glad to have you here," he said, curled like a C in his swivel chair, staring at his screen.

"Thank you."

"New blood, just what we needed. You're considered something of a godsend."

"I'm very happy to hear it—"

"But, unfortunately—"

Unfortunately?

"Yes . . . ?"

They *were* glad to have me here, I *had been* considered something of a godsend, but now they'd realised their mistake. If I'd be so good as to pack my things and . . .

"Well yes, unfortunately we have hit a bit of a snafu . . ." he said, blinking his narrow pink-rimmed eyes at me now. "Simon Peters, you remember him from the interview? One of our poets? Well, he's been signed off for four months . . ."

"Signed off?"

"By his doctor."

"For four months? What's wrong with him?" I was trying to remember which one of the two panel members Simon was—the one who looked like a whippet and dressed like a mod, or the one who had more of the air of a Shetland pony about him: short, stocky; glowering out from under unkempt hair.

"I'm afraid that's confidential."

"Of course."

"But you see it does leave us in a bit of a pickle."

"Mmm?"

"Well, to put it simply, Simon ran the undergraduate lecture strand. And now he's off sick, he can't . . ." He made a face, as though it pained him to ask, but was at a loss as to what to do otherwise . . .

"You want *me* to do it?"

"Well, that would be wonderful. That would be such a help."

"But I . . ." am drastically inexperienced, have no idea what I am doing ". . . don't know."

"Oh, I'm sure you could do it standing on your head. They're only first-years; they don't know a thing: they'll just be impressed to have a novelist in the room. You really are a godsend." He reached over and patted my arm, like he was applying a sticky label to me.

"If I talk it over with Simon; see what he used to do with them . . . That might help."

"I'm afraid that he can't be contacted on work matters, not while he's on sick leave."

I bit my cheek, nodded.

"You just do your own thing; have a bit of fun with it. Look," he said, off my embattled frown; he leaned in, elbows on knees, hands dangling, long fingers intermeshing. "The fact is, I hate to give you more to do; you're just finding your feet, and all that, I understand, I really do; but I'm going to have to ask you to be a bit—flexible, particularly while Simon is unwell. Things will settle down when he's back."

I tilted my head. I could be flexible. Flexible was not a problem. Preparing and delivering an entire lecture strand out of the blue, when I had never so much as taught at a university before, was. Everything I had to say about writing would fill the first ten minutes of the first lecture. Maybe fifteen, if I spoke very slowly.

"I noticed that my PGCHE course has a three-hour session on time management coming up," I said. "In a month or so."

"Well, that sounds wonderful," he said, and beamed at me, his face folding into crevasses. "I'm sure you'll find that very helpful."

I nodded. I'd meant it as a joke.

The bus reeled out of the university, wove round suburban estates, then chugged into the clogged arteries of the town centre, windscreen wipers creaking. It was crowded and I'd had to fold and stow the pushchair; we sat at the front, Sammy sideways on my knee. He smelt of Plasticine and milk and his long day. We called Mark. I told him about the lecture strand, the teacher-training course, the reading list. Mark sympathised; he had got a bucket-load of marking himself to do. But still, he'd be up at the weekend, was looking forward to it.

The bus emptied itself at the stops through town, grew quiet. We passed a last row of redbrick semis, crossed the motorway flyover, and were out into the countryside. Straggling grass, damp sheep, looped pylons, the moors like sleeping monsters. No more gabbled conversations now, just the faint hiss of someone's headphones.

When we got off at the crossroads, the rain came at us sideways. The bus pulled away with its one remaining passenger. Grey jacket, beanie, headphones, angles of jaw and cheekbone through the misty dirt-grained window. By the time I'd got Sammy into the pushchair and hauled the weather shield down over him I was soaked through. We trudged up towards the house.

At the farm, the cowshed was full of steam and shifting black and white; here and there a head was raised and huge dark eyes stared back at me. Sammy had gone quiet; I bobbed down to check on him. He was wide awake, sitting forward in the pushchair, his little fingers pressed against the inside of the rain-cover, following the glittering raindrops down with his fingertips. He smiled me a big wet smile. We rattled on through the yard, past a huddle of crates and pallets and an old timber barrel lying on its side. A dog leapt out at us. We both yelled in shock, matching the noise of its barking; I swerved the pushchair aside. The dog stopped just short of us, right out on the end of its chain. Sammy wailed; I held a hand out towards the dog, palm up.

"Easy there, easy."

"Moss!" someone yelled. "Moss!"

A man came pounding up towards us in his cut-off wellies, a shotgun case on his shoulder.

"Moss, now, that'll do."

She went silent; the chain slackened and snaked on the ground as she turned to go to him.

"G'lass." He touched her head with his free hand, and went to let her off her chain.

"Please no—"

"S'alright." Released, she just sat down, and looked up at him. Her tail swept the wet tarmac. She was matted and dirty, and her coat sparkled with water.

"I'm John Metcalfe," the man said, and offered his hand. "This is my farm."

His face was deep-lined, lean, shadowed by upturned collar and the brim of his cap. I shook his hand. It was hard and cold. The dog watched.

"She dun't know you, is all," he said. He pushed his cap back, the brim dripping. "You've not been properly introduced."

I tentatively offered her the back of my hand, and she sniffed it.

"Is that her kennel?" I saw now that there was a dim bundle of blankets inside the barrel.

"Aye."

"Isn't that a bit cold for her?"

"She's a working dog; you don't keep pets on a farm. Though happen you could do with one."

"One what?"

"A pet. A dog. For company."

"Oh we're fine as we are."

"It's lonely enough up here."

"We moved here for the peace and quiet." I could hear my southern vowel sounds. I hadn't realised before that I had an accent.

"Aye well. Happen you'll change your mind, come winter-time. Think on."

We got indoors with a fumbling of keys and straps and clips and zips and shoelaces. Set down on his feet, Sammy waddled up the hall and into the kitchen and was requesting juice while I was still peeling myself out of wet clothes in the hallway. Back in London I'd never got beyond the nod and hello on the stairs. Here for a fortnight and the neighbours were already making free with their advice. Like it was any of his business. Like I had time to look after a dog. I stripped down to my bra and pants, grabbed a jumper off the radiator and slung it on; in the kitchen I bundled my wet clothes into the washing machine. I sorted Sammy out and gave him a cup of juice, then hitched him up onto my hip and opened cupboards and he stared over my shoulder and sucked on his drink.

"What'll we have for dinner?"

But he leaned away to peer past me, over towards the window, and chewed on a finger. His cheeks were flushed. I touched his forehead. If he got ill he couldn't go to nursery, and if he couldn't go to nursery I couldn't go to work, and I had to work. I checked the Calpol bottle and there was a good inch in the bottom, which would have to do, but I'd save it till it was absolutely necessary.

"We could have . . ." I was almost out of food and totally out of ideas. "Beans on toast, or pasta and pesto. Or . . . I dunno."

He still didn't answer. I turned to look where he was looking, and he shifted in my arms to keep his eyes on the window. It was dim outside, overcast and getting on for dusk now, and with the kitchen light on, the window was sheened over by our reflections: my pale bare legs and baggy sweater and scrubbed-up hair, and him, small and beautiful on my hip. I hitched him up higher and went over to the window, and I stood him up in the empty sink and held him round his belly as we stared out together at the over-grown garden, the leggy shrubs, the battered bare lilac branches, the dwarf wall and stone steps up towards the fields and moors and woods and sky. It was all wind-tossed and moving, still teem-ing down with rain.

"What were we looking at exactly, Sonny Jim?"

He took his finger out of his mouth and pressed it damply against the windowpane.

"Out dere," he said.

"No way, sweetheart. We're not going out there. We just got in."

He slapped his palms flat against the glass and stared out. I peered with him, out into the wet garden: it had a livid intensity to it, all shadows and yellow light, but I couldn't see what in particu-lar had captured his attention.

"What do you see, Sammy?"

He leaned in closer, breath misting the pane, eyes narrowing. And he said, "Man."

I scooped him back, grabbed the light switch and flicked it off. The two of us stood in the sudden dusk, him warm against me. We stared out into the weather-battered garden. I couldn't see anything. Couldn't see a man.

"Was it the farmer man?"

Sammy didn't respond.

"Did you see that farmer man out there, Sammy?"

He blinked at me, bewildered.

I set him on the floor, then rattled the blind down. I stood listening. Then I thought to check that the back door was locked. Sammy, though, pulled a tea towel off the front of the cooker and took it upon himself to clean the kitchen wall.

"You were just making it up, weren't you, Sammy? I don't mind if you were."

He stopped what he was doing and looked at me. One of his assessing looks. Then he nodded, and pottered off to the living room, where I heard the television come on. Gentle chat, and the theme for CBeebies bedtime hour. I stood, shaky, in the kitchen, looking at the dimpled glass panels of the back door. Then I switched the light back on, and made our dinner.

That night, Sam woke yelling from a nightmare. I stumbled into his room and picked him up and carried him back to bed with me. He whimpered and mumbled then drifted off again; I lay awake, listening to the empty distance and the weather and the indoor emptiness of the house. I thought of Mr. Metcalfe, his face craggy and cold, saying, *Happen you'll change your mind, come wintertime.*

Think on.

NAME	STUDENT NO.

Gordon, Richard. 9056325002
Checked shirt, grey hair, hefty; works at the Power Station. Didn't quite catch exactly what he does. Writing "a romantic novel with a twist."

Haygarth, Steven. 9056325003
Solicitor. Nicely turned out. Writing crime fiction, set locally.

Harrington, Tim. 9056325004
Awkward, loud fellow. Seems like a sweetheart. Dystopian novel.

Morgan, Karen. 9056325005
Social worker. Writes magical realist short stories. She's all soft colours and meaningful-looking silver jewellery; a sharp eye, though.

Palmer, Nicholas. 9056325001
Bildungsromane/Künstlerroman: "Chemistry." "Dark," "edgy," "art."

Sharratt, Meryl E. 9056325007
Sweet American kid. Seems smart and very committed. Work on her YA werewolf novel already well under way.

Postgraduate Mixer. It was held just down the corridor from my office, in the Senior Common Room, which was a grand title for a kitchenette, two seminar tables pushed together, half a dozen chairs and a fake kumquat tree in a pot. As I worked at my desk, I'd been aware of people passing, of voices gathering there and the noise swelling. I'd been trying to finish writing my first lecture, but was beginning to suspect that it'd never be finished, not even after I'd delivered it. By the time I threw in the towel, and went to join the fun, the room was packed and loud and smelt strongly of damp coats, old coffee and wine. I had to tap elbows and excuse myself and nudge my way through.

I found myself next to Professor Scaife at the refreshments table. I lifted a glass of orange juice, said hello.

"Have you seen Professor Lynch?" I scanned the crowds. Michael Lynch was the other poet; the whippety one: I'd checked his photo on the departmental website. If I could pick Michael's brains I might stand a chance of getting through this year alive . . .

"Oh no. Mike doesn't come to these."

"Oh?" and I had *so* much work to do: "I didn't know it was optional . . ."

"Oh it isn't. It's mandatory. It's just Mike never comes."

I was just about to ask how that worked, when Scaife volunteered: "And even if he did, he couldn't."

"Why's that?"

"Well, he's in Canada."

"Canada?"

Scaife picked up a bottle of white wine. "Top you off?"

I shook my head, showed him the juice.

"Did no one tell you? I thought someone would have told you." He filled his own glass to the brim. "He landed a year's residency at the Irish Centre in Toronto. Sounds like a nice little jaunt for him, don't you think?"

"A *year*?"

He nodded.

"So this year Creative Writing is just *me*?"

"Hey what's that?" He leaned even closer to hear me.

"This year, I'm all the staff there is, for Creative Writing?"

"Well, when you put it like that, yes. Until Simon gets better, you *are* the only full-time member of staff. Let's hope four months sees him right."

All these new students, paying so much money, to be taught by *me*?

"Maybe he'll bounce back," Scaife said. "Quite unpredictable, isn't it? Stress is such a tricky creature."

"Isn't it," I said, though I wasn't supposed to know about Dr. Peters's stress. "But the thing is, I'd assumed one of them was going to be my mentor . . ."

"Hmm?"

"It's in the teacher-training manual. All new staff are appointed a mentor. But it looks like everyone who does the kind of thing I do is suddenly *hors de combat*."

"Tell you what. I'll do it. I'll be your mentor. It'd be a pleasure." He patted me on my arm, then his hand curled round it, and gave it a little squeeze. "It'll be good to get to know each other a little better. And I do need to get a firmer grasp on Creative Writing."

I stood stiffly, in his grip, then I shifted slightly so that his hand fell away. "Thanks."

I raised my glass and said I'd better go find my new students, and he acknowledged this with a dip of the head. Maybe it wasn't actually a *bad* thing to have the Head of Department as my mentor. He must at least know what he was doing.

As I weaved my way across the room, I spotted that kid I'd given the brush-off on the square, the good-looking almost-ugly guy with the cigarettes and the scar through his eyebrow. He was in the company of a stout lad in leather blouson jacket who seemed to be bending his ear. Our eyes caught, and he half-smiled, half-winced. We both knew who we were now; we even had the name tags to prove it. I smiled at him. At the moment there was no way through the knots of people, so I just raised a hand and moved on. I found three of my new students, who had already found each other: Steven, Karen and Richard. We bellowed at each other amicably for a while. A little later, when the crowds had thinned and it was quieter, I got talking to Meryl, whose name tag revealed her to be also one of mine. She was eating Cheesy Wotsits from the buffet table. I liked the way she did it, determined, thoughtful, as though the eating of Cheesy Wotsits was a cultural experience to be considered in its own right.

"You know," she said, "these are pretty much the same as Cheetos."

I asked her about her work, and she was off on a wild delighted gallop through her novel-in-progress. Her book was set in small-town Oregon ("I'm from Halfway, Oregon; well, I'm from a coupla miles north of Halfway, and a coupla miles north of Halfway is really just a coupla miles north of the Middle of Nowhere"). Her heroine has just moved to an isolated house outside town, with an overprotective mother; Dad is absent. She doesn't fit in at her cliquey high school; her mom won't allow her to do any of the usual high school social things, and her dad is not *just* absent, but actually *missing*. . . . It's only when she finally makes a friend, and gets to go to one of the high school parties—that she discovers that those cliques and gangs are in fact *packs*. The local kids are *werewolves*.

"It's called *Halfway*. After the town. And because it's about being in-between."

"Woah."

Her face split into a grin. She had Wotsit gunk on her teeth. "Yeah."

"I look forward to reading it."

"I'm super excited to be writing it!"

I really loved Meryl right then, her enthusiasm, her openness. She seemed so fearless. She even asked me what I was working on. I drew a breath to tell her, but then the kid from the square was with us.

"Hey," he said.

"Hello again."

"Yeah. Huh. Awkward." He was the picture of flustered good manners. "I didn't realise you were staff; I'm new here. Obviously." He tapped his name badge. *Nicholas Palmer.* "I thought you were a student, that day, on the square."

"It's the way I dress, isn't it. I'm just too scruffy to be staff."

"You can't be too scruffy to be staff. Actually you just look too young."

I laughed.

"Seriously," he said. "Doesn't she"—he peered in at Meryl's name badge—"Meryl?"

Meryl smiled, happy to be drawn in. "Totally," she agreed.

"I'm thirty-three," I said.

"You don't look it."

"You should see the portrait in my attic."

Meryl laughed delightedly at this; he smiled, but looked at me steadily with those pale opaque eyes, as if he was checking me for signs of thirty-three-ness. I felt a little pink under his scrutiny. I felt a little flattered. What was he? Twenty-four, twenty-five? No older than that, certainly, and with the sheen of money on him. And then he turned to Meryl, and offered her his hand.

"It's good to meet you, Meryl."

Meryl lifted her hand to take his, then noticed that the fingers were still dusty with Wotsit pollen. She set her glass down and brushed them clean, and offered her hand again. He took it, met her gaze steadily, and with a smile climbing one cheek.

"Back home you get a bunch of napkins with everything," she said. A blush blotched her chest, rose up her neck and flooded her cheeks. I wondered if Nicholas knew that he was doing it, if he did it deliberately, this thing of making women think that he really, really noticed them.

"Ah well, you see, they're still on ration here," I said.

She boggled at me: "Really?"

"Not really." I turned to Nicholas. "Meryl was just telling me about her novel: it sounds great. What are you working on, Nicholas?"

"It's not so easy to talk about."

"You're going to have to get used to it, now you're doing the MA."

"Well, yes."

"And there's no time like the present," I said. I suppose I wanted to put him on the back foot, after he'd backfooted the two of us by being all interested and noticing.

He hesitated, placing his words like they were seeds in a tray: "I've been working on it for a long time. I have a good part of it written. The idea of the MA, for me, is that it'll give me structure, that it'll enable me to finally complete it."

"And what's it about, your novel?"

"I don't even know if it is a novel. It really depends on what you mean by 'novel.' And as for 'about,' I think that's a bit limiting, don't you? I mean, as a question."

"Oh-kay." I was so conscious of Meryl's assessing gaze, the way she drank everything in. "So, how about this. Tell me three things about what you're writing."

"Yeah," he said slowly. "Okay. So. I'm interested in experimentation . . ."

"Are we talking GCSE Chemistry here, or are we talking Hadron Collider?"

"Definitely Collider," he said. "I'm interested in pushing the form, pushing my writing as far as it will go. People rehash Beckett or Joyce every day, and that's . . ." He shook his head.

"That's not your thing?"

"No. Because I'm not a fucking impressionist. What I'm doing here hasn't been done before."

The swearword made Meryl flinch. I found it quite charming, though, this innocent arrogance; he was shooting for immortal transcendence, with no idea of how difficult it is to achieve even mediocrity.

"So what is your thing?" I asked. "It's not a novel. It's experimental. It's not like Beckett or Joyce. So what is it?"

"It's . . ." He shrugged. "Well. I guess it's Art." And then he grinned: "That's your three things right there now."

I laughed outright. "I look forward to reading it."

"I look forward to you reading it too."

Meryl opened her mouth to add her enthusiasm to the chorus, but Nicholas spoke across her:

"I've read *yours*," he said.

I kept my poker face. I stared him out. "Oh yes."

"It's quite a read."

"Thanks."

"Based on your own experiences, I imagine? It has that feel about it."

"Not really. It's fiction."

"Come on. You can't write it unless you've lived it. You can't write it *well*, anyway."

I took the compliment with a tilt of the head; I'd had few enough, God knows. "Maybe. But there are different ways of knowing, aren't there?"

"How do you mean?"

"You can know something emotionally, without having practical experience; you can put yourself in someone else's shoes. Otherwise how would anybody write sci-fi, or historical novels?"

"Yours wasn't sci-fi."

"It's more or less historical by now."

I wished I'd had the sense, all those years ago, to lift my head out of the total absorption of its writing, and consider what the book might have been saying about me. It didn't occur to me, literally didn't once cross my mind until that excruciating phone conversation with Mum, to whom I'd proudly sent one of my comps, and who'd taken the whole thing so very literally, and couldn't forgive me my own darkness, or the blame on her that she felt it implied. She hadn't yet got over it. I'd lost my (touchy, stubborn and sharp-as-lemon) Mum to two lukewarm reviews, pathetic sales and near-complete loss of confidence in my own writing.

"It had the ring of truth about it."

I leaned in close, as if to tell a secret: "That's the trick, you see." He leaned in too, to hear me. "To make the whole thing up, and still to tell the truth."

"That's not my deal," he said.

"What is your deal?"

"Wait and see."

He raised his glass, to show us its emptiness, then headed off towards the drinks table. I turned to Meryl, eyebrows up: a "What about him, then!" expression. Her face, though, had gone all compressed and difficult.

"That guy is so . . ." she said, and she hesitated and wafted her hand around, and we left the sentence hanging unfinished between us. We watched Nicholas over at the drinks table, where Lisa refilled his proffered glass.

"What he's doing, the scale of that," she said, "kinda puts my little werewolf story in the shade."

Bless her. "Don't worry, Meryl," I said. "There's space for all of it. Whatever he's up to, it doesn't diminish what you're doing; it doesn't have any impact on you whatsoever." I leaned in and whispered to her: "Thing is: we don't even know yet if he's any good."

Chemistry
By Nicholas Palmer

A flame licks at the lump of hash. Alex's tongue slicks out over his lip like there's something living in his face. The game flickers over the three of them; the music turns over and over. This, this is what Nick wanted all along not the jostling and the drinking but the softening at the end of things, when they all just quit lying to each other for a while.

But Gideon drags out a baggie, and drops it down on the glass-topped table. He is tapping out the coke, starts to chop it into lines. Coke is all lies but the hand flicks and taps and Nick knows Gideon is trying to be nice is lobbing more and more into that evening filling it up till it is so full that it has to spill over till they have to smile have to laugh at the excess because Gideon is trying to make his little brother happy or at least make him forget. Nick doesn't do happy and he doesn't do forget, not this day of all days.

It was supposed to be just a quiet one, Gid, he says.

Gideon grins his big white grin. Nick snorts a line of coke to be nice back.

The soundtrack of the game loops and roars and the lights flicker and Alex smokes his spliff and splats zombies and Nick grinds his teeth and watches the spittle stick and catch on his brother's lips as Gideon just keeps on talking talking talking. Nick should come down to London yeah and come out with him in London and yeah go clubbing yeah, this girl just last week, in the toilets, her mates laughing outside, and because London he'll never see her again, doesn't have to, not like round here where everything you've ever done follows you round like cans tied to a car. But fucksake not a word to Hannah cos she'd have his balls. Nick nods as though Gid is right and an easy fuck would solve *everything, while he's thinking Just fuck off Gideon. Fuck off back to London why don't you, and leave me here alone.*

He's done with it. He gets up and his head swerves and yaws. He flaps a hand to stop Gid following. He goes down the back stairs into the kitchen. There's a mess of crumbs and open packets and the fridge stands open, spilling light and cold, humming. He heads out, into the February cold and leaves the back door wide behind him.

He climbs the lane out of the village, disturbing the rooks, sending a few flapping up into the sky. Farmyard dung and a dirty tractor and the dog staring from the darkness. Tarmac crumbles to grit and grass splits the track. He climbs the blue heath to where the limestone scabs over the hill and the few trees are twisted little dancers and the moss drips in the grykes. There on the cold stone he hunkers down. From there he watches the motorway's red and white river, watches the streams of streetlamps blink out in the town beside the bay. The sea beyond goes silver. It's morning. And he is through it, through that night and out the other side.

He rolls a joint, sinks back, lies on the rock. He smokes, and lets the smoke fall up into the air. Rocks of dope crumble and flare and he brushes them away. The cold is hard against the back of his head, against his shoulder-blades. The fresh new blue is dizzying. He rubs the roach out against the rock. He stares into the pit of the sky. He misses her he aches with missing her his lost girl he feels untethered with her gone. He feels that any moment he might fall headlong up into the sky

Don't get me wrong: I liked it. I didn't see how it was smashing subatomic literary particles, but I liked it. I figured that either its radical nature would emerge as the work went on, or it wouldn't, and that it didn't really matter. It could be good without being revolutionary.

Tim nodded and pouted along like he was listening to jazz. Karen clacked a silver ring against her teeth and twisted a curl around her finger, thinking. She said it wasn't what she looked for in a novel these days, grit; she found she encountered plenty of grit in real life, but she thought it worked well here; he did a good job with his grit. Meryl was fulsome in her praise of the *mise en scène;* Steven wondered if the non-standard syntax might be off-putting, and where it was going; it seemed to be looking backward rather than moving forward: Was Nicholas coming into his story arc in the right place? Richard sat back with his arms folded over his plaid belly and didn't contribute anything, apart from the faint whistle his nose made as he breathed.

"Where do you want me to start?" Nicholas asked.

"Well, the beginning *is* traditional."

"Or," I said, "you could decide not to think in arcs and lines. You might think of it as a pool in which narrative pebbles are dropped and we watch the ripples roll outwards. Or a spiral, where a key event is returned to, and seen differently each time."

Nicholas fixed his gaze on me; I noticed Steven and Richard exchange a quizzical glance; I felt hot.

Meryl said, "Is that more female though? A more female way of writing?"

"Does it have to be about gender?" Richard.

"All I'm suggesting is that we can think in other shapes. And that it might be particularly helpful for Nicholas, who's already set out his stall as an innovator, to think in other shapes. Not lines and arcs, maybe, but circles, or spirals, or anything he wants."

Nicholas still looked at me, long, considering: those silvery eyes. And then he slowly nodded.

"Okay," I said. "Good. We'd better move on then. Lots to get through."

I shuffled pages around to find new work, and my cheeks burned. We had a piece from Richard's "romantic novel with a twist." Our protagonist was a spurned husband who had taken to spying on his estranged wife. He'd positioned himself at a pub window so that he could observe her at work in the estate agents across the street, eat pies, drink pints of bitter and ruminate. A meat pie got a good deal of descriptive attention, as did the wife's despicably hipster lover, as did the very attractive barperson, who provided, along with beer and pies, a sympathetic ear, and who would, I was pretty certain, turn out to be transvestite.

Nicholas said: "I expect we'll be hearing more about that pie."

Richard craned round to him, eyebrows up.

"You know what they say," Nicholas explained. "If there's a pie on the table in the first act, it's going to have to go off in the second."

I snorted. I probably shouldn't have. It wasn't kind.

"Actually that's 'gun,'" Richard pointed out unnecessarily. "Chekov."

Nicholas nodded his thanks.

We moved on briskly to an extract from Meryl's werewolf story, *Halfway*. A house in the birch woods, a yellow school bus, the casual cruelties of the schoolyard; a promising friendship and the dawn-breaking glimmer of a world that offered more than our protagonist could yet grasp. It already worked; you could feel it working. It was clear what the character wanted, needed—to belong—and we watched how she struggled to make that happen, and how the bullies, poverty, how her own gaucheness got in her way. I thought, simply, *This kid is a writer.* Nicholas didn't join in with the discussion that followed. I noticed Meryl's gaze drifting back to him from time to time, at first hopefully, and then anxiously, and still he didn't say a thing.

"Nicholas, you're very quiet," I said eventually. "Don't you have anything to add?"

He shook his head.

"Not a dicky bird?"

"There's nothing to say."

"Literally nothing?"

"Well no, because you know, it works. It does what it needs to do. It's good. So there's nothing more to add."

Her eyes went huge. "Thank you."

He shrugged. "It's true."

"Well, when you think that," I said, "say so, out loud please, because it helps."

Meryl was speaking, her voice lowered, privately to him. I caught the phrase: *it means so much to me.* She was still talking to him, *sotto voce,* her shoulder pressing against his shoulder, while I wrapped up the class.

"Tim," I said, "next week, can we have some stuff from you?"

Tim nodded. "Yep, no worries. No worries at all. I'll get that to you soonest."

The room emptied. The door fell shut.

I slumped in my seat. First day of teaching over. It had gone okay, hadn't it? I locked up and dropped off the key with the porter. And then I had to run and pick up Sam.

Dr. Peters had titled his lecture series *How Writing Works*, which was helpfully vague. For today's first wild stab at the topic, I'd written ten pages of lecture notes, I'd prepared a shower of Power-Point slides, and I was dressed like a grown-up in black jacket and trousers—not quite a suit, since I didn't own a suit, but it could pass for one at a distance. I'd run the lecture through in full, twice, in front of the wardrobe mirror. I muttered passages of it as I went about my day; I'd included instructions to self as to where to click the PowerPoint slides along, and where to smile, and here and there I'd even scrawled a handwritten reminder to breathe. I was as prepared as I could be, but even so, as I clumped down those hollow-sounding steps to the front of the lecture theatre, my heart banged in my chest like it wanted out, and I wanted out too. The lecture theatre had a capacity of a hundred and fifty people, and it was pretty much full. The kids were chatting in clusters and/or staring at their smartphones; a few watched me coming down the staircase towards the black drapes at the front. The data-projection screen glowed and a NO SIGNAL message bounced around. As I reached the desk, the room grew quiet. I rummaged out my reading glasses, scrubbed my hand through my hair. The room was properly silent now. I smiled up at the ranks of faces, my specs making everything soft and indistinguishable. I began to talk; some of the students began to make notes. This seemed at once alarming and encouraging.

I got into my stride, set my notes aside and took off my reading glasses. My distance vision sharpened, and I spotted Nicholas and Meryl, sitting together in the third row from the front. She was tiny beside him, hunched over her notes, scribbling; he was sitting back, hands clasped on the writing ledge, looking at me with that half-smile. And then up towards the top, near the projector, were Richard and Steven, shoulder to shoulder, the former in a plaid shirt, the latter in his suit jacket. They looked like they'd come straight from work, had probably taken time off specifically to be there. From their expressions I wasn't sure they considered it time well spent.

MA students were allowed, but not obliged, not even expected to attend. This was a first-year lecture, after all. I faltered, put my glasses back on, went back to my notes. I read out my thoughts about finding one's own unique voice, and it sounded lame. I talked about everyone's individual perspective. I talked about the use of one's own senses, to see (and touch and hear and smell and taste) what you see, not just recycle what others have already seen (and touched and heard and smelled and tasted) and already written down. That this was a first step in experiencing the world anew, and communicating that newness, and making something that nobody else could make. And I felt like I had exposed myself somehow for saying it.

I concluded the presentation with a picture of Marcel Duchamp's *Fountain*. At the sight of a glossy ceramic urinal blown up on the huge screen for their consideration, some of the audience sniggered. I said we'd talk about this more next week, about exactly that uneasy laugh, and the act of defamiliarization that it was a response to, and its implications for us as writers . . . though I hadn't written a word of next week's lecture yet and wasn't sure myself what the implications were, though I was pretty sure there must be some.

And that was it. Fifty minutes done.

I logged out and gathered up my things, letting the students clear the hall before I followed. I didn't want to risk overhearing any informal feedback on the way.

Someone was still lingering by the door, though, as I clumped up the stairs towards it. I peered over the top of my specs: Patrick

Maloney. He held the door open for me and we walked together back towards the department, rain like a bead curtain either side of the covered walkway. He hoped I didn't mind him coming along; he made a point of attending the Creative Writing lectures; Mike and Simon were always so insightful and entertaining that it was a joy to listen to them. He didn't say whether I had been insightful or entertaining, or if it had been a joy to listen to me. We turned out of the quad and joined the main route down the length of the campus. The covered walkway was packed solid with staff and students; Mina dodged past in the opposite direction, notes clamped fluttering to her chest; she was dressed in a beautiful peacock-blue dress and an orange jacket, an exception that proved the rule of her usual gothic blacks. She said hello and was past us.

"Gorgeous dress," I called after her, and she waved and mouthed thanks. "Mina's a lot more colourful than usual," I said to Patrick. I imagined a shared wardrobe, him in the shower while she's picking out her clothes.

"Yeah, she must be giving a lecture."

I didn't follow: "Is that a luck thing?"

"Hey?"

"All that colour, is that for luck somehow?"

"Well no, it's just if you wear black against those black curtains you just kind of . . . disappear."

I stopped in my tracks. Someone stumbled behind me, tutted, slid past.

"Oh God," I said. I glanced down at my own serviceable black.

"No, really it was fine." He gestured me on: people were ducking out into the rain to get past us, swearing.

"How could it be fine?" I said.

"Well, I could see your face and hands. And you did wave your hands around a lot, so that helped."

"Oh God." We swung in through the doors into our building, climbed the stairs towards our floor.

"I would've thought someone would've told you," he said.

"No one tells me anything."

"You can always ask me."

"But I don't know what I don't know, so I don't know what to ask. It's all a bit Donald Rumsfeld. All the unknown unknowns."

We stopped at my office door. He looked at me a long moment. "I think of anything you should know, I'll let you know, I promise."

"Thanks."

He headed off down the corridor, then turned again, walking backwards as he spoke: "Great lecture, by the way."

I covered my hot cheeks. "Thank you, thanks."

And I went into my office and put my head in my hands and howled with embarrassment. Quietly, because the walls are very thin.

Gill House was in a mobile-phone black spot; I had to cross the lane and stand by the field gate to make a call or send a text. I should have got onto BT and had them hook the landline back up, but I rather liked being unreachable. I dropped out of social media like a stone; I didn't miss the cud-chew of memes, the snapshots of all those perfect lives, the flares of temper, the cod spirituality, not one teensy bit. And I couldn't pick up work emails even if I wanted to. I felt insulated. Time at Gill House soon took on its own particular rhythm. I'd work while Sam napped, or played, or watched a bit of TV. At the weekends, we'd walk in the woods, we'd throw stones in the river, we'd read books, feed the birds.

The maid was in the garden, hanging out the clothes, when down came a blackbird . . .

I already recognised the blackbird, the little cheeky sparrows and the blue-tits. But that big dusty-pink and slate-blue one that clung to a branch and swayed there and never joined the others feeding: I didn't know what that kind was called.

Some days, Mark leaned in the doorway and watched the birds with us. It seemed to do him good, this place. In London, he'd spend the weekend fretting about school politics and pupil welfare, or just chipping away at a mountain of marking. Here, though, he seemed content to drift along with the current of our days. He'd play with Sam, take him for a walk down to the village shop; I'd hear their chatter as they trundled down the lane. He seemed somehow more present, here, with us, than he ever was when we were together all the time in London. I became hopeful. I started conjuring up fantasies. It's a bad habit of mine. That he was coming around to the idea of this place. That he saw its benefits for all of us. That the three of us would be together again, and it would be easy, and comfortable. We'd have family life and good work and a proper home. A pipe dream, perhaps, but also not that wildly ambitious.

Some Sundays, Sam and I made the lunch together; it took forever, with Sam's assistance, so that on this one particular afternoon we were sitting down to an undercooked gratin of aubergines and courgettes and potatoes at half two, and not one o'clock as I'd intended, and Mark was getting antsy. By the time we got onto the apple crumble it was pushing Mark's drive back late, into darkness. Four hours in the car. Prep for school when he got home.

"You could just stay," I said tentatively. "Take another day here; phone in sick and drive down tomorrow."

"You know how it goes. Someone doesn't turn up, it all goes to sh . . ." A glance at Sam, a smile. Same as ever. Can't let anybody down.

And so we finished lunch and he slung his stuff in the car, and we stood in the fine rain as he squeezed Sam and kissed me and clambered into the driver's seat. He turned the car, windscreen wipers squeaking. Sam and I stood at the gate to wave him away; I caught a glimpse of his face, profiled, for this last moment still physically here. He looked so different. He looked already exhausted. Trying to do his best by everyone was wearing him threadbare.

I was chewing at my cheek and we were both still waving after him as the car slowed and then pulled over to one side, to avoid some obstruction in the lane. When the car had gone, a woman peeled herself away from the hedge, and stumbled out onto the tarmac. She was wearing a long blue coat, all the way down to her ankles, and she stood there uncertainly for a moment, as if she had forgotten what she was doing. Then she saw us, and flapped a hand to keep us where we were, and came beetling towards us. I waited, puzzled, Sammy on my hip. As she came nearer, I saw that it wasn't a coat she was wearing, but a dressing gown; navy blue fleece with a quilted yoke. Her feet were bare. There was rain on her hair. She wasn't that old, late fifties, maybe; probably a bit younger than my mum. She had an agitated, urgent air about her. She came up weirdly close. I went to step back, but she wrapped her arms around us, held tight.

"Thank goodness," she said. She smelt indoorsy and sour. She rubbed my back. "There now."

Sammy wriggled and protested. I held him, and she held us, and my eyes filled up. Then she took a step back, released me. Her expression shifted, went out of focus.

"You're. You're . . ." She was trying to place me and couldn't.

"Hi, yes. We're new here."

"Where's Sarah?"

"I don't know. I haven't met Sarah yet."

I assumed a grown-up daughter. I assumed that this sometimes happened. That finding her mother gone, Sarah would be scooping up the car keys and heading for the door, to go out looking for her.

"It's so cold," the woman said, but it was mild and wet and grey.

"You're just not properly dressed for it. We should get you home, get you warm. Do you know where you live? What's your name?"

She drew breath to speak, but another voice called out: *"Gracie?"*

She turned towards the sound, her pale feet padding round on the tarmac. John Metcalfe strode up the lane. He had on an old tweed jacket and blue overalls, folded down wellingtons, Moss ghosting along beside him. He was scowling. He reached out towards us, and the woman put her pale hand in his.

"There you are, Grace," he said.

She smiled faintly.

"You have to tell me when you're going for a walk, then we can go together. Or else our Jim will take you." Then he turned to me and said, "I hope she's not been mithering you."

He was gentler now than I could have supposed. "No, not at all. She just mistook me for someone else. She said she was looking for Sarah. Perhaps they missed each other."

He blinked, then turned to her: "This is the lady who lives here now, Grace. We talked about it, remember? And this is her little boy, remember? We said it was nice to have neighbours, and we'd go and say hello, one of your good days. Remember."

It was like an invocation, like a prayer. *Remember. Remember. Remember.*

"You could come by for tea one day?" I ventured. "Sammy loves to meet new people."

"Oh, I'm not new," Grace pointed out.

"No," I said. "I suppose not."

"Well," he said, and seemed to be about to say something more, but he just said, "Thanks, lass." And he drew his wife away.

A hard and lonely road to walk, that one, and only leading to the dark.

Winter's Blood
By S. D. Haygarth

Part One

DCI Winters got out of the Ford Mondeo, stuffed his hands deep into his gilet pockets and sighed. He might have been twenty-five years in the service but it didn't make it any easier. Death was never easy.

The woods along the riverbank were a popular dog-walking area, only recently accessible again after winter floods. The call came from a middle-aged woman who'd pulled a stick from a tangle of jetsam to lob it for her Labrador, but saw skin and hair and a brown eye blankly staring back at her. She had to drag her dog away and scramble up the bank to get a signal and call the police, and tell them that she had found a body.

No. Not a body, he reminded himself. A girl. Because the first step to finding out how she died was finding out how she had lived. You have to work your way back from the body lying on the ground, follow the threads of her life to find out how she died.

All this was running through Winters' thoughts on that chilly November morning as, followed by his partner, Detective Constable Lauren Clarke, he ducked under the police tape and slithered down the bank to where the SOCOs were at work under their white tent; Dave Kitchener was taking photographs. Soon she'd be bagged up for transportation to the mortuary.

"What've we got here, Dave?"

The girl lay there, naked on the stones. She was white as porcelain, as smooth and flawless, and as cold. Kitchener took a pen from a pocket. He lifted her hair aside, to show her throat. There were blue bruises on her white skin.

Winters bit on the inside of his cheek; it was the cold weather that was making his eyes water; that's what he told himself. DC Clarke peered over to take a look, and then turned her face away.

"I'll get onto arranging an ID, boss," Lauren said.

"You do that, Lauren."

She began the climb back up the bank, getting out her phone.

Everyone knew who it was already; they just weren't saying. Posters of her smiling face were on every parish notice board and stuck in every village shop window; they were pinned to telegraph poles all through the town. Her image was shared and reshared, tweeted and retweeted. Rachel Powell was seventeen, medium height, slender build, brown hair, brown eyes. She attended Youth Club in Kirkby, she'd been a Guide and then had helped out with the local troop. Her lovely family were distraught; it was ten days since she had been last seen, nine since she was reported missing. He'd been expecting the worst. She just hadn't seemed the type to up and go.

"She didn't die here?" Winters asked.

"Doesn't look like it. My guess is she was washed downriver in the floods. It's likely all we'll get off her is silt."

"Do your best."

"Always do."

Kitchener crouched to photograph her hand; the nails were torn. He looked up at Winters. "You okay?"

Winters nodded.

"You don't have to be here, you know."

But he did. They both knew he did. He couldn't run away from this. Not anymore. He couldn't keep on running and still stay in the one place.

. . .

I didn't anticipate the explosion; I was not prepared. It felt like a fairly familiar but also fairly uncontroversial piece of genre fiction.

"So," I asked the class. "Any thoughts?"

Nicholas had his sleeves rolled back on dark skin. He'd been running the edge of one thumbnail over the flat of the other, back and forth: "Couple, yeah."

Steven settled in, pulled an *I'm listening* face.

"First thought is," Nick said, one thumbnail still scraping at the other, "does it *have* to start with a dead woman?"

"Well, that's how these stories work," Steven said. "That's the story engine that powers the novel, so yeah, it does really."

"So, it couldn't be an old, fully dressed woman then?"

"Well."

"Or a naked man?" That thumbnail still scraping, started pushing at the cuticle. "Could it be an old man's body, an eighty-year-old naked *man* washed up with the floods?"

Steven looked to me, baffled; I widened my eyes at him, half shook my head, as surprised as he was.

"Explain, Nicholas."

"Okay then, so, what about this," Nicholas went on. "I don't *know* this woman. She could be anybody. Literally, Any Body. Sure, Girl Guides and yeah whatever the background bullshit we're given, but she has no agency, she's not a character, she's a device. She's not *real*, so we don't care."

"You don't *care*?" Steven said laughingly, looking round to scoop up approval from the other students. "What are you, a psychopath?"

"It's your subconscious we're talking about here, pal. Not mine."

"*What* did you say?"

I raised a hand. "Let's keep it about the work, gentlemen. Okay?"

"It's not my fault if you read it the wrong way," Steven said.

"*Totally* is," Meryl leapt in. "That's actually your job."

I caught a glance then between Meryl and Nicholas. Spotted the crackle there.

"Let's put a pin in this for now," I said. "We can come back to it fresh at a later date. One more piece to look at."

Which was Karen's short story. "Empire Line" was light on its feet but dark at heart. Her protagonist, off work to nurse her mother through her last days, puts on a ton of weight from comfort eating. On her first day back in the office, she wears her favourite, most forgiving dress, and is mistakenly thought to be pregnant. People treat her differently, generously; she realises that she likes it; she plays along, accepting kindnesses and advice and second-hand baby gear, preparing for an arrival that will never happen. And all the time she keeps feeding herself, feeding her grief and loneliness, so that her shape swells and softens; as the months pass, she no longer feels able to do anything, go anywhere, see anyone. She no longer even wants to eat, but wants to sip sweet milky drinks and to sink into a bath. She no longer even looks pregnant, but has become a grotesque version of the baby she will never have.

Karen might not have liked grit, but she did like acid. Her stuff was vinegar-sharp. I felt a bit overwhelmed by it, to tell the truth, all the female flesh. All the darkness, too, from this and all the other stories. All these female bodies in flux. Dying and decaying, awakening and transforming, washed by floods, ballooning, returning to the womb. And I was struggling with my own question of whether there was a way to write female without writing body, and whether there was a way to be female without being reduced to body, and how you would think a life in books would be one way to live like that, but that there were still days like that sweltering June day in London, an event at the bookshop for an author I'd long loved, me a sweaty sheen of fangirl bookseller nerves, a long shift's grubbiness upon me; telling him my first book was going to be published the next year, and him congratulating me and wishing me all the best of luck with it, welcome to the club, I'll teach you the secret handshake later, making me laugh; and then how, after his reading—moving, funny, full of intelligence and warmth—he had come over and taken his seat beside me, and his foot had knocked against my foot, and he leaned down, as if by way of apology, and just touched the toe of my shoe with his fingertips, and then ran his fingertips up my bare summer leg, from ankle to the tenderness just inside the knee, and left his hand there and leaned his damp shirted shoulder against my bare shoulder, and didn't say a thing at all, and I didn't say a thing at all either, but after a moment I got up, and made myself busy, picking up glasses and talking to customers and tidying books until he left, with his publicist, who had seemed like such a lovely woman, and I felt hot and chastened and shaky, and have never since read another word that he has written.

People were being complimentary about Karen's story. In a quiet moment, Nicholas said that he'd really enjoyed it.

Steven smiled, irritable. "Not exactly constructive criticism we're getting from you today, is it?"

Nicholas looked at him; his jaw slid sideways and his eyebrows went up: "Is that what you think? You think I'm being *difficult*?"

Steven shrugged. "I didn't say that."

"Because what I had to say about your work was not about being difficult. It's about asking you not to repeat the lies you've heard before; it's about you telling the truth."

"Is that what it is?"

"Fellas," I said, "we gotta finish up here. Tim, next time, be good to see some work from you?"

Vigorous nodding from Tim. In all the chat and business of departure, Nicholas was still. Meryl followed the others out; she glanced back at him before allowing the door to fall shut behind her. And still Nicholas sat there, his notes still on the desk, his jacket still on the back of the chair, his hands clasped in front of him, one thumbnail scraping at the other. I could hear the students in the corridor, their loud and lively chatter; I was willing Nicholas to go and join them.

"So, um. Sorry about all that. But, bit of a rush here, so . . ." I had to lock up and drop the key back with the porter before running for Sam. The nursery had draconian rules: fifteen minutes late and they'd charge you for an extra hour. Half an hour and they'd phone Social Services. "Do you think you could come to my office hour in the week—" A quick glance at my watch. "I really have to run."

"I won't keep you," he said. "And I want you to know, I'm not going to make a complaint. Not at this stage."

My attention snapped sharp: "What's that?"

"Maybe it didn't occur to you. I get that you're new, I mean this is all new to me too. But work like that, like Steven's submitting." He blinked his pale eyes. "He needs to put a trigger warning up before it."

"Trigger warning?"

"So you can choose to absent yourself, if you need to. If you feel that it would do you harm, that it would set you back, to be exposed to it."

I just said: "You're right."

He raised his shoulders. "I just can't stand people telling lies."

I said, "Leave it with me."

I followed him out the door. Karen, Tim and Meryl were waiting there.

"Coming for a drink?" Karen was still sparkly with her story's success.

"Can't. I have to pick up my son."

"Just a quick one?"

I shook my head. "Sorry. If you're five minutes late for pickup they sell the kids for vivisection."

I left the key with the porter, who bounced the keys in his big palm and told me "Safe home, kid." But I felt uneasy; I couldn't even smile at being called a kid.

I strode past the bar, through the blurt of voices and music; I glanced in, saw them among the glinting glass and red upholstery. Karen said something funny. I watched her smile spread in satisfaction at the laugh she'd got, and the way she raised her glass to hide it. Tim made some comment, glancing sidelong at Nicholas; Meryl touched Nicholas's arm, tweaking his attention to her. And then I was past the window and off into the darkness.

I barely slept that night. No sooner was one worry—trigger warnings, Nicholas, Steven, lectures, Mark—put aside than another popped up in its place like a duck in a pond. The final and most distracting of these ducks was my desperate need for sleep; it swam around and around in circles till well after two. Then they all bobbed up together at five a.m., crashing through the surface and shattering all possibility of further rest.

I was up with the lark and in with the secretaries, Sam already dropped off at nursery at opening time, while most of the university was still in darkness. At nine I bumped into Lisa in the corridor: Hello there, Lisa, that's a lovely jumper, and filthy weather isn't it. (She always had a lovely jumper and it was always filthy weather.)

When I went to make coffee, Mina's light was on. Patrick's wasn't. It struck me as odd that they'd come in separately, but then people had such wildly different timetables. Through the cross-wires of the glass-panelled door I could see her hunched at her computer, peering at the screen; she had a tired-already look about her that I recognised from my bathroom mirror. So I made her a coffee and on the way back tapped her office door with my toe. She jumped, looked round, smiled, and opened the door for me.

"Milk or no milk?"

"Ooh, no milk, thank you."

"Good cos I don't have any."

"You want those crib notes? I'll find them for you." She set the coffee down, turned towards the filing cabinet.

"It's not that, actually."

We sat down. She was wearing a loose black blouse over a vest patterned with brightly coloured Mexican death's heads. Her fingers were tightly interlaced, and squeezed between her knees, and her collarbones stood proud and tight. Pushed for time and chasing deadlines but, well, being nice. Being lovely.

"Maybe I should go to my mentor about it."

"Who's your mentor then?"

"Christian Scaife."

A flicker of an exquisite eyebrow. "Oh-kay."

"But the thing is with him as Head of Department. As my boss. I don't want to, well. Flag up this kind of thing. Because I can cope, of course. It's just I need a little guidance."

"Who suggested Chris as your mentor?"

"Well . . . he did."

She seemed to be on the point of saying something, and then didn't. I told her about the conflict in the last class. Nicholas's taking down of another writer for his depiction of a female murder victim. How he'd said that that kind of material needed a trigger warning, and that whilst I realised this was valid, I also knew the content was no worse or better than the kind of thing you'd see on Sunday-night teatime telly. That it had occurred to me that he, Nicholas, could well have experienced some kind of trauma, since he was asking for a trigger warning, but I didn't know and didn't want to go prodding around where it might hurt. In short, I didn't know how to handle it without making it worse, seeming to take sides, or censoring content you could find in any bookshop in the country.

Mina properly listened. She said, "First things first. Okay?

This needn't be such a big deal. Send a round robin email to the whole group, attach the class protocol document, make it as neutral as you can. Just a bit of admin, nothing personal. Tell them they all have to reread before next week."

"Good. Yes."

"So that's your arse covered about trigger warnings. If the older guy chooses to ignore protocol then it's not your fault: you told him. He gets a final warning, and if he's a dick about it, you pass him on to the Head of Department, and if that doesn't solve the issue, Chris can refer him to the Disciplinary Committee."

"So I can just pass the buck?"

"Totally. That's what all that bureaucracy is there for. So you can pass that buck and get on with your job."

"I don't know, wouldn't that seem a bit . . . nuclear?"

"But it might do this guy good. Some students are tender little plants and they need sunshine and careful watering and even a touch of frost'll do for them. Others are more like walnut trees and what they need to make them bear fruit is actually a damn good thrashing. Could be he's one of them."

"Is that true?"

"You can always tell him that: say you're challenging him because you see something in him. He'll love it."

"No, I mean, is it true about walnut trees?"

"It's what my granddad always used to say. He used to go out in the garden of an evening and hit it with a stick."

"Did you get many walnuts off it?"

"Come to think of it, I don't remember there ever being any."

Trigger warning: Contains violence against people and animals.

Chemistry

Like a rock lobbed into a stream, there's the smash and split
and then the water rejoining and smoothing itself again so
that the surface is barely troubled but underneath there's the
remaining solid lump of stone that must be slammed into
always after. It will take more than a life to wear it down to
smoothness.

Around him the college bar is thick with drinkers and he
drinks sitting at the counter and when someone talks to him
he finds that he is blinking at their face and wondering not
so much what they are saying but why they are bothering to
speak. He turns away from the moving mouth and he looks
down at his hand there on the wooden countertop and it is
dirty he is filmed with dirt he will always be she was the only
clean thing in his life and he can't write clean with his dirty
hand.

His head sinks over his glass and he closes his eyes.
And when he closes his eyes he is with her, it is more than
memory he is there and the day is arid, blazing, and they
find each other by the river, and they swim and the water
beads on her skin; and it drips from her hair stretching out
the curls and he kisses her, and their bodies are cold against
each other, and their mouths are warm.

Come with me?

And she takes his hand and they are climbing up the
bank, dry earth attaching itself in sprays up their shins, past
dusty nettles and fat balsam stems, up into the sunpatched
beech woods.

This is where I come, she says, when I want to be
alone.

She toes off her squelching tennis shoes and upends them
and the river water pours out and she laughs and the cold

wet clothes are peeled off like skin leaving them more than naked for each other. There in the darkness of the college bar he touches his fingers to his lips in echo of a kiss. There is frost on the grass outside there is a snap in the air like it could shatter into bits like it could cut you up.

Someone leans in against him at the bar. He opens his eyes and sees some guy.

You look proper wasted there, mate, the guy says, and he nods slowly because this seems like the first sense he has heard since the phone call and the news, since that carefully casual Maybe you've heard, as if the girl were just someone he might have seen around, as if her death were just a scrap of gossip that had drifted upwards from the locals, and was nothing much at all. But she had chosen death, had taken it to her, body and soul, as she had once taken him.

A girl leans round the guy and he just stares at her treacle-coloured curls and her freckles and she smiles at him and he blinks a slow sick blink and he knows it is not her because she is two hundred and more miles away and cold as stone. He knows he is to blame. Without him there would have been no darkness in her. He touches something and it can't stay clean.

Later and he is in someone's room. A rumpled bed, identikit posters and books. A bong passed from hand to hand murky bubbling. All this edgy conformity.

Some girl the girl with the treacle curls crosslegged on the floor beside him is talking and he nods but he doesn't like it and he doesn't care what she is saying it's all empty words weightless and they drift like ash

He draws in the smoke again, and he holds the smoke deep inside him, and it snakes through his lungs and into blood and it creeps and slithers into his bones and for a moment nothing happens, and he thinks, Fuck this,

*fuck this, fuck this, and goes to get up. The world goes
white.*

*He comes round to circled faces, pushes up and away.
Outside the night is ice and the ground seesaws beneath
his feet and the air is hissing and whispering and there
is a hand on the back of his neck pushing him forward
pushing him on. He has to get out, get away. He steps out of
college through the little door in the big door, and along the
pavement comes a man and a dog, the dog solid muscle and
jowls and straining on its harness and the man shaved head
puffed jacket. The man gives him a look he doesn't like and
so fuck him he aims a kick at the dog and the dog crunches
in the ribs and it flings to the end of its lead and the man is
jolted with it and the dog yelps, hits the ground on its side,
scrabbles and whines and the man is close up face broken
veins and blackheads and creases narrowed pinky eyes. The
man spits You little shit what did she ever do to you, and this
is the best idea he's had in ages. He smiles. A fist smacks into
his face and the pavement swings up to meet him and*

*The night porter leans over him. There's blood in his
eyes. He hauls himself over onto all fours pavement beneath
hands belly heaving vomit onto the stones and blue lights and
huddled in a blanket and A&E and softening of pain and a
woman leaning over him breathing dabbing sticking and her
breasts close in blue scrubs and no sign of concussion the smell
of her of disinfectant and sweat and washing powder and
deodorant and he closes his eyes and feels her breath on him*

*She leans away and says Well you are going to have a
scar there young man.*

He shrugs

*You have been a silly boy haven't you. Getting tanked
up, getting into fights; you've got off lightly, you know. Could
have been much worse.*

But this is all that was ever wanted, to feel something
and be in the moment feeling it, to be right now in the
present moment, here. The smell of her and the warmth of
her and the pillow of her breasts and the pain of the cut and
of its stitching. But the moment is gone as moments always
are and she is saying something about what to expect what
to do if pain painkillers and if infection and then there is a
phone in reception where he can call for free

Call what

Call a taxi. Taxi home.

Home?

A shuffle of images the big house with the gravel drive
two hundred and more miles north of here and the cold
kitchen with the fizzing light and Margie's steak pies,
and the attic rooms of childhood Gideon and nanny down
the hall, and the common room at school with its sagging
armchairs and its chessboard and the day-old Times and
Telegraph, or the polish and dope smell of his college rooms
and clutter of books and mugs and clothes and the books.
Home is in none of these places it slips through his fingers
like water and is as ungraspable as Now. Home was her and
she is lost.

Are we done, he asks the nurse and she says I should
say we're done, and he says Can I go, and she says Of course
you can but call a taxi and he says I'll walk as he swings
his legs off the table, and she says You won't walk you need
a cab and straight to bed and a good night's sleep sleep it off
because that head my god that head is going to hurt you in
the morning

He says, Okay okay mum, I'll get a cab and he leaves
her there backstage in A&E and he walks out through
the waiting-room hopefuls and front of house and past
the receptionists behind their security screens and he goes

through the swooshing doors and across the yellow grid where
the ambulances swim in and out again and he crosses the
carpark and he is out into the city. Headlights stream and
flare and there are halos round the streetlamps. Not back to
his rooms no not with his things in them no, all the evidence
that adds up to him. A hotel. He could sleep in a hotel where
he can be absent from himself as well as everybody else. He
thinks of the girl with the treacle-coloured hair and he could
go to her he could go to her and be let in and be taken to
bed, if he remembered who she was and where she lived but
he doesn't remember not even a name. There is pain in his
head and his eyebrow stings and he walks through the night
city past the kebab vans and the closed shops and the tourist
junk and the sugar-crumbling medieval walls and the bikes
piled against railings and the terrace houses and the gates
are locked but he scrambles over them, cuts his hand on the
rust. Beyond there is dew on the grass, and he switches on
the torch on his phone and the headstones slope and rabbits
freeze spotlit and their burrows dig right through the graves
and out again ivy trails and a car's turning headlights make
Caravaggio shadows, he sucks blood and dirt from his hand.
He turns the light and swings it yes this is the right one it
is his. The man buried here with his wife Anne you can
barely make it out but the man buried here lived to be fifty-
two and have two of his children buried before him and he
died in 1843 and he had married and had children and the
children died and his name was Nicholas Palmer. He alive
there lays his head down on the cold earth on the pastness
of this other man, the over and doneness of him, eternally
over. Arm crooked behind his head he looks up into the
filthy city sky filmed with streetlamps and car fumes and he
finds his cigarettes and he smokes a cigarette and he thinks
of the beech wood green and alive and the leaves stirring

*and dripping water glowing moss and birds in the trees and
sometimes a deer and here and the patch of light, always
moving, always changing, never still: her in that place, her
being and belonging there. And that is the choice, between all
that life and growth and pain, and this stillness, this failure,
this darkness.*

"Is this chronological?"

"What do you mean?"

"Is this set before or after the first piece you showed us?"

"Oh, yeah, it happens before, but comes after . . . You see I'm
thinking in circles now." This with a half-smile for me. But I was
preoccupied not so much with the work itself, or the structures
of his novel, but with fitting it into a pattern with his gut-punch
reactivity to Steven's work, what he'd said about death and telling
lies and trigger warnings. Then Steven lifted a finger for attention, like he was summoning a waitress.

"Yes, Steven?"

"Dead girl klaxon," he said.

"Sorry?"

"Didn't you notice?"

"What?"

"She's dead, his girlfriend or whatever, that girl in the story.
You not going to pick him up on it?"

"I don't follow you."

"He was going on like I was some psycho, so how come he
gets away with it?"

"I don't think anyone meant to imply . . ."

Nicholas tilted his head.

Steven leaned in to glare at him: "You don't have a leg to stand
on, pal."

"Okay. I see. So Steven's reminding us about Nicholas's

questions about using a young woman's death as an initiating incident for his story. Which, it seems, this story also does. Any thoughts?"

Karen leaned in. "It's not leering over a naked dead body"— Steven visibly baulked at that—"it's about grief for a lost loved one."

"Is that a genre difference?"

"Could be."

"Is it murder here though? I don't think so." This was Meryl; she traced through the piece with a fingertip. "*'She had chosen death, had taken it to her, body and soul'*—that sounds more like suicide to me."

I looked to Nicholas; his dark head was bent now, his face obscured, but he slightly nodded.

"So I guess she has a degree of agency that Steven's victim didn't have . . ." Karen twisted a lock of hair around her finger, let it go; it bounced back like a spring. "The boy blames himself, but at the same time the narrative implies that he is not to blame. She made the decision; she chose."

Steven, scowling, tipped his chair back, his suit jacket swinging open. Richard leaned back too, the buttons of his plaid shirt straining to reveal patches of hairy belly. Their eyes met behind Karen's back. That's all there was to the interaction, but observing it, I got the distinct impression that a moment of this sort had been foreseen, discussed between them, and a strategy agreed. Because as Steven landed the front chair legs back on the floor, Richard cleared his throat, picked up the baton and ran with it.

"It doesn't seem right," Richard said, "that some of us are criticised and others get praised for the same thing. You're not even writing crime fiction. You don't *need* someone to be dead. You could just choose to do something else."

"No, Nicholas said. "I couldn't."

Steven scowled round at him. "Couldn't what?"

"Couldn't do something else."

I leaned in: "Why's that, Nicholas?"

"That's the rule," Nicholas said.

"Rule?" Steven asked, folding his arms. "What rule? What are you on about now?"

"My rule."

"*Your* rule?"

"The rule I've set. The rule of the work."

"What is it?" I asked.

Nicholas looked at me. His strong dark face seemed congested, full, as though something was about to spill, as though he was only just managing to keep a lid on things.

"I'll only write what happened," he said. "I'll only write the truth."

I flicked back through what he'd written, the drugs and drink and darkness, the scar on his eyebrow, the lost girl.

"I'm so sorry," I said.

Meryl put her hand on his arm, gave it a squeeze.

"Dude." Tim got up, gestured for a hug; Nicholas didn't get up. Tim just stood there, clasped Nicholas's shoulder, rubbed it. He said, "Ah, man," and went back to his seat.

"You've signed up for the wrong course," Steven said. "This is fiction."

"Okay," I said, holding up my hands. "Let's think about process here."

I talked then, probably the longest I'd ever spoken uninterrupted in class. About the decisions we make when we are writing. About what we choose to include and what we choose to exclude, when summoning stories out of the ether or digging them up from the past. About subjectivity. About emphasis, lexis, point of view, voice, tone. About how our own experience influences all those decisions. That though our material might differ it was a difference like the difference between sandstone and limestone, say, and that we're all still always using the same tools to shape it.

"So, what you're saying is that it's still fiction, even though it isn't actually *fictional*?" This was Steven.

"I'd say it's still a novel. Or it will be. Or it could be. And that this is exactly the right place to work on that."

I looked to Nicholas, but he was slouched in his chair, not making eye contact with anyone. That was the experiment, then; that was what hadn't been done before. To write a novel using only what had happened. To write a novel that's the truth.

"Hadn't you better rein it in a bit though, mate?" Richard asked, all faux bonhomie now. "Can't be doing you much good."

"I said that it was true," Nicholas said. "I didn't say that it was good."

I turned my wrist conspicuously to look at my watch. "We'd better move on. Let's take a look at Karen's new story."

Karen's story was about a woman who fell in love with owls. It started when her eye was caught, in a charity shop, by a ceramic ornament of a snowy owl sitting on a branch. The detail beguiled her: the grain of the feathers and the glint of the eye and the small blue flowers round the base. It was only a pound, so she bought it, brought it home and set it on the mantelpiece, and would stand looking at it, tilting it and turning it the better to admire it. Then she saw owl-shaped cushions in Primark, and she got these too, but couldn't decide between the colours, so ended up buying all four. Then she found an owl scarf, and a sweater with owls on it, and gloves, knickers and socks. There were earrings and a necklace. Then there was owl-print bed linen, and an owl rug, and then curtains for her bedroom. And it still was not enough. Or not quite right. In fact it was all wrong. These things in the shape of owls, or decorated and patterned with owls: they were tawdry, cartoonish representations; they were an offence to the natural dignity of owls. She stripped off her jewellery and her scarf and socks and dressed with satisfaction in cream and beige and brown; she couldn't settle in her owl-stuffed sitting room and couldn't even consider going up to her bedroom, which was a travesty, festooned with owl-printed fabric. Instead she climbed into the shrubbery at the end of the garden, and started to fashion herself a nesting site. She lined it with dryer-fluff and cushion-stuffing and shreds of fabric, having ripped up her offensive soft furnishings. That was quite tiring, and she was sleepy at work all the next day, and so when she got home from the office she climbed into her comfy roost and dozed in the sunshine. That was enough for her while it was summer—brain fog at work and then snoozy afternoons in the shrubbery—but then in September she slept all through the afternoon and evening and when she woke, it was dark. She was chilly but she felt good. In fact, she felt awake, alert, more alive than she had in years: and she felt hungry. Then a mouse ran past and, well, that was that.

"Does she start coughing up pellets next?"

"No."

"Does she learn to fly?"

"No."

"So what happens next?"

"Nothing happens next," Karen said. "That's where the story ends."

"It's a bit mad," Steven said.

"No madder than my werewolves," Meryl pointed out.

"No, no madder than that," Steven agreed.

It was five to the hour. "You know what, let's draw things to a close there. Plenty to think about for next week."

They left in their little factional clots, and I packed up my stuff, then locked up. I felt like a kid riding a too-big bike, teetering on the edge of disaster the entire time. I'd forgotten to nag Tim about his work; we still hadn't seen anything from him. But that seemed a small concern, next to what was going on with Nicholas. Everything he'd been through. I couldn't fathom it. But then, maybe, that was the point of his writing. To sound out the depths, to map this darkness.

The next morning, I spotted Mina in a swirl of teal-blue military-style coat, striding in long black boots. I ran to catch up with her. Our breath plumed. The rain was mizzling, half-hearted, cold.

"Can I buy you a coffee and pick your brains?"

She shuddered. "Oh that expression. But coffee though."

The college bar was empty. We sat down on the creaky vinyl stools, and she selected a little paper tube of sugar and shook the contents down.

"This is more of the same or something new?"

"Well, I sent the protocol document round, and didn't get a peep back from them; you'd think that was all good. But then Nicholas produces a piece and *he* gives a trigger warning, which is just right because the stuff is dark. But it's about grief, really; self-destruction, the psychology of bereavement. But Steven, the old fellow, he has a proper go, about the fact of there being a dead girl in it, and I don't know if he's being deliberately obtuse and disingenuous, or really means it. And *then* Nicholas said that he only writes what happened. He only writes the truth."

We both watched the spill of sugar grains into her coffee and I realised that when I'd brought her coffee before I hadn't thought of that.

"Did you call bullshit on him?" she asked.

"Eh?"

"The more a writer says 'It's all true' the more inclined I am to think I'm being messed with."

"He has a scar, through his eyebrow. This was about how he got it."

"Yeah, but what about 'How the Leopard Got His Spots'? That's not true. In fact it hardly bears looking at."

I nodded, uncertain, and sipped my coffee.

"Look," she added. "Obviously I don't know this kid. But it seems to me that he's probably playing some tricksy postmodern game. It must be that or he's totally naïve. The truth!" She chuckled, shook her head.

"I don't think he's totally naïve."

"Well, there you go then. It's bullshit and he's messing with you."

I loved Mina, I realised. "But, you know. The thing is, I really think he's processing some trauma. That he's got a real problem there."

"Not your job."

"Well, yes, but—it's happening in my class. So I do need to manage it somehow."

"You get too tangled up in this one kid, you're asking for trouble. You have to protect your time; you have to protect yourself."

"I get that. I do. I'm not suggesting anything more than, well, basic kindness, I suppose."

"Well, first up, go check if the kid is stickered."

"Stickered?"

"They put a yellow sticker on the kid's file if there's a declared mental health issue. Ask Lisa; she can show you."

"Nobody told me there were stickers."

"It's not exhaustive: kids don't have to declare anything if they don't want to, but they tend to, because then it can be taken into account with exams and whatnot."

"So if I check his file, and it says there was some tragic event . . ."

"No. That information's actually held confidentially, in Central Records. We just get a sticker."

I sat back. "So what you're saying is, that I can check his file, and if there's a yellow sticker, I'll know there's something I should know about, but I can't actually know what it is?"

"That's about the size of it."

"Brilliant."

LISA DARBY

DEPARTMENTAL ADMINISTRATIVE OFFICER

Statement

We don't let the academic staff into the records store. You'd think they didn't even know the alphabet, the way they stuff things away any old how. So I fetched the file for her, and waited while she read it in my office. It's the only way you can be sure you'll get it back in the right place.

She flipped through it, seemed kind of puzzled, so I asked her if there was a problem, and she said that she had thought there might be a yellow sticker. I took it back off her and had a look myself. Then I explained to her what the file meant.

He was not a run-of-the-mill postgraduate student. His A-level results were all spaced out. That means he had to re-sit. Probably a crammer, because he didn't just scrape by; he got As, eventually, and then had gone on to Oxford, but had only got a third. And that was five years after the A levels were all done. No mention of what he'd done in the intervening years.

To me, that kind of pattern indicates a student who's got problems *and* money, I told her. Poor kids mess up like that, they crash out and they don't keep on getting hauled back in. Re-sits, Oxford, and now a postgraduate degree with us: that's tens of thousands of pounds in fees alone.

We don't usually take applicants with a third; we do stipulate 2:1 or first. The student would need to be exceptional, or there'd have to be extenuating circumstances. The decision would have been made by Professor Michael Lynch, who was in charge of admissions at the time, on the basis of a portfolio of existing work. I took a quick look for her, but there was no portfolio on file: we don't have the storage to keep everything.

She was telling me, meanwhile, about how he was writing some pretty dark stuff, and how she'd had a request from him about trigger warnings in relation to other people's work. Around forty per cent of our creative writing students have declared mental health issues, and those are just the ones that choose to let us know, so I wasn't overly surprised. I suggested she tell him to get in touch with Student Services. We have trained counsellors on staff. It's their job to help.

And that was it. She went on her way, and I went to re-shelve the file. I looked at his photo. Striking-looking lad; clearly had everything going for him. But you never really know, do you, what's going on with other people. You can't tell by the shiny wrapping what's really inside.

After that, I emailed her the Safeguarding and Harassment Policy document. She should have had it in her welcome pack, but turned out nobody had remembered to give her a welcome pack. We're understaffed. It's not surprising that these things get overlooked.

Safeguarding and Harassment

The University has a zero-tolerance policy towards harassment. Harassment may be defined as discrimination, verbal or physical abuse, or inappropriate behaviour towards an individual, on any grounds, including but not limited to gender, gender-identity, race, sexuality and religion. Harassment must be reported, in the first instance, to the relevant Head of Department.

The University has a proactive policy towards safeguarding. Members of staff have a duty of care towards each other and towards students and a duty to report any concerns regarding safeguarding, in the first instance, to the relevant Head of Department.

To this end, the University actively discourages physical relationships between staff and students. Any such relationship must be reported at the earliest opportunity to the staff member's Head of Department, and be noted in both the staff member's and the student's file. The individual student shall not then be taught or their work assessed by that member of faculty from that point until the end of their studies.

In all instances where a safeguarding or harassment complaint is made, the relevant Head of Department will act as a first contact and liaison between the individuals concerned. Only if a resolution cannot be reached to all parties' satisfaction will the complaint be referred onwards to the Faculty Disciplinary Committee.

I rounded the corner to find myself on a collision course with Scaife. He stopped dead in front of me, one hand extended towards me, offering me a smile, asked how the teaching was working out, how the teacher training was working out, how my writing was going, how my son—it was a son, wasn't it?—was settling in at nursery. I started to answer his first question, but he was already nodding and drawing breath for the second, and before I'd finished a sentence on that, he was on to the third. I realised he didn't actually want to hear what I had to say; he just wanted a brief, positive remark from me, so he could move on to the next thing, and the next, and then have done. I supposed that this was him mentoring me. I provided the brief, positive remarks, and then, speaking over his next enquiry only because I had to, I mentioned the desperate hurry I was in and he said, "Of course, of course," and turned three quarters so I could slide past him. I went to go by, but then he put his long fingers on my arm.

"Oh, but just one other thing."

I managed not to look at the hand. I stared up instead at the open pores across his cheeks, his pale-lashed eyes.

"Yes?"

I felt the pressure of his hand. The nerves tingled all the way up my arm and into my neck and all the way down to my fingertips. I wanted to shake it off, *get off me, get your hand off me,* but what I did was stand there, and wait for him to speak.

"I've just had an email from Mike." Off my blank look: "Mike Lynch."

"Oh yes."

"What it is, is, annoying this, but he was in charge of Admissions, you see. And of course he's in Canada, and nobody gave it a second thought till now."

This was where the "conversation" had been headed all along. I changed my stance, as though settling in to listen, but really to make his hand slide off my arm.

"It's good we can all work remotely nowadays," I said.

"Ah no, not Mike, he can't. Not his kind of thing at all."

"Don't they have Wi-Fi in Canada?"

"Ah well, you see, the thing is—we do have to protect his time."

I pushed my hands into my pockets. "*His* time?"

"Mm-hmm, yes, so I'm afraid we're just going to have to shoulder this between us. But it's the simplest thing in the world. The new software should make it even easier. Just don't ask me how to navigate around it! Lisa's your man for that, she'll show you the ropes. Oh, and you'd better come along to the meeting."

"The meeting?"

"Two o'clock tomorrow, the Gaskell Room. If you could just read through the guidelines before that so you're up to speed, they're on the website, on Staff pages, and take a glance at the current batch of applications on the Admissions page. Mike said there were a dozen or so posted there already. I think he must have got an email alert. But you'll want to get cracking on them; you won't want to let them build up too much."

What I wanted, I thought, seemed to have very little to do with it at all.

The term continued in that fashion, like a game of Buckeroo. First the lecture series, now Admissions, then an essay to write for my teacher-training course; more and more students' work to read, another lecture to write and deliver, and then another, and with every new role, more meetings to attend. I managed occasional coffees and grabbed sandwiches with my new colleagues, and mad dashes to pick up Sammy from nursery before they sold him for organ harvesting. Mark came for half-term but had to bring so much marking with him we still took Sam in to nursery anyway so that we could get our work done. We managed one day out, and a supermarket shop, while we had access to the car. I scattered crumbs for the birds, and we watched them swoop and hop and hustle, watched the blue-and-pink bird swing on its branch.

From time to time Scaife would pull me into his office and look sincere and ask how I was getting on, and in my brief, positive answers—keen to get away from him before those long fingers landed on me—I tried to tread the delicate line between coping splendidly and inviting him to hoist another bag onto my saddle.

And so the term went on. And then there was this. No trigger warning. Just this:

Winter's Blood
By Steven Haygarth, LLB

Midnight, and there was frost on the fields and patches of
black ice on a road notorious for its accidents—there were
bunches of dead flowers tied to fence posts and telegraph
poles, and torn gaps in hedges, like some kind of failed crop.
And yet the man drove down the narrow winding lanes
at a steady speed, not slowing for the bends but dropping
down a gear and heaving the car round them, careless of
his safety, and that of other road users, and of his tyre wear.
He loosened his silk tie, and unbuttoned his smooth cotton
collar. His hand rubbed at his expensive haircut.

The car—a black Audi RS6 Avant—hurtled round
the bend. He was driving too fast for the road conditions,
and he should have known that—formal suit, old-fashioned
briefcase, the cut of his hair; everything about him indicated
he was conservative, careful, considered. But not tonight.
Safety did not seem to be of any concern to him right now.
At this time of night the valley roads were usually deserted
and he was counting on that being the case. He rounded a
bend, and at that moment, a fox stepped out into the road,
and the man did not hesitate or swerve, he just drove on. The
Audi hit the fox on the shoulder and sent it spinning back
towards the verge to die there, in the cold grass, its mouth
trickling blood.

How was he supposed to have known who she was?

As he drove, he drummed his fingers on the wheel and
scowled at the road as it flung itself towards him, the big
spreading bare trees against the stars, the telephone poles
and lamp posts and the signposts. At the junction, he heaved
the car round to turn right onto the A road without even
checking for oncoming traffic. Perhaps he would have seen

headlights approaching, had there been any. But still, this was careless and he did not have the appearance of a careless man.

How was he supposed to have known who she was?

It was only this evening that he'd seen the poster, pinned to the office board. A picture of the young woman, in walking gear, high up on some hillside, straggling hair and a gap-toothed grin, fresh and outdoorsy and un-made-up. Someone's friend, that's what she looked like. Someone's friend from off the netball team. The girl who helped at Brownies.

And the details underneath. Rachel Powell. Seventeen. Last seen on the seventh of October northbound on the A81 bus. Any information. Etc.

He didn't know if he should study it carefully, or just glance and look away. He didn't know what would seem more normal.

It was her, but that wasn't what she had said her name was.

The poster had been pinned there by Charlotte, the paralegal, with her hair up in a fluffy ponytail, who had started on about the poor girl, friend of her sister's; family a wreck with worry.

"I hope they find her soon," he mumbled.

He had poured his last cup of coffee of the day and had gone back to his office and shuffled up his court briefs and he had tried to concentrate. But his head had spun, the words blurring as the memories of that night had come back to him.

He dialled a number. Then he hung up before he'd even finished dialling. Because phone records could be checked. But he wanted to warn, to confer, to settle a story. He wanted to complain. He bit his lip, shook his head: idiot. What was he thinking. He was alone with this. They were not the kind of organisation to have a complaints procedure.

He swung the car round and spun onto the gravel and up the drive. The security light flicked awake. He killed the engine, and he sat there for a moment, breathing, his hands on the wheel. He looked up at the top window; it was dark. She was asleep. He had allowed himself those risks when driving home, because part of his mind was hoping that he would crash, and that would be that, problem solved. It would all be over. And that in a few weeks, all that would be left to mark the spot would be a few dried stems and rotting petals.

Perhaps if he had more nerve, if he was a stronger man, he would not have relied on chance. He would have put his foot down and driven headlong into a telegraph pole.

He got out of the car. He went around to the front and peered at the bumper where he had hit the fox. There was a smudge there, a print, like the mark left by a football on a garage door. He crouched down, got out his handkerchief and breathed onto the paint. He polished with the handkerchief and leaned away to look. The mark was gone, or so it seemed at least in the light of the security lamp, on the gravel sweep in front of his home. He straightened up and pocketed his handkerchief. He got his briefcase from the car, and keyed his way into the house.

If only every accident could be cleared up with so little fuss, he thought.

He took off his shoes and climbed the sweep of stairs. He slipped into the bedroom and his wife turned over in bed.

"It's late," she said.

"Yes."

"You must be exhausted," she said.

"A bit."

"You work too hard," she said.

"I know."

"I never see you," she complained.

But she didn't mind the big house, the holidays, the car, the clothes.

He slipped out of his suit and got in between the cool cotton sheets. His wife's body was warm and soft—she had put on weight after the second child, and had showed no signs of making an effort to shift it. He eased himself close to her, enjoying the warmth of her body. He thought to himself, perhaps this is alright. Perhaps this could be enough. Perhaps if I just settle for this, and don't go looking again for anything more, then all that trouble would just go away.

He slid a hand around her waist, and then up to her breast. She breathed out. She hardly ever let him nowadays, but he took this as a signal that he could.

He thought, Maybe I can get over past mistakes. Maybe I can be forgiven. Maybe if I go on just pretending to be the man that everybody thinks I am, then I will actually become that man. And then it won't be me, anymore, who's done those dreadful things. It will have been someone else. And so there will be no guilt, no case to answer, because it wasn't even me.

But as they lay there, side by side, afterwards, and his wife snored quietly, the other thoughts pushed back through and tangled into a briar patch.

He would be good.

But it was too late to be good.

He would change.

Too late.

He wished that it had happened differently.

Wishing changed nothing.

It was an accident.

One girl, you could call one an accident; you could make

a case. But two. Two is not misfortune. Two is not even carelessness. Two is intentional. Two is too late.

And if it was too late for him, then he might as well enjoy himself.

Jenny stood in the shower. The hot water cascaded round her, running in rivulets down her naked body. She let it run through her bleach-blond hair, darkening it, and soaking and cleansing her. She soaped her fingernails and hands. She hated the smell that lingered round her from the mushroom farm. Who would have thought that mushrooms would be so smelly—but the stink of the compost, and the white, almost corpselike odour of the mushrooms themselves became overpowering. It lingered in her hair, and on her hands, and she always dumped her overalls at the back door when she came home, because they stank so badly.

But work was work, and there wasn't much of it round here, not for young people just starting out. Most of her friends had left; they were studying in cities all across the country, or had started jobs or internships in London or Manchester or Birmingham. Those that remained, had remained because they had jobs waiting for them: straight out of school they went full-time on the farm—which is what they'd been itching for, all along, school having been an inconvenient obstacle to getting their day's work done. Or they joined their dad in the plumber's van, or haulage company, or joiner's workshop. You had to have good grades to leave this place, and to stay you had to have a niche already carved out for you in the family firm, and Jenny, with her mum in and out of hospital, and her dad in and out of touch, throughout her teenage years, had neither.

Hence the mushroom farm. Jackson's Mushrooms, out on the Carnforth road.

But she wasn't going to be at Jackson's forever. No. Jenny wasn't going to settle for that. She was going to make something of herself, she was going to have nice things, and a comfortable lifestyle, and for however long her mother had left—she was on her third round of chemo at the moment—she was going to have nice things for her mother too.

She got out of the shower, and her skin bristled in the chilly bathroom. The house was empty, and so she hadn't bothered putting the heat on. She wouldn't be home for long herself—and when her mother was at home, slowly shuffling from bed to sofa to kettle and back, they had to have the heat on high and the bills were scary, so it was better to do without it for a bit. She wrapped herself in a skimpy towel and ran through to her bedroom, where she pulled on her dressing gown and towelled dry her hair. She got out her hairdryer and her makeup case. She had plenty of time. She wasn't due at the place until eleven. But she had to look— and smell—her best. Tonight, she was going to start her new job. She was, she thought, with a smile, moonlighting.

Moonlighting paid far better than the mushroom farm.

A little later, she was done. She turned her head side to side and looked at herself in the mirror. Her bleach-blond hair was ironed to a flat papery sheet. Her face was matte and a few shades darker than her throat. She blinked false eyelashes and smiled a lipstick smile. She pulled the straps of her skimpy dress up her shoulders. She could do with a coat—a fur, she thought, luxuriously—but she would have to put the purchase of a fur off for the time being. Because there was the gas bill to pay. And her mother needed a fur if anybody did; she was getting so thin. Perhaps—the thought delighted her into a genuine smile—someone would fall in love with her and buy her a fur coat. Would buy her all sorts

of things. Anything she took a fancy to. That would make
a very pleasant change from having to scrape the money
together to buy things for herself. It sucked, having to buy
things for herself. But she was looking forward to treating
Mum.

She lifted her perfume bottle—a knockoff she'd got from
the market, though the fiver it had cost had seemed a lot to
her. She sprayed it in great gusts around her, over her hair,
and under her arms, and on her wrists and behind her ears,
and then, as a last thought, up her skirt so that she shivered
as the chill spray hit her thighs. The fragrance was sickly
sweet and cloying, but she snuffed it in and thought herself
delicious. She slipped her little feet into her killer heels, and
then realised she'd need her trainers too, and tottered round
in her heels till she found them, stuffed under her bed. She
couldn't drive in heels, and she had to drive—all in all, it
would be a thirty-mile round trip up the valley, up the back
lanes past Kirkby, to the big house where she was expected.
She'd been past the place before, on nights out, to parties in
friends' houses, but neither she nor anyone she knew had
ever been inside. A different level of society, that kind of
place. There was a glamour to this, there was an excitement.
To be expected. To be anticipated. To be wanted at a place
like that.

Best to keep to that kind of client, though. They had the
money, and she wouldn't be bumping into them in Aldi or
the Rugby Club. That was partly why the mask of makeup,
the ironed-out hair. In the normal run of things she'd be
barefaced and ponytailed and therefore barely recognisable:
being herself by daylight would be her disguise.

Dangling her trainers from her hand, she stood in front
of her mirror. She turned from side to side, examining her
appearance. Her hair was perfect. Her makeup was perfect.

*Her heels were perfect. Her dress—skimpy, clinging, just
revealing enough—was bloody gorgeous.*

*He doesn't stand a chance, she thought. I'll knock him
dead.*

"Here's a thing," Karen peered round at Steven. "My daughter,
she's seventeen, she's like, I hate my thighs, I hate my bum; she's
living off SlimFast; she can never be thin enough. And she's gorgeous; the way she sees herself is a crying shame. I'm twice her
size but I'm more at home in myself than she is. Maybe if you
wrote your character like that, she'd be more—realistic."

Steven said, "Okay."

"I think there's a bigger question here," Nicholas said. His
fingers were meshed together on the tabletop. It was like he held
himself deliberately still, but couldn't stop that thumbnail from
scraping at the other, pushing at the cuticle.

Steven leaned back in his seat. He folded his arms. "Here
we go."

"Yeah, here we go. What it looks like from what we've got here
is that your killer is punishing women for their sexuality." Steven
looked pleasantly surprised that his intentions had been understood. "They dare to feel powerful, however briefly, but he proves
them wrong. And he punishes them for having dared."

Steven nodded.

"But here's the thing. Is it him punishing them, or is it you?"

"*Excuse* me?"

"Because that's something you need to consider, don't you
think? How big a leap of imagination this is for you."

"What exactly are you implying?"

"You need to ask yourself that, mate, not me."

"This is censorship. Your whole attitude. Jesus."

"Lookit, write whatever you want. I'm serious, go right ahead.

Far be it from me to dictate what you do. But take some fucking responsibility for what you let come crawling out of your subconscious."

"Nicholas," I said, "that's enough."

"It's just a story," Steven said. "What's your excuse?"

There was a moment's silence.

"You know what? Fuck this." Nicholas grabbed his bag and shoved back his chair and was gone. The door slowly closed behind him. Steven asked, eyebrows up in astonishment, "What's his problem?"

Karen said, "I think we could be a bit nicer to him."

Steven snorted.

"If you paid any attention at all," Meryl said, "you'd *know* what his problem was."

"Can we just cool it, d'you think?"

"So, what, we all have to tiptoe round him now?" Richard asked.

"I'm not tiptoeing round anyone. He can tiptoe round me," said Steven. "Maybe I'm offended now."

Meryl *tsk*ed. She went to get up, to follow Nicholas, but I waved her back down.

"You guys take a break, grab a coffee; we'll start back in fifteen minutes."

He hadn't gone far; he was smoking a cigarette under the tree in the quad. I sat down beside him on the bench; he flicked a scowl at me.

"I'll go if you don't want me here."

"Stay."

Just that one word, but it felt loaded with meaning. I felt like we understood each other.

"You were making good points, you know. Though you kinda blew it by swearing. And then storming out."

"You know what?" he said. "I don't care. I'm done. He's never going to understand. It's always going to be blah blah blah, dead girl, blah blah blah sexy girl. Blah blah blah terrified sexy girl. Blah blah blah sexy dead girl. And so it goes on, so many dead girls, and it is such *bullshit*. He has no idea the lies he's telling." He raised his shoulders, then lowered them; a slow, heavy shrug. The air was wet with drizzle, a grey misty curtain around us.

"I wanted to say," I said, "you could talk to someone."

He was already shaking his head.

". . . they have counsellors here and maybe if you were to go and see one of them . . ."

"No."

"Just, no?"

"Talking doesn't help. I know it doesn't help. It might help some people but it doesn't help me."

"You've tried counselling before?"

He drew on his cigarette, blew smoke, nodded.

"It didn't help even a bit?"

"Torture," he said. "And still." He swung his hand round, including the situation he was in. "I realised some time ago that all I can do is write it out of my system. That's the only thing that works."

"If that's what you need," I said, "then I'll do my best to help."

He nodded his thanks.

"And I'll—talk to Steven. See if we can get him to tone it down. See if we can't work something out."

He sucked his cigarette into a hot coal, then he flicked the stub away, out into the rain. It hit the grass and sparked and faded out.

"Good," he said. "Because otherwise I'm just going to have to stay away from class."

"Try to not let it get to you," I said, though I knew how inadequate that was. "Look, I've got to get back. Are you coming?"

He shook his head. He picked up his pack of cigarettes from the bench, tucked his lighter into it.

"Have you got somewhere you can go? It's maybe not a good idea to be alone right now."

"I'll be fine," he said, and then he said, "I'm not great company anyway."

He sloped off through the fine rain, and I ran back to class.

"That kid is such a . . ." Richard glanced round at me as I came in, and looked caught out, but finished his sentence anyway, sheepishly: ". . . snowflake." I took my place at the table, rubbed my hand through my wet hair.

Meryl was red and shiny and blinking. "Actually I think that term is super-unhelpful."

"It wouldn't exist if it wasn't necessary," Steven said.

"He's traumatised; you've read his work."

A snort. "'Traumatised.' He's not traumatised, he's a nutjob."

"Okay," I said. "We do have rules here. We have responsibilities towards each other. This is not a free-for-all."

"Tell that to the prima donna out there."

"I don't accept swearing in the class and I have spoken to him about that. But from now on, if you present violent or explicit work, you post a trigger warning. You've all had access to the protocol document. If things don't change I will have to refer this to our Head of Department, and you could both end up in front of the Disciplinary Committee."

"But nothing happened," Steven said.

"What?"

"Nothing happened to her."

For me, the pronoun kept slipping between Steven's character and Nicholas's lost girl, and I couldn't pin it down. I shook my head. "What?"

"Nothing violent or explicit. Jesus. Trigger warning for cheap perfume now? Or that fox?" he hissed out a breath.

"Let's not be flippant here," I said.

"I'm not being flippant; I'm being deadly serious. This is PC gone mad. We've got to post a warning that a story may contain conflict and jeopardy now? Of course it bloody might; it should, it *has* to. Otherwise what is it? Not a story, that's what. And what about his stuff? That's properly weird; even if it's true. In fact it's weirder *if* it's true. What if I decide that his stuff is upsetting me? What if my dog just died and I decide to throw a hissy-fit because he kicked a dog that reminds me of mine? What then?"

"Same rules would apply. I'd say I was sorry for your trouble, and suggest you seek help if you need it, and I'd ask the class to be alert to your issues. I'd also expect you to get on with your work here and respect class protocol. Just as I did with Nicholas. Okay? Now can we do some actual work now, please?"

My cheeks were hot. I spoke more sharply than I should have.

We had one more piece to look at; a section of Meryl's novel *Halfway* in which it became clear that the love interest was not only a closeted werewolf, but was also bisexual, much to the fascinated confusion of our heroine. Which set Steven off again. About ticking PC boxes.

Meryl had a talent for the sudden blush: "I'm really not ticking any boxes."

"Then why does he have to be bi?"

"It makes him the more mysterious and exotic, in a conservative, heteronormative culture."

Steven rolled his eyes, and Meryl narrowed hers. I made the right noises to cool things and nudge them along, but all I could think about was that there really shouldn't be this level of conflict in the class, and that I didn't know what I could do to defuse it, and that I still hadn't managed to winkle any work out of Tim, and was it all my fault? Next week was the last week of Michaelmas term, and scheduled for personal tutorials. As we closed the discussion I passed round a sign-up sheet.

"What about Nicholas?" Meryl asked as she handed the sheet back to me. I glanced down at the list; there was one space left, the last appointment of the day, six p.m.

"I'll pop him down there. Could someone let him know?"

"I will," Meryl said.

I pencilled his name in with a question mark.

Patrick was in the common room, waiting for the kettle to boil. I filled a pint glass from the tap and stood at the counter to drink it.

"You okay?" he asked.

Still drinking, I held up my left hand to show that it was shaking.

"Christ. What's up?"

There, in that weirdly corporate common room with its red-and-purple furnishings and fake kumquat tree, in the smell of old coffee and instant soup, I spilled everything to Patrick. All the stuff I'd drip-fed to Mina, plus the new stuff; I felt sure he'd have heard some of it already from her. I told him about Nicholas's rule, his lost girl, the talk of trigger warnings, his storming out of class and threatening to stay away. I told him about Steven's fictional murders, his accusations of censorship, snowflakedom and PC gone mad.

"Crikey. In Eng. Lit. we just read a book and talk about it. Or at least some of us read the book. Or at least I do. And then I talk about it."

"I guess it gets more personal when you're writing the book yourself. You're laying out your soul for other people to dissect."

"You can refer him to Student Services yourself, you know. You don't have to wait for him to go to them. They'll chase him up."

"Maybe I should."

"Call Sian Cutler," Patrick said. "She's brilliant."

"Okay," I said, "I'll look into it."

"Sometimes they really get to you. But you can only do so much."

I grimaced. "I first met him, I thought, arrogant rich kid. My own prejudice, you know. But I see the mess he's in, and I feel just so sorry for him, and really feel like I've let him down."

"I don't believe that for a minute."

"I can't let him drop out."

"He's the real deal then?"

"Yeah. I think he probably is."

"Well, then he'll write it anyway, won't he, MA or no MA."

"But if he drops out it'd really mess up my retention rates."

Patrick laughed. "So cynical already?"

I shrugged. "I'm a quick learner."

SIAN CUTLER
STUDENT SERVICES

Re: Nicholas Palmer

We have no record of an enquiry or referral from anyone from that department regarding this individual at this time.

When students are referred to us, or concerns are raised about a student, a file is opened on that student, even if no further action is taken.

We have no such file on record for Nicholas Palmer.

I should have realised that tutorials would overrun. That students arrive late, or won't leave when you need them to. That you should schedule breaks and buffers to accommodate this and your own need for coffee or the loo. I'd seen Karen and Richard and I was chewing my teeth and trying not to look at my watch while listening to Meryl, who couldn't believe that we were already a third of the way through the MA, everything was going so fast, so much had happened but there was still so much to do. An MFA back home in the States was actually two years, which gave you time to grow, as a person, as well as learn, as a student, and learning mattered but growth was so important, wasn't it; and here, she felt she was learning, but she wasn't sure that she was actually *growing* . . . I wasn't sure how I could do anything to help with that. I reminded her we still had a good way to go, and the work seemed to be going well, and that what we were doing here was about a lifetime's writing and not just about this one year.

"Yes, yes, I know that. But—"

Steven loomed outside, peering in through the glass panel. He came in without knocking as soon as Meryl got to her feet, so there was an awkward jostling and shuffling in the narrow space as they negotiated their way past each other.

"Steven."

"Meryl."

He was all professional, straight from the office, suited and pinstriped and creased straight up and down. I asked him, with some apprehension, how he thought things were going. And he was blithe and businesslike about it. He had written twenty thousand words, which meant he had another forty thousand words to go and that was where he expected to be by now: a third of the way through, of both the course and the novel. On target, so. Happy enough. As he spoke he looked round my little office with a frown. I watched as the thought solidified: that getting published might not mean being handed the keys to a magical kingdom, but rather to a dim little office considerably less salubrious than his own. No mention of the classroom conflict, though—maybe some of what Nicholas had said had hit home. I didn't bring it up.

Tim was ebullient. He was psyched, he told me; the writing was just pouring onto the page. Was he annoyed with himself for not submitting more to class? Of course he was. But was he raring to go for next term? You betcha. He felt he'd really just hit his stride, and was insanely keen to get the guys' feedback on as much as possible in the new year. I told him I was relieved to hear it. I reminded him to follow guidelines in the coming term, with regard to length and frequency of submissions. But he was already brushing that aside—yeah, of course, yeah, no worries . . . ; anything you had to say he already knew; he was way ahead of you . . . Thing was, he now had ten thousand words or so that hadn't been looked at in class yet, so could I just take a glance over the Christmas holidays? I could email him any feedback. That would be fine.

"Aah, no, sorry. I can't."

He baulked.

"Thing is, if I did this for you, I'd have to offer the same thing to everyone, and I just don't have the time."

"Yeah, no, course I get that, totally I do."

My eye was caught by movement outside the door. Nicholas was leaning against the wall there: the sleeve of a battered grey jacket, and his quarter profile were visible through the glass panel.

"That's my next one now."

Tim peered over his shoulder. "Oh, Nick, cool."

He waved, and went unnoticed; he leaned back to tap the glass. Nicholas was waved in; he entered, taking out earphones. He accepted a fist bump as Tim got up to leave.

"So, party then," Tim said. "Should be cool."

I blinked, assumed this was not to do with me.

"Dude, you did tell her about the party?"

"I was just going to."

Tim teetered on the verge of going but didn't go. A small end-of-term gathering for the MA crowd, Nicholas told me. Nothing major. Round at his gaff. Would I come?

"Everyone's invited?"

"Yeah. Everyone. So you have to come."

It sounded like a disaster. "I can't really get out in the evening; there's my little boy, you see."

"You can get a babysitter."

"I don't know any round here yet."

"I'll sort it for you."

"Huh?"

"There's always cards up in the village shop window, advertising. I'll text you some numbers."

"The village shop?"

"Yeah. You know it."

"I'm just surprised you do."

"I'm staying with my folks out there, at the moment. Place near the river."

"Oh," I said. I remembered then, through rain-streaked window, a glimpse of jacket and jawline as the bus pulled away. Had he seen me struggling with pushchair and tired child? Did we pass his place when we went to throw stones in the river? Did he overhear me talking nonsense to Sammy, or on my mobile complaining to Mark about work?

"Give me your number," he said.

I recited my number, watched him tap it into his phone. I felt flustered. He flashed me a look, tapped in something else, and my mobile, in my bag, went *ping*.

"There you go," he said. "Now you've got my number too."

"Thanks," I said.

Nicholas turned to his friend. "Tim, mate?"

"Yes."

"Off you fuck, now."

Tim hesitated, then decided to laugh.

"No worries. Laters."

"We should get started." I busied myself with papers, shuffling Nicholas's feedback sheet to the top. I felt hot. "You've had a bit of a tough term," I said.

"The work is going well, so." A shrug.

We talked about the challenges of the rule he'd set himself, about how he was going to shape and frame reality, because the reality of reality was that not everything could be accommodated. That the human brain itself is constantly editing—otherwise we'd be incapacitated by sensory overload, lost in a constant LSD trip. And was there a worry that he might actually catch up with himself, with his current lived experience, and if so what would he do about that? In brief, did he know where he was going?

It would fall into place, he was confident of that. There was a kind of inevitability about it by now; he was following his narrative thread through the labyrinth, towards the Minotaur. He'd just let it happen.

I asked, "What did happen, Nicholas?"

He half shook his head.

"To her?"

It was none of my business. He turned to look out of the window, silvery eyes on the grey evening. "I don't want to talk about it," he said. "You know that. Talking makes it all shrivel up and shrink."

"Just in terms of the story. So I know. Is that something you're going to give us? Or will you leave it unresolved?"

"Don't try and skip ahead," he said. "You have to give it time."

Which made me glance at my watch: a thrill of panic. "Oh my God. I've really got to go."

"We were about done anyway."

The motion-sensitive lights rippled on down the length of the corridor. I struggled into my coat, fumbled my keys, locked up behind us.

"You can always call by my office hour," I said, "if we missed anything."

I paced alongside his easy lope until we came to my turning.

"Well, goodnight."

"I'm coming your way."

There was nothing out there but empty offices, the nursery, the perimeter road, carparks.

"Where you headed?" I asked.

"You don't want to be walking on your own after dark."

Then we were out at the perimeter road and there was the pedestrian crossing and the hobbitty nursery building, and I didn't know what to say to him apart from "Thank you."

"So I'll text you," he said. "About babysitters."

"And your address too, cos I'm not sure which house?"

"Will do."

I started onto the crossing. Then he called out after me: "Hey."

I glanced back.

"Safe home, yeah?"

I raised a hand to him. I arrived at nursery at the very last moment, and scooped Sammy up and squeezed him and shoved him into his coat. We rattled down the underpass for the bus. I'd expected, half-expected Nicholas to be waiting there, but he wasn't. The bus was almost empty, and smelt of booze and damp. I stowed the pushchair and sat Sam on my knee, and held him close, and kissed his head, and felt—well, unsettled. By Nicholas's kindness and his brusqueness and his arrogance. By the tangle that he was. I remembered that text he'd sent me earlier, and fished out my phone. It just said

Hey there you.

And that made me smile. Reaching round Sammy's small warm body, I texted back.

Hey there you yourself.

I didn't refer him to Student Services. I thought, *He doesn't want to talk; why try and make him. The writing helps.*

MERYL E. SHARRATT

Complaint

One thing you should know about me straight off is I'm greedy. I want everything. I want to work my ass off and write the most amazing books, and to goof off and go dancing or bake in the sun on a beach. I'm a complete cynic and a desperate romantic. I can be so selfish and I can be so generous too. And I'm persistent; I'll pursue something like a Terminator if I really want it. And more than anything I want *experience*, I want to clutch it to me stuff it down my throat make it part of me, all these opposites and everything in between. I know that that's crazy-impossible. Life can't be like that, not all the time. That's why I write. That's why I came here.

This place, the university, the town: it has a very British kind of melancholy and I drank it in. There was a charm to the damp campus, the narrow dorm room, the way the bed creaked and the spots where Blu-Tack had pulled the paint from the plaster, the way someone had doodled initials—MW 4 EJ—on the underside of the bookshelf above the bed and drawn a heart around it, and you could only see that when you're lying down. I loved the way the rain glittered on the windowpanes and pooled on walkways and dripped through the awnings and here and there the ceilings too. I was not unhappy here. This was a place for meditation, for introspection, for kind of cerebral solitude which was, at first, productive. I would go days writing and reading and not speaking to a soul, holed up in my room with my novel or trailing out to get coffee or food. I'd sit in cafés working on my novel. I'd sit in the library working on my novel. For a while I was very much alone here, with my novel, and I loved that way of being.

I loved it but only because I knew it wasn't forever. This was a strictly time-limited situation. Once the course was over and I'd handed in my dissertation, I was off to travel Europe. My plan was to keep going until I found wherever Paris in the 1930s was these days—I was hearing good things about Croatia—then I'd settle there and live cheaply until I started making decent money as a writer. And then I'd go wherever I wanted.

It was a big deal, me making that decision, coming here. I don't just mean the money; I mean love. I'd had to gnaw off the part of me that was trapped back home, in Halfway. The wound was still raw, and hurting, but I knew I'd done the right thing. If I'd stayed there, with him, gotten all settled and comfortable, I was never going to be the writer that I was going to be. After that, I was determined not to let myself get tangled up with someone again. I was done hurting people, including myself. I had places to go. Things to do. Books to write. Someone to be.

But Nicholas was a locked box and that got me; I kept tugging at it, tweaking it, trying it from different angles. If I wasn't careful I would soon be sticking a knife in to lever it open . . . I asked the others—Tim and Karen—whether they'd figured him out, had they managed to prise the lid off yet?

"That's just the way he is," Tim said with a shrug.

"But doesn't it bother you?"

"What would bother me?"

"That he seems, I don't know, so closed off, so self-contained?"

"You don't know many English people yet do you, sweetheart?" Karen laughed.

"What do you mean?"

"Americans are peaches, soft and sweet on the surface, tough at heart. The English are coconuts: there's sweet stuff there, only you have to make a bit of an effort to get to it."

Maybe it was that, the difficulty of getting into anything sweet that made me so determined. If he had been a peach I'd have eaten him in three bites and been done. I wouldn't have felt the need to keep tapping, knocking, banging my head against the shell. In class I'd get so little from him. I mean, she clearly thought that he was the star; she made that obvious from the beginning. He got so much attention. I guess he deserved it, but that doesn't mean that other people didn't deserve it too.

We'd be in the college bar, and I'd get goosebumps just standing next to him. I'd catch myself daydreaming about him, when I should have been daydreaming my novel. It occurred to me that if I wasn't careful I'd be tangled up again. I told myself getting tangled up with another writer could, paradoxically, be liberating.

I started hating those after-class drinks. We'd just be there together but not together, and everyone except me would get drunk, and I'd be alone sipping a soda and wondering what was so funny. Eventually I got up the nerve to say to him we should go for coffee sometime, just the two of us, so that we could talk, since it was impossible to really talk in the noise and crush of the college bar. Maybe we weren't entirely on the same page at that point; maybe he thought of me more as a friend, but I could take that. Like I said: greedy and persistent.

"Study group," I suggested. "Just you and me. Special study group for the gifted and talented."

He laughed. We started going for coffee. The talk was always about work. He never opened up to me about any other aspect of his life, although I knew his writing was strongly autobiographical. I remember he told me that a work of art, in whatever form, should say something about the world *and* something about the form itself, whether it be the novel or sculpture or music or painting. And that anything that doesn't do that wasn't art. And that that, ultimately, was what he was trying to do. Make a work of art.

It wasn't what I was trying to do. I was just trying to tell a story. And along the way, to process my own experience of growing up where I grew up, of high school bullies, of feeling like an outsider and a freak, that kind of thing. I wanted to make some sense of my own existence. I began to wonder if maybe I should have thought the whole thing through more, before I even started. If I should have aimed higher. Was good enough. I began to wonder if I was wasting my time.

After those coffee dates, I'd sit and chew a pen, or stare at my computer screen, the little cursor line flashing in and out of existence and the words not coming. Or I'd write a sentence, or a paragraph, reread it, and delete. In the face of his certainties, I lost all conviction.

I kept submitting work to class, though. Earlier work, stuff I'd written while I was still home. Stuff that I was now cutting away at with a scalpel every day, so that it got leaner and leaner. I'd cut away the fat, and the flesh, and was down to the bones. I hated it.

And she didn't even notice that I wasn't writing. She didn't even care. What mattered was him, and his work, because she saw that he was special. Nobody else was ever going to get noticed.

I'd lie on my bed and stare up at that scrawled heart on the underside of the bottom shelf and daydream future-us. Maybe I should have started writing about that, the two of us living in Split, or Dubrovnik or Zagreb, or wherever Paris in the '30s would be by then, writing side by side at separate bistro tables, me acquiring a taste for tiny bitter coffees, and becoming the new Simone de Beauvoir and he my Jean-Paul Sartre. I certainly spent more time in that imagined future than in the world of my supposed novel.

And if I didn't get the novel written, then I wasn't a writer at all, let alone Simone de Beauvoir.

I started to have fantasies about dying. I wasn't actually suicidal, I'm pretty sure of that, but the way he grieved for that other girl for years, feeding the pain and feeding off the pain, made me jealous of her, of the way that she was perfect and dead, whereas I was imperfectly alive.

And then there was that day he ran out of class. The discussion had gotten out of hand, and he had had enough, and left. Frankly I didn't blame him; sometimes the best thing you can do is take yourself out of a situation. I'd wanted to go after him, but she told me straight-out not to. I guess it was her responsibility to make sure he was okay. But then it was also her responsibility to manage classroom discussions in such a way that students didn't feel they had to run out of the room. If she'd gotten that right, none of the rest of it would have happened.

As it was, she didn't manage to persuade him back for the second half of class. We just went on without him, as if it wasn't that big a deal. She was a little snippy with the troublemakers but that was it.

I went looking for him as soon as class was over. Maybe I could "just run into" him in the bar, or a coffee shop, or in the library, or in the student union shop. But I didn't. Disheartened, I gave up and went back to my dorm room and made myself a cup of hot tea and lay down on my bed. I was pretty unhappy right then, but the walls are so thin here and my neighbors are not what you would call *congenial,* so I didn't make a noise about it. After a while, there was a knock on my door. I got up and straightened myself out.

"Come in."

He stood there, soaked to the bone, bruised-looking. He had come to me. When things were really bad, it was *me* he wanted.

"Come in," I said, "come in."

I handed him my towel and he held it, just stood there dripping. I took it from him and stood on tiptoe to rub his dark tousled hair.

"Are you okay?" I asked.

He shook his head to clear it. "No." Then after a minute he asked me, "Are you?" noticing maybe the smudginess around my eyes.

"No."

He touched my face. His hand was cold, and my cheek was hot. I leaned in to him, and then—well, let's draw a veil over that. The detail isn't relevant in this context. What matters is to state, for the record, what we were to each other. To have it acknowledged that we were together, that we mattered to each other. It was early days, but it was real.

That last week or ten days or so of the Michaelmas term, he'd find me in the library in the afternoon, and we'd head back to my dorm room. The rain dripping outside. We were discreet. No one realized, except for maybe those uncongenial neighbors; we didn't have another class till January and I certainly didn't tell anyone in the MA group; I didn't need anyone's validation. We sent texts back and forth, like little love notes. We spent hours in my dorm room. There was always the chance of running into him on campus. That brightened those rainy days.

And then this party.

As far as I was concerned it was him and me in our little bubble, and the rest of them were on a scale of irrelevance from "nice enough" through to "complete pain in the ass" and I could take them or leave them. I had gotten the impression that he felt much the same way. So I couldn't fathom why he would drag the whole crowd out to his family home, and host a party there.

But like I said: *greedy, determined,* so I figured I'd take it in stride, because it would be an experience.

Karen said she'd give me a ride, which was sweet of her, but then she was late, and I'm always early for everything. I was jigging and fidgeting in the entrance hall of my building for fifteen whole minutes before she pulled up in her little soda can on wheels.

We swung out of campus the back way, heading into the countryside. We raced down narrow winding lanes, high hedges flickering past in the headlights. She kept wrenching the stick shift around; I had no idea how much trouble they were. The countryside was so empty; there seemed to be nothing for miles except the occasional home. The rain swept the windshield; we went grinding and dipping over the hills, weaving around curves, those big looming moors above us like something out of a Brontë novel. I tugged my good dress down. I don't like wearing dresses; I look like a boy in a dress, all shoulders and knees. But it was a party, at his house, and that seemed like a special occasion. I wanted him to see I'd made an effort.

We reached a village—a scattering of homes, a pub, school, village store—Karen made the turn and we drove down the street and pulled onto a gravel drive. The car crawled up it, then stopped outside this house. Karen whistled.

"Is this it?" I asked.

"SatNav says yes."

It was the kind of home you would expect the Bennet sisters to trip out of in an adaptation of *Pride and Prejudice*. It was set back from the road; there were high laurel hedges, and the drive swept around an immaculate oval lawn. Karen pulled her little Matchbox car over and we got out and picked our way up to the door, the two of us huddled under my umbrella, Karen clutching a bottle of wine. I pressed the doorbell; I could hear it ringing inside. Dogs started to bark.

I'd had no idea Nicholas came from this kind of background. That he had money. But now the idea of it began to grow and sprout and bloom. Maybe I had been narrow-minded, thinking that European exile was the only way to live as a writer. This way of living—the steady, deep-rooted growth that came with old houses, lawns and gravel drives—could be creative too. There's something inherently authentic about *belonging*, isn't there?

"I didn't know," I said, "that it would be like this."

"Like what?"

"Like, uh, well, all BBC."

"You didn't know that Nicholas was posh?"

"No."

"Posh is written all through him, honey; like *Blackpool* in a stick of rock."

The Englishness of England still had the capacity to charm even after all these months of rain. I rang the bell again. I was shivering in that dumb dress. Karen insisted that we shouldn't wait any longer, and so we made our way along the side of the house. Climbing plants were twisted veins up the side wall; gravel crunched underfoot. We came through a side gate into a big paved yard, and the dogs, wherever they were, barked even louder. I couldn't imagine that all of this went unheard. We knocked at the back door, but still no one answered.

"Do you really think we're in the right place?" I asked.

"Yes, hon."

"Then why isn't anyone answering?"

"It's a big house; could be they've got music on."

"But he's expecting us."

"Maybe we're not his top priority."

I could have said something sharp at this, but I'm glad I didn't. She tried the door and it opened.

"Here we go."

British manners are sometimes baffling—at times excessively ornate, at others careless to the point of rudeness. I followed Karen into a huge kitchen, with a big blue stove and dark wooden fittings and a fizzing fluorescent light. The sound of voices and music took us through to a large living room. Chairs and sofas clustered by a fireplace. Nicholas was lounging with a tumbler full of ice and whiskey in his hand. He was wearing his blue sweater; it was my favorite; it brought out the color in his eyes. Tim was asking him about the Wi-Fi password, he had a specially made party playlist on his phone, wanted to get it synched up with the Sonos; but Nicholas ignored him. He'd seen me, and raised his glass and smiled, and that thrilled me. Then she leaned out from a winged armchair, and I faltered: Who invites their professor to a student party? I guess the short answer to that is *Nicholas*.

She said, "Hey there, Meryl; hi, Karen."

She got up to greet us. She was wearing a shortish skirt and thick black tights, and for once was wearing makeup—I particularly remember her dark red lipstick. She seemed unlike herself. Her work uniform of buttoned-up shirt and pants was kind of asexual, I suppose. But to tell the truth I hadn't really thought about her appearance until it changed. Until then it hadn't seemed relevant.

There was a fire burning, but the room was chilly. There were drinks and cigarettes and cans and ashtrays and smoke in the air and loud talk and music and I could still hear those poor dogs barking out there. It felt chaotic, dismal; there was no sense that someone was in charge, was hosting. I felt so far away from home.

I looked to Nicholas, but he'd gotten Tim occupied with the tech, and then after that he wrapped himself up in conversation with her; they had their heads together like they were plotting something; he was clinking that ice around in his whiskey glass like he was paid to advertise the stuff.

Karen said, "Hey, posh boy?"

He glanced around him as if to say *Whoever can you mean?*

She raised the bottle of wine that she'd brought. "Corkscrew?"

"*You* bought wine with a *cork*?"

"I did, yeah. Special occasion, innit."

He pushed himself up to his feet, and went off to the kitchen. Karen followed him. I heard her talking with him, teasingly, and his jokey replies. I wished I'd had her nerve; I would never have dared tease him; it all mattered far too much for that. Tim went after them, puppy-dogging for attention, still brandishing his iPhone.

Which left me alone with her. I perched on the arm of Nicholas's now empty chair. She lifted her wine glass in salutation. I didn't have a glass so I just smiled and nodded.

"Did Steven and Richard come?" I asked, for the sake of something to say.

"They're out back. There's a pool. I think they're seriously considering a swim." She widened her eyes. "Can you believe this place? Oh, but maybe everyone has a pool where you come from?"

"Not really, no. It gets kinda cold."

She nodded exaggeratedly, "Of course, of course. Mustn't generalize."

"How is your son?" I tried. "Does he mind being left?"

"Oh, he's fine; he was quite excited actually. The baby-sitter seems uber-competent. Teenage girls are just brilliant, aren't they? We should let them run the country. They'd soon have it all sorted out."

If I can't give myself to something one hundred percent, then I don't see the point of doing it at all. That's why I don't plan to have children; it wouldn't be fair. I figure, if you have a career, a social life and a child, one of them is bound to suffer. If not all.

When Nicholas and Karen returned, he handed me a glass of wine that I hadn't asked for. Richard and Steven came in from the back of the house clutching beer cans, and seemed positively jolly: alcohol's not always so good at smoothing over differences; sometimes it emphasizes them. I took a sip of wine to be polite. It made me wince. I tried again. I was really trying. I was trying to fit in. Trying to belong. I looked to Nicholas, wanting his attention. In the end I had to put my hand on his arm.

"Are your folks not home?"

"Not tonight."

"Where they at?"

"Just. Away."

"You been by yourself awhile out here?"

"I suppose."

"It's just, I could have joined you."

"I've been writing. Working flat out. So."

"Of course, me too. Yeah."

He shifted and my hand fell off his arm, and he lifted the wine bottle and refreshed people's glasses, and returned to his conversation with our professor.

I guess this is a digression, but I wanted to show that I expected—and was due—something different from him. I didn't ask for much. I didn't want his heart and soul and hand in marriage; I only wanted a grain of kindness. But that night, he just kept shutting me down.

I wasn't used to English drinking. I'm still surprised by it sometimes. The determined pouring of alcohol into the body, the deliberate achievement of drunkenness: I couldn't see the appeal of it at all. That's one thing I am not greedy for, maybe because it's so limiting. Alcohol parks you in the constant present, makes you unsubtle, makes you repeat yourself. At least Karen was taking it easy. She sipped at one glass of white wine, rather than chugging it down like the others. She was driving, so I could rely on her.

I took myself out to the kitchen and helped myself to a soda from the refrigerator. It was a kind of Italian lemonade, and it turned out to be really sour. I stood at the kitchen island and heard the voices and the music from the living room, and the dogs barking outside, and I sipped the lemonade and choked on disappointment. Was just a little sweetness too much to ask of something that was, after all, supposed to be sweet?

I shook myself, then went back through. Karen spotted the soda can.

"Ooh, are you not drinking, hon?"

"I don't really, no."

"That lets me off the hook then," she said, and rifled in her bag. She handed me her keys, a big jingling bundle, with a furry pompom and a Smurf dangling off them. "You don't mind, do you?"

"Driving? Oh-kaaay," I said, and weighed the keys in

my hand. Those narrow winding roads, and everything on the wrong side. And that persnickety stick shift. Karen slugged her wine back, and refilled her glass eagerly.

Soon it was like everyone else was in on a joke that I didn't get and they weren't going to explain. Someone would say something and they would all just find it crazy funny, and I'd look from one reddened laughing face to another, and wonder what the big deal was. And then I remembered that they were drunk, and I was sober, and that was it. I wanted to go back to my dorm room. I wanted to actually *be* alone, rather than just feel it, because that would be less lonely. I elbowed Karen but she just gave me a sloppy grin and got right back into whatever earnest conversation she was having with Richard.

"We should play a game," I suggested.

"What game?"

"Scrabble? That's literary."

"We don't have a Scrabble set."

"That's disgraceful. How can you call yourself a civilized human being and not have a Scrabble set?" This was her, recrossing her legs.

"Who said I called myself a civilized human being?" Nicholas countered. Tim guffawed. I didn't like the way Nicholas was looking at her. But she didn't seem to mind. She smiled.

She said, "Good point."

She seemed at once blurred and emphatic. Drunk as any of the rest of them. Drunker, even. It was disappointing, to be frank.

"Sardines," Karen suggested.

"Too energetic."

"Spin the Bottle?" Steven offered.

"Are you kidding me?"

"There's a snooker table out back," Tim said. "Anyone fancy a game?"

"Oh, I've never played," I said, lighting on this. Tim nodded to me, insecure and grateful. I really felt for him. But I felt for me more.

"Billiards," Nicholas said, just enjoying the word.

"Language!" Tim guffawed again.

I'd never played, but I'd seen it played. And for a moment I entertained the thought of a closeness and warmth with Nicholas as he taught me how. The lean of our bodies against each other. And then I told myself to grow up, get real; wasn't this what I had insisted on myself? No getting tangled up again. It wasn't Nicholas's fault if he felt the same way.

She said, "I'm not playing."

"Why not?"

"I'm just no good at that kind of thing. And I don't do anything I'm not good at."

"Is that true?"

She held Nicholas's gaze and smiled. "Yep. Don't let that stop you, though; you go on ahead."

"Truth or Dare then," Nicholas said.

Mostly people say yes to Nicholas. You might hold out for a while, but people tend to fall into line.

"So, Meryl," he asked me. "What'll it be. Truth or Dare?"

And this was the moment, the communication that was just for me. I melted at it, in spite of myself, in spite of all the disappointments of the evening. It was an intimate question, because of what we were to each other, what we knew that nobody else knew.

I said, "Dare."

He was still looking at me, half smiling, and I blinked

and looked away. Everything about him seemed heightened, overblown, projected. "So what'll we dare young Merry here then?" he asked.

I ended up having to extemporize a blues song about writing my novel.

I wonder now if he did it deliberately to embarrass me; it did embarrass me, but I did my best to pull it off. *Woke up this morning, my computer done crashed. Hard drive's corrupted, massive data loss. I'm calling China, I'm calling half a world away.* . . . They laughed themselves silly, because they were drunk, and being sober in the company of drunks is like having a superpower.

When it was *her* turn, she opted for a truth. I imagine she expected it to be more dignified than a dare. I'm always hungry for something useful: I would've asked about the realities of getting her book published, about getting an agent. The kind of stuff we haven't touched on in the master's at all, and is, frankly, almost equally as important as the writing itself, because it's no good having a fantastic piece of writing if you don't know what to do with it when it's finished. Not that I was writing, at the time; I was cutting.

It was on the tip of my tongue to ask her, but then Nicholas spoke before I could spit it out.

"So, your boyfriend?" Nicholas asked.

"My husband," she corrected.

"Husband, even better. What's the deal there?"

"There's no deal."

"So why's he not around?"

"He's around quite a lot, actually," she said. "But he works in London, and I work up here, so."

"That's one hell of a commute."

She inclined her head. Her throat was coming out in big pink blotches. "It's not that unusual. London being what it is. And work being what it is. These days."

"But you must find it difficult, all by yourself out here."

"I'm not all by myself. I've got Sammy."

"Oh yes, of course. How old is he now?"

"Three."

I glanced from her to Nicholas and from Nicholas to her. The way that they were looking at each other. Her cheeks angry-red, eyes fierce; his expression cool and composed. He *looked* cool and composed, but I felt a stab of concern for him. Whatever else he was, he was vulnerable. That's one thing nobody understands about him: his vulnerability.

Richard announced that he had drunk as many beers as he could reasonably drink and still drive back, and so he and Steven would now make tracks.

"Maybe we should all hit the road," I said.

"Ah no, you have to see the lake," Nicholas said.

"You have a lake?" she asked. "You have a swimming pool *and* a lake?"

"Yeah?"

She just laughed and shook her head.

We slung on raincoats and took umbrellas from the stand; we walked down wet lawns, flashlights skimming across the grass. Trees stood out against the sky; the pond—it was a pond, not really a lake—not a lake by American standards anyway—was in a hollow at the foot of the lawns. There was a pale mound on the central island, which Nicholas said was a pair of swans. I felt that this was, more than ever before, really and deeply England, and that I would never be at home here, and that my heart was breaking.

The jetty was slippery underfoot. I picked my way down it in my heels, my arm hooked through Nicholas's. He handed over the umbrella stem and got out his cigarettes. He offered them around and we all shook our heads, except for her. She paused and then said, "Better not." She wrapped her arms around herself, looked out across the lake and shivered. She yawned deeply.

"Tired?" Nicholas asked.

She nodded through the last of her yawn, and then said "Always." She looked at her watch.

"The night is young," Nicholas said, with a gesture to the rain, the dark, the dimpled pool ahead of us.

"But I am not," she said.

"Ah now," said Karen, slightly slurred. "Don't you start that. You're just a slip of a thing."

"Who right now really needs her bed," she said. "I'd best be off."

If she left now, I thought, then maybe I'd get Nicholas back. I couldn't blame him for wanting to charm our professor, or even for being a little fixated on her. But with her gone, we could curl up in front of the fire, just the two of us, and watch the flames. If it wasn't for Karen and Tim; I couldn't exactly curl up on the couch with Nicholas while Karen and Tim were still around, knocking back drinks and yammering. Maybe one of them could drive the other home, but they were each as drunk as the other . . . Whichever way I played it I couldn't quite make it work out so that Nicholas and I were alone together for the night and it was good.

Then Nicholas said—and remember, this was to his *professor*—quite casually, "I'll see you home."

"That's okay," she said. "I know the way."

"It's dark," he said.

"I'll be fine. I brought a torch."

"I'll give you a ride," I offered. "It's no trouble."

"Ah, fresh air, though, to clear the head. That's what's in order," Nicholas said.

They argued it back and forth between them, but he won. He always does. But then, she didn't try that hard.

I watched them crunch down the drive under a big shared sports umbrella, setting the dogs off barking again. The ground turned to Jell-O underneath my feet.

"We'd best be off too," Karen slurred, a hand to the door frame.

"We'll wait until Nicholas gets back."

She pulled a face. "Really?"

"Really."

She sighed, and went inside.

The kitchen was cold; the light buzzed. Karen filled the kettle clumsily and looked in cabinets. I chewed my nails. I wasn't supposed to feel jealous. Jealousy wasn't supposed to come into this.

Karen leaned into the refrigerator; the light made her face glow white.

I said, "Is that all right, to do that in somebody else's home?"

"I don't think this is really anybody's home."

"What do you mean?"

She just shrugged.

"You don't think Nicholas really lives here?" I asked. "You think he broke in and all this, it's, what, a lie?"

"I think he lives here *and* it's all a lie."

"You're not making sense."

"Just look around you. All the horrible expensive furniture. This horrible expensive kitchen. There's a great big fuck-off Aga there, but it's not on, I bet it's *never* on; there's no warmth to it. There's no warmth to this house at all. I'll grant you it's a house—a very expensive house—but it isn't really a home."

She gave a little shudder, and rubbed at the back of

her neck, and said that was all she had to say about it. She made us hot tea, and we went back into the living room and found Tim there asleep in an armchair. She put more wood on the fire, but it must have been damp because it didn't burn too well. We sipped our tea and watched the fire smoke and listened to the rain. She seemed significantly more sober. She yawned.

"You know, I think I'm probably okay to drive."

"What's keeping them so long?" I wondered.

"It always seems longer when you're the one waiting."

She rested her head against the wing of the chair and when I glanced at her again she'd dozed off. The rain was churning in the guttering and tumbling down the downpipes. I dozed off too, my head pillowed on my folded arms.

I woke to the dogs barking. I heard a door slam, and the sound of him moving around the kitchen. The fire had died out, the new wood unburned, but the lamp was still on. I peered at my watch; it was almost two a.m. I felt cold and nauseous. I got up and smoothed my hair. I nudged Karen with a toe; she blinked awake.

He came into the room. I remember his expression. The composure. The lid firmly on the box. "Still here?"

Tim stirred and woke and wiped his face. "Hey, dude."

"What's wrong?" I asked Nicholas.

"What do you mean, what's wrong?"

The way he said it, it was like the shard of ice in the boy's heart.

"Where've you been?"

"Just saw her home."

"It took forever."

"It took as long as it took."

"Maybe you shouldn't drink so much."

"Is that what you think?"

"You're not a pleasant drunk."

"You're not so pleasant sober right now."

Karen got to her feet. "Gimme back the keys, hon," she said. "Let's be off."

"It's okay," I said. "I'll drive."

And so I drove us back to campus in a storm of misery, crunching gears and taking curves too fast and there was one moment when we rounded a curve and headlights glared straight at us and Karen squealed and I swerved and the oncoming car blared its horn at us.

"Christ on a bike, Meryl!"

"Sorry."

But I wasn't sorry; the oncoming headlights had drawn me towards them and I had wanted that crunch, the smash, the annihilation. If it hadn't been for the people in that oncoming car, and Karen sitting next to me in the passenger seat, and Tim in the back, swaying and cursing and swallowing spit, I might have just closed my eyes and held on to the steering wheel and let the worst happen. Then I would have joined her, his dead girl, and been perfect too.

But I was more careful for the rest of the trip, though Karen still clutched at her seat and hissed and winced, and would say from time to time, gently: "I'm sure I'm safe by now," or "Pull over, if you want? I can drive."

And I'd shake my head and crunch the stick shift around. I was determined to do it. I would master this stupid, strange, needlessly complicated thing, that you're just expected to understand without anyone ever really explaining it to you. I wasn't going to let it beat me.

And so we got back in one piece though my hands were shaking and my heart was pounding. We dropped Tim off at his dorm and I drove on a little further to mine, and pulled over. Karen sat there in the passenger seat, a hand on her heart. She gave me such a look.

"Are you going to be okay, love?"

"Yeah, sure, why not?"

She had that befuddled look that people have when they've been drinking, but she also looked so concerned for me, and that made me blink back tears. I felt bad for nearly killing us.

"For what it's worth," she said.

"What?"

"Forget about him. Before it gets too messy. He was never going to make you happy."

"He did make me happy."

"Maybe, for a little bit. But not in the long run. And maybe it was you making you happy. Bouncing your own happiness off him. Not him doing it himself."

"Bullshit."

"Take my word for it, love, you're better off without. In ten years' time, you'll struggle to remember his name."

"Oh fuck you, Karen."

I slammed out of the car and ran; I tumbled up the stairs and into bed in a fit of tears. I woke up in the morning chilled to the bone and still wearing last night's dress, last night's makeup smeared with tears onto my pillow.

I didn't have an ounce of doubt that the two of them were together, and that night was the night that it really happened, that things changed between them. I didn't blame him; it wasn't his fault, and it wasn't, strictly speaking, a betrayal. We had never said what could and couldn't happen with other people; we'd never said that we would be exclusive, but then I'd never thought there would be a need to lay it out so explicitly.

I had no trouble understanding what she saw in him—

his looks, his youth, his talent—I can understand the temptation. What I could not understand was what he saw in her. Presumably he decided to hitch his wagon to her star, at more or less the same moment I realized her star was really just space junk falling back to earth. He didn't have the courage, he didn't have the faith to see what *we* could have done together, me and him. What we both had was *potential*. And the thing about potential is that it has a use-by date. And that, I think, was his failure, more than anything else. That was the betrayal, that he didn't see what we could have been. I blame him for his lack of faith, but I don't really blame him for anything else. I blame her.

I was drunk. Suddenly, really quite drunk.

And I didn't drink that much that evening. Just a couple of glasses of wine. Maybe three. I don't know how I ended up so blurred and slurry.

He wouldn't let me walk home alone. I didn't want his company, didn't want any company at all. But he kept insisting, and I went along with it. It seemed quicker, easier to give up, to stop saying no.

He brought a good torch—a hefty Maglite, a different beast entirely from my faint pocket-sized thing—and a decent umbrella, and so I was better equipped on the way home than I had been on the way down.

He held the umbrella and offered his arm to me, and I took it, because it seemed easier than bumping along side by side unlinked. I held the torch. We walked up the main street and past the shop and school and pub and up the hill following its beam. The rain flickered through the light, drummed on the umbrella skin and soaked through my boots. The fresh air was cool on my face.

He talked. I remember a stream of words, a hallucinatory dream-logic coherence while the water pounded on nylon and hissed on the tarmac. I remember the trees laced overhead and my wet feet and the drag of his arm and his voice beside me, just above me, telling me how he was sent off to boarding school when he was seven, how he couldn't even tie his own shoelaces, how you learned to cry quietly and soon learned not to cry. *It was like my heart was cut right out of me.* Desperately lonely but never alone, except in his own head. And when he did come home it wasn't home, everything was now parched, arid; everything was separate as statues in a desert and the air was full of unsaid things, things like grit, like stones in the air; hard and jagged and stinging. There was Gideon before him and there always would be Gideon before him, an older brother who sailed over every obstacle and made money casually, heaps of it, mountains, and was getting married, was accumulating things, was perfectly content and got on with filling the air with more rocks and grit and things.

Understand me, he was saying. *Know this about me. This is what I need you to know before I can be understood.*

I listened and nodded and thought that it was important to try to understand.

He told me about local kids playing rounders on the village green, the long dusk; him lingering on the bench with a cigarette, then waved into the game. The look of her, the way she swung for a ball, so focussed and fierce, and the thwack of connection. It was instinct and accident: he caught her out, stood there with the ball stinging his palm and she shook her head and laughed. Ask him before that moment and he'd have said he didn't believe in love at all, thought it was a lie people told each other and themselves, that it was a lie that calcified into just more grit, more stones in the air between them. Ask him after that evening on the village green, and he knew differently. That September she started at the local college and in October he was due to leave for Oxford, but they had an understanding. He left for Oxford but he didn't leave her, he'd have never left her. He doesn't know what his parents said or did or what her family said or did, but after that it all went to shit. He blames them. He blames himself. He blames her. She should have trusted him. Even if nobody else did. She knew better.

He looks back on that time, the aftermath of her death, and it is like looking into a pit. He considers the person he was then, and that person is a stranger. He was not himself. The only thing that kept him going was the anger.

Anger pulled him back together, got him through it. Anger helps.

And all that he can do now, is write. He has no illusions. The writing doesn't matter, it changes nothing, but he has to do it anyway.

It was so sad, I thought. I was sorry for him; I thought I understood.

Our pace was slowing; we passed through the farmyard and the dog growled from her barrel but stayed put, green eyes reflecting torchlight back at us. I felt as though I was a step away from myself, as if this was all happening to someone else. Maybe that was the wine.

The security light flashed on, and we stood floodlit under the shared umbrella. The babysitter's little silver car gleamed beside us in the rain. He'd talked himself out, now; he stood there beside me, breathing quietly. He said, "Thank you."

I told him not to mention it.

"I thought I didn't want to talk. But somehow it's different with you."

I told him he was welcome, and I told him good night.

"Oh," he said.

I ducked out from under the umbrella, raced through the rain for the door. I glanced back as I fumbled for my keys; he was still there; he raised a hand to me. I waved back.

I pulled myself together for the babysitter, complained about the weather and commiserated about homework as she gathered up her books. Sammy had been good as gold, she said. Any time

I wanted, she said. I watched her to the car and then closed the door. I imagined Nicholas stepping up onto the grass verge to let the little car past on the narrow lane. Maybe she'd give him a lift.

The kitchen tiles were cold under my wet stockinged feet. I filled a glass at the sink, leaned against the counter to drink it. The water was good; straight out of the hills. I padded back up the corridor in damp tights, and there was a knock at the door.

A quiet knock, the kind that seems to expect that it's expected. I went to open it. I imagined that the babysitter had forgotten her scarf or textbook or pencil case. I cracked opened the door, tired but patient. Nicholas stood there, a shadow against the security light's brightness.

I glanced past him. No car: she'd gone.

"I—" he said. "I needed . . ."

I just shook my head at him, already half-asleep.

"I know," he said, "you're tired, I'm sorry."

I said that he better get off home; I'd see him some other time. I went to close the door. Night.

"I can't. Face it. Can't face them all. They're all still there, in the house and I—I should never have. Can I—" He wiped his face with a hand. "Can I just come in for a bit?"

A swoop of fatigue; a stare at my watch; it was after midnight.

"No, I don't think so, no. I'm going to turn into a pumpkin."

"I didn't know what else to do. I have nowhere else to go. I've got. No one."

And so. I creaked the door wider, and he slipped through.

"Be quiet."

He closed the door behind him. It clunked shut. I winced.

"Be *quiet*."

I waved him through to the sitting room, from where the sound wouldn't travel upstairs quite so easily.

I offered him a glass of water, cup of tea.

He perched on the sofa. "Water, please."

In the kitchen I glanced at my watch again. Sam would be up in . . . six hours? I really needed to sleep. I was shattered, and drunker than I would have thought from three glasses of wine. Should I give Nicholas a blanket and let him kip on my sofa? What would Sam make of that in the morning? He might tell his dad, and what would Mark think, Mummy's new friend coming for a sleepover . . . And there'd be a student in my sitting room when I staggered down with Sam, bed hair and a hangover in a few hours' time. And then there was the rest of them, back at the party, and what they might think of him not coming back at all . . .

I brought through a glass of water, sat down beside him and handed him the glass. He took it, didn't say anything.

"So . . ." I said.

He set the water down carefully on the floor, then he put his hand on the small of my back, leaned over me and kissed me. I sank back under the weight of him. It hadn't even crossed my mind that it would have crossed his . . . I gave him a still-friendly shove.

"Yeah. No," I said. "Sorry. Can't happen."

He cupped my shoulder, held me still, leaned in again to kiss me again. I wasn't yet afraid. But he was big. There was heft to him.

"Seriously, Nicholas. No." I twisted away.

He pushed me back against the sofa; ungentle now. I pushed back at him, not friendly either anymore. Getting scared.

"Nicholas, no. Jesus. What's wrong with you?"

He was strong, that's the thing. Bigger than me, and just insistent. There was no one to call out to. No neighbours near enough to hear me yell. Just a little boy asleep upstairs. Who could stumble sleepily downstairs into this. And I didn't want to get hit. I gave up before Nicholas did. I let it happen, because it was going to happen anyway, and this way it would happen without me getting hit.

While he fucked me I was cold and sore and tired and also

kind of bored. I waited it out. I felt old and fat and ugly and disgusting. I thought about my stretchmarks, my stubbly legs. How strange it is that being wanted can be so horrible, can make you feel so disgusting.

Afterwards, clothes pulled back into place, he stroked my cheek, and went in to kiss me again. A sticky print landed on my mouth.

And he said, "It's okay, it's okay." He touched my chin.

It really wasn't okay, it was very far from okay, but I wasn't going to say that.

"I'd better go," he said.

I heard him go out the front door and shut it behind him, heard the Yale lock slick into place. I went to the window and lifted the edge of the curtain and peered out. I went to the front door and pushed the bolts into place. I trod my way upstairs.

Sammy was breathing softly, curled on his side. The floorboard creaked and he stretched out his arms and spread his fingers, turning them with easy grace. Then his arms went soft and his left hand hung over the edge of the bed. I eased myself down to the floor and rested my face against his soft little hand. I stayed like that for ages.

I wondered whether Mark would be angry with just Nicholas, or with me, or with both of us.

I ran a bath. I creaked into the bath. I stared at the condensation and the drips and I listened to the rain outside and I felt stupid and already hungover and wondered how I was going to face Nicholas again in class. And the class: what if he told Tim, what if he told Meryl, what if he went back to the party chuckling . . . *Guess what—no, who—I've been doing . . .*

What if they all *already* knew?

I lay awake in bed for hours—flashes of earlier in the evening, flashes of the walk home, the crook of my arm around his arm, the way I'd felt then—patient, trusted, a little bored. The moments when I could have done things differently and it would not have happened. I must have slept a bit, because when I woke Sammy was standing at the bedside staring at me, and I squeaked in fear, and that made him jump, and then I reached out and wrapped my arm around him and hugged him close.

That morning I put on normal like I used to put on my mum's shoes when I was little. I jollied my little boy along. I got him dressed and gave him Weetabix and juice and helped him brush his teeth and pack his bag for nursery and I stayed out of the sitting room. I threw my toast crumbs out onto the path and the birds swooped in from the hedge; the blue-and-pink bird swayed on a branch, then dropped to the grass and picked its way around the edge of things.

We went to catch the bus and I was afraid that Nicholas might also be there, but the bus was empty when we got on and stayed empty for the first few miles; I got Sam settled on my knee and then we were on campus and walking to nursery and I was handing him over to Jenni and telling her he was in good form today, and she took my word for it, and was all smiles.

Then I was walking in the rain across the perimeter road towards the tipped-out-toy-box of the university. One foot landed in front of the other foot and the bag knocked against my hip and the doors heaved themselves open at me, which meant that I or someone at least was there, and a passer-by caught my eye and said "Morning," to me which confirmed it, but I did not feel that this thing moving through the world was me. I heard myself say hello Patrick, hello Chris, hello Mina; and then doubt the truth of even that. Then in the corridor, Lisa stopped and frowned, and reached out a hand as if to still me there.

"You okay?"

"Yes, fine, thanks. Nice jumper."

I smiled at Lisa's sweet face with her freckles and her almost auburn almost curls and her clean hands with the sweet pearly nails, her soft green jumper, and I thought how nice she was, and how clean, and that I would never be as nice or as clean as she was again.

I opened up the *Safeguarding and Harassment* document she had sent me earlier in the term, that I had shared with the MA group. I confirmed that even if I made no complaint or accusation, I was still obliged to report the events of last night to my Head of Department *at the earliest opportunity*. My Head of Department, Christian Scaife.

Later, in the campus pharmacy, I asked the pharmacist—a lean, sallow man in his fifties—for the morning-after pill, and watched the shift in his expression as he tried hard not to judge me.

It cost thirty-five quid. I paid and took the little paper bag and left and would never go in that pharmacy again, even if it was the only health care available for fifty miles. I'd sooner sew my own severed leg back on with a darning needle than go back through that door. And thirty-five pounds: I couldn't afford thirty-five pounds. I couldn't afford any of this.

I bought a coffee at Greggs and locked myself into the ladies' loo near University Reception, so as not to be near the department. Beyond the doors I could hear the receptionists chatter and the phones ring, and whenever someone came into the loos the outside noise flared louder; women came and went and peed and flushed and washed; hand dryers roared, and there were voices. I read the instructions and read them again and read them again just to be sure. I dabbed the little tablet onto my tongue and swallowed a swig of coffee. The pill was a dot of almost nothing. It was already dissolving in my swallowed coffee, in the slosh of spit and stomach acid. The hormones would be tugged into my blood and be shunted round my body, through arteries and veins and capillaries, letting my uterus know it ought to get a shift on and shed all that accommodating blood, so that if there happened to be a drifting cluster of cells falling through that inner darkness, quietly multiplying, it will be waved along on its way, and wouldn't settle down and find a home in me.

And I had a meeting to get to. I dropped the packaging into the sanitary disposal bin and flushed the loo because it seemed odd not to, and let the cubicle clang shut behind me. I caught my own eye inadvertently in the mirror when I washed my hands. I saw the hollows underneath my eyes. I got out my concealer, and smudged it on.

I thought, *You fucking idiot.*

I thought, *Fuck you, Nicholas. Lumbering me with this.*

In the meeting, I nodded and noted things down, but I could feel a separate layer of thought, like fresh water flowing over salt water, flowing over the everyday of it all. Flashes of that night. Of the blue corduroy of the sofa cushion, his mouth on me, my face turned away. Of the shove of him into me, the tear of it. The time it took. The time he took to come.

"It'd be good to hear what Creative Writing has to say about that."

And I was back in the room, Christian and Patrick and Lisa there taking minutes. Patrick was looking at me, brow creased. I tried: "I don't foresee that that would be too much of a problem." And Christian said, "Well, if it's alright with you then . . . ," and I nodded and returned to the shallow drifting waters and my hand drew spirals on the page.

"Hey."

It was after the meeting. I was unlocking my office door. Patrick jogged up to me. "Are you okay?"

"Yeah, thanks."

"Are you sure?"

I touched my face, wondering what I was giving away. "Didn't sleep well, that's all. How are you?"

"But what you agreed to back there."

I looked at him, drew a blank.

"I thought you were up to your eyeballs already?"

I just looked at him.

"You've just agreed to update the postgraduate handbook."

I swallowed. "Well, I expect it needs doing."

"Yeah, but by you?"

"Who else is there?"

"Simon should be back next term; he could look at it then."

"He'll need easing back in though, won't he?"

Patrick pulled a sceptical face.

Then I was in my office and I sat down, and then got back up again and turned the snib so that the door was locked. Patrick had gone; I wondered if I'd been rude. I felt a bit bad about that. And I felt uneasy too about the door being locked because people can still see you through the glass panel, and if they can see you then they can try the handle and find out that it's locked, and then why are you sitting there in full sight in your office with the door locked like a madwoman?

I dragged my chair so its back was up against the wall beside the door, parallel to it, so that I was out of the line of sight and the office looked empty. I put my face in my hands. Swallowed back a heave of acidy coffee; I had to keep that tablet in me. I took a few shaky breaths, then I unlocked the door, went to my computer and switched it on. The rain fell on the window and dripped from the tree and the room grew dark.

My phone pinged. I jumped. A text; the generic alert, not Mark's double ding. I scooped it out of my bag.

It was Nicholas.

Hey there you.

I dropped the phone. It hit the floor, lay there glowing. The screen dimmed and blinked out. I leaned out of my door, glanced up and down the corridor. It was dark, so I came out completely and waved my arms around, waking up the lights. They rippled on in sequence, fizzing: the corridor was empty, greasy breeze block and worn carpet from end to end. I slipped back into my office, peered out of the window and scanned the quad. Patches of orange lamplight, the glow from the porter's window. Dark arches, doorways. Nobody visible, but that didn't mean there was nobody there.

The phone pinged awake again. I scrabbled it up. Just the reminder. I fumbled to delete the message, deleted too the back and forth about babysitters that came before. That first *Hey there you*, and my chummy reply. As if deleting that changed anything. His fingertips on my cheek. His mouth on my throat.

I gathered up work to take home with me. I locked up. I passed the college bar, heaving with end-of-term festivities, the sound of Slade blaring out over yelled conversations. I kept a determined profile. I walked fast. I ducked past the porter's lodge, and there were a couple of girls in the passageway there, in team hoodies and leggings, drinking from plastic pint glasses and laughing.

Term was over. I was going back to London.

The blood started the following day. I felt it come, and took myself off to the drippy little bathroom in the cottage. I sat there with my pants around my knees, and blew a breath and laughed a little bit and teared up too. It wasn't a guarantee I wasn't pregnant, but it meant that things were probably headed that way.

On Sunday, we got the bus into town, and then the train down to London.

Our train was overcrowded, smelly, running half an hour late by the time we got on it. I managed to get our stuff stowed and find us a seat. We were diverted via the Midlands due to theft of signal wire on the West Coast Mainline. I was bleeding heavily. I had to take Sammy with me to the loo, and distract him with talk and pointing out the poster in the little room while I swiftly changed my tampon. Back in our seat, I persuaded him to put his head down against my chest and have a little sleep. I put my hand over his exposed ear, to block out the noise. He blinked slow blinks. I got out my phone, was going to text Mark. But there was another message waiting there.

You busy? Thought we could meet up. Go for coffee.

And then a blink later:

Bring the boy.

I deleted the texts. My face went red.

I waited for a patch of signal as we chuntered through Rugby. I texted Mark.

Can you meet us at Euston? Expect to get in at 4ish.

I'd just clicked Send when I remembered that school didn't break up till the end of next week, and his phone would be on silent anyway, till home time.

My son slept on my lap. My tampon swelled inside me. Time, and the train, inched on.

In the ladies' loo in Euston, I left Sammy in his buggy outside the cubicle, kept his little foot and the pushchair wheel in sight under the door. I made him sing to me the whole time too, so that we both knew that he was safe and wasn't being stolen.

By the time we got back to the flat, he had fallen asleep. The fried-chicken eaters stood up to let us pass, and I bumped him up over the threshold and lifted him out and left the pushchair in the hall, and clambered up the stairs. Mark closed his laptop and got up, and I put the boy in his father's arms, and slid my backpack off my shoulders, and lifted up the neckline of my top to peer in at the red marks where the bag straps had pressed and chafed. Mark carried Sam through to the bedroom, then came back and put his arms around me. I closed my eyes, and smelt the familiar smell of him and leaned against the familiar flesh and breathed there.

"I missed you," I said.

"I missed you too."

We just stood there, arms around each other, my head resting on his shoulder. I could feel his heartbeat. I could smell him; coffee and school and skin and a faint remainder of the morning's cologne.

"Sorry I couldn't come and meet you," Mark said.

"Don't be daft."

"You must be tired."

"Shattered."

"Sam seems to have settled anyway," Mark said. "So that's good."

He let go of me, and went through to the kitchen, and started to open a bottle of wine.

"We'll have to get him up later and put him on the loo," I said. "And get his PJs on."

"Okay, no problem; I'll do that. You hungry?"

"Always."

"We'll have to order something, sorry. Mad time at work."

"It always is, coming up to Christmas."

"Shall we get a Chinese? Or Indian? Pizza?"

"So long as it's not fried chicken," I said, "I don't mind."

He handed me a glass of wine. I took the faintest sip and set it aside, and went to fill a glass at the sink instead.

"Thirsty," I said.

He asked about work and I waved the topic away: I said it was all too boring and annoying, and I really wanted to think about something else. What's going on at school? Mark recounted the tale of a controversial promotion to the Senior Management that had the staffroom in disarray. He could see the sense in it, thought the woman—Amy, did I remember Amy?—Oh yes, Amy; a little wince at the awkward memory—would do an excellent job, but he could see that it was upsetting for those she had just leapfrogged.

I went back into the sitting room and sank down on the sofa.

He gathered up takeaway menus and followed me, dropping down beside me. I rubbed at my arms. He handed me the menus, then reached down and scooped up my feet, so that they lay across his knees.

Sammy woke round five and would not go back to sleep; he bounced and chattered and fizzed. Mark rolled over, muttered, had to leave for work in a few hours, so I dragged myself up out of bed. Pitch-black outside. I tried to mute the noise, but Sammy was so excited. It was an age, as far as he was concerned, since he'd last been here. And so I acknowledged all his rediscoveries, and tried to quieten the opening and shutting of doors, the heavy little feet on the hall floor. We had downstairs neighbours to think of, as well as Mark's day at work, and so there was nothing to do with Sammy but put the telly on quietly, and sit on the sofa with him, and lean my head back and close my eyes, and let Ben and Holly take over for a little while.

I must have dozed off; I woke to hear the sound of the shower and then Mark moving around in the bedroom. I had to break the skin on it; I had to squeeze the words out. I knew that whatever else happened, there would be some kind of absolution for me here, with Mark; that he would do his best for me, that he would be kind, because he was always kind. But he also had to go to work.

"There's a Christmas do on Friday, after school. Just drinks down the pub; you fancy it?"

"What about a babysitter?"

"You could call Esther? Or that old lady, Joyce?"

"Jean."

"I'd do it but I've got—look, I gotta go."

And he was out the door and heading down the stairs. I lifted Sammy up to my hip and we waited at the front window to wave goodbye. The mildew had grown under the windowsill. Mark paused at the crossroads, glanced back, raised a hand. We waved back at him.

There were presents to buy, and Christmas food. And everyday food too, because the fridge was more or less empty— there was just Mark's signature collection of crumby margarine, mayonnaise, open tins, and the dry end of a lemon. I supposed I should get Sammy in his pushchair. Head up to the Triangle. Greengrocers, Iceland.

Blue Anorak Man.

I gave Sammy some breakfast. He spooned Weetabix into his gob. I stared out the back window. Next-door's yard and plastic chairs and wheelie bins. The rain running down the pane, making clean lines through the city dirt. A gust of wind shook the double glazing.

"We'll stay in and make some biscuits, shall we, Sammy?" Though we'd have to pick the crumbs out of the margarine first.

An upstairs neighbour slammed a door. Raised voices, footsteps back and forth above. A young couple, Mark had said; they'd moved in back in October. Seemed to row a lot. He worried about them. But what could you do?

I told Mark that Esther had gone back to Madrid and Jean was booked up into the New Year. So Mark went to that work Christmas do without me, and I got Sammy to bed and drank a cup of night-time tea in front of a stupid film. Mark came home late and silly, and tried to tell me about some new scandal at work; he was very exercised and amused about it. I persuaded him to come to bed, and he responded enthusiastically, but when we got there he flopped a heavy arm around me, kissed my neck, then fell instantly asleep, and started to snore. I heaved his arm off me, took a blanket through to the sitting room, still couldn't sleep. If I couldn't sleep I may as well write: I got out my notebook but that took me back to Nicholas; what if I wrote what happened there, I wondered. What if I wrote that out of my system. I woke up in the morning curled up cold on the sofa with a stiff neck, notebook lying splayed face down on the floor.

Over the long Christmas weekend, Mark drank a lot. I don't know if it had always been this way, and had only become more apparent now because I didn't want to drink at all, but it certainly seemed that drinking was his main leisure activity. Nothing scandalous, not a vodka on his cornflakes kind of thing, but of an evening he drank his way steadily through whatever alcohol was to hand until it was finished. When the Christmas stock of wine was gone—and I hardly touched a drop of it—and a Christmas gift of whiskey, he discovered a liking for the cheap Cointreau knockoff I had bought in Aldi for a dessert recipe, and when that was gone, he realised that the Co-Op was open again anyway, and bought more wine. Once or twice he commented on my not drinking and I said I just didn't fancy it; I hadn't been drinking during term and didn't really feel like starting again now. He pulled a face and said I should really try to relax and enjoy myself a bit. We should enjoy ourselves together, while we could, since I'd be gone soon enough.

I said that he was right. And I really did agree with him. But I did rather feel that drinking had the opposite effect to the one he suggested. If anything, it was distancing. It kept me at arm's length. It also rendered a difficult conversation more or less impossible.

Then I noticed that he was acting differently with his phone. Again, perhaps, it was only because my attitude to mine had changed. I'd stuck it on airplane mode and only checked it when Mark was out of the flat. Mark kept his in his pocket, and when it wasn't in his pocket, it was left face down on the arm of the chair right by his hand. Sometimes it would ping and he would just ignore it for a while and then turn it over and casually glance at the screen. Sometimes he'd pick it up with superhero speed. Sometimes he'd scowl at it. And the thing is, it turns out he's easier to read when he's been drinking. It all gets a bit more caricatural, bigger.

"Who's that?" I'd ask.

He'd harrumph and say, "Really annoying. Junk." Or "Just Steve," or "Mum. Gimme a minute, better get back to her."

And then he'd maybe answer the text, frowning, like it was all too much trouble. And I realised that I didn't really believe any of it—neither what he said, nor his manner of saying it—but that I couldn't bear to pick away at it right now to find out what was going on underneath.

Sammy, though, was uncomplicatedly delightful. It was the first Christmas that he had really got, and he was just caught up in the magic of it, enraptured by the decorations and thrilled by the presents. He clearly felt it reflected well on him, all the bits and pieces he'd acquired, the cheap wooden train set and *The Pop-Up Book of British Birds*. He felt that he must be a very good boy indeed.

On Boxing Day, I met up with my dad in the park. The morning was cold and blustery. Dad had a present for Sammy—a little Playmobil set. Sammy was delighted, got out the plastic little man from the box, and started off on adventures with him round the playground. I huddled on a chilly metal bench with Dad and watched the boy bobbing the little man up the handrails and sending him rattling down the slide.

"Can we come see Mum sometime, d'you think?"

Dad made a characteristic dad-face, the lines deepening from nose to lip. "I dunno, love. I would leave it. For a bit."

I blinked. I'd been leaving it for a bit for years now: she was a stubborn old bag, my mum. Just like me. She'd torched our mutual bridges; I was determined, though, to keep heaving boulders, dropping them in the water. One day there'd be stepping stones.

"Tell her I love her," I said. "Tell her I'd love to bring Sam round whenever she wants to see him. I can just leave him there for a while. I don't have to stop there or anything."

"I will," Dad said. "I'll tell her that."

But his tone was *I don't know what good it'll do.*

I kissed Dad, and he hefted up Sammy by the armpits for a hug and kiss, the little guy all hoicked-up parka and dangling little legs. Then Sammy and I and the new Playmobil guy went back to the damp little flat and the slow hours.

On New Year's Day, locked in the bathroom while Mark swilled wine in the sitting room, I flicked my phone off airplane mode. I scrolled down the midnight texts from old friends, smiled at the giddy crepuscular snaps; paused over a message from my sister in Berlin; she said she missed me, and I welled up a little over that. Maybe we could go, the three of us, a trip to Berlin . . . And there was another text from Nicholas.

Happy New Year.

It didn't have quite the jump-scare of the first one, but still, it got to me. Those three conventional words. But what did he mean by it?

I deleted the message, just as I had all the others. And, this time, I blocked the number.

I ordered groceries online before we left London. On the mainline train we coloured in and played I Spy and wove our way to and from the on-board shop for tea and juice and biscuits, and I tried not to think of what went on in the tight-packed terraces, in that strange house by the edge of the woods, and in the cars and coaches and lorries that beetled up and down the M6. I tried not to look beyond the moment, Sam and me there, colouring in and chatting. Because what came next was a brick wall, and we were hurtling towards it, and I had no idea how to get through or over or past it.

The cottage was cool and quiet. I took some calming breaths. The Asda van drew up as I was heaving my backpack off. Sammy ran back and forth to the kitchen with supplies and made the delivery man smile.

Then I locked the door. I took our bags upstairs, and bundled up my bedspread and brought it down with me and threw it over the sofa, so that now it was covered in marled white cotton, and I didn't have to look at the blue corduroy any more. If it had actually belonged to me, and not to the landlord, I'd have chucked it out.

I lit the fire. We toasted crumpets. I sat with Sammy on the rug and there was too much space behind my back. I inched round so that I had my back against the wall. Even so, every creak and tap and drip, my head went up. I put Sammy to bed, *round and round the garden, like a teddy bear, one step, two step . . .* I went back downstairs to check the doors were locked. Then I made a cup of camomile tea and I went back up and closed the curtains and got into bed with some students' work, and started reading and making notes. There was no reason to be afraid right now. I had been foolish and pathetic and that was why things had happened the way they had happened. But I was hyper-alert to the sounds of the house, to the creak of floorboards as they eased themselves out and the scratch of branches against the eaves in the wind. There was a lock on my bedroom door, and there was a key in the lock, and I was tempted to turn it. But if I locked myself in, I'd be locking Sammy out, and so I couldn't lock my door.

The beck, shrinking in the cold, leaves fragile growths of ice on rocks and banks. The ice is thin as paper, curved like fungus. The moon is full and bright. It casts stark shadows on the crusted snow.

The discarded clothes are sculpted into hard folds, their colours bleached out by the blue-white moonlight. Boots tumbled, laces stripped, tongues frozen. In twisted singlet, tangled underwear, as though sweating through a summer night, the body lies. The skin is rimed with frost, and laced with shadow, as if this is a kind of kindness. As if this is a kind of grace.

LENT

It was like those times when you cut your hand washing up; you're just getting on with what you have to do, thoughts freewheeling, not even paying attention; then you feel the slice of a tin lid or broken glass into your hand. And then you lift up your hand and there's a clean line on your skin and then it wells blood, and then it's streaming, and you realise what you've done. The thing itself was just being what it was: you hurt yourself on it.

In Greggs, after dropping Sammy off: "Coffee please. Black. And a Belgian bun."

And there was post-Christmas Patrick with a Greggs bag in each hand, one oozing grease into the paper, the other one sticking to the iced bun inside. The usual greetings and then:

"D'you want to hear my New Year's Resolution?" he asked.

"What's that then?"

He weighed the bags against each other in his hands, as in a pair of scales. "To have a more balanced diet."

I paid for my bun and coffee and then we walked together, crossing the main square.

"Did you see the round robin about Simon?"

"No." I'd been avoiding email.

"Still unwell, unfortunately. He's been signed off for another four months."

No respite for me then. "God."

"Heavy term ahead," he commiserated. "Are you going to be okay?"

"I didn't get any writing done this vacation."

"Too busy?"

"Distracted. Just. Couldn't focus."

"Well, you have a kid, so."

But exactly *none* of my problems were Sammy's fault. I stopped halfway up the stone steps: "D'you know what, having a kid has never got in the way of my writing. Having no money has got in the way of my writing. Having a full-time job has got in the way of my writing. But the kid, no, never. He's not a problem."

"No, course he isn't. Sorry."

I opened my eyes wide so as not to let them drip and when that didn't work I said, "Hold this, would you?" and he grabbed my coffee off me and I rifled for a tissue and dabbed under my eyes.

"I'm just really tired."

"That didn't look like tired to me."

I pocketed my tissue, took my coffee back, and we climbed on, heading out of the square together.

"Is it possible that you've never seen really tired before?" I asked.

He gave me a sceptical look, but decided not to push it. We walked past walls stuck with last term's tattered fly-posters, past concrete planters full of bare earth and cigarette ends.

"First year in the job is the worst," he said.

"Good."

"It's all new, you're on a steep learning curve, you have all these new lectures to write and new seminars to plan. But once you're through it, it's just repeat until retire."

"You don't mean that."

He shrugged. "That's how some people do it."

"Right now, the only way I figure I can do everything I need to do is if I give up on sleep entirely."

He hesitated, and then he said, "I have this theory."

"Oh yes?"

"I reckon there's two types of people in the world."

"Everyone has that theory."

"Yeah, but bear with me. I reckon with one kind of person, you do them a favour and they're not comfortable till they've reciprocated in some way, or thanked you properly—like, bought you a drink, or chocolates or something."

"Yeah?"

"The other kind, if you do them a favour they'll decide that favours are just what you do. You become the person who does them favours, and they'll keep on asking and asking, and you'll keep on doing and doing, till you notice that they just don't ever reciprocate, they don't even properly thank you, and your goodwill is all used up. It's not even that they take you for a mug; they just don't recognise that you might have other things going on, that there might be other things you want to do other than favours for them."

"So what you're saying is, some people are complete narcissists?"

He laughed. "I guess. But the point is more, that you have to recognise what's happening before it's too late. Because it's not just goodwill that gets used up."

We had reached the doors into the department; his voice, I realised, had been dropping as we got closer.

"How do I look?" I turned my face to him for inspection. He didn't say anything.

"Panda eyes?" I asked.

"You look lovely," he said. He gave me a wonky smile. He said, "I hope your day gets better."

I peered at my face in my phone, touched away smudges. I

felt a little better, for Patrick saying what he'd said; for noticing. I could trust him, I felt, not to tell anyone about tears on my first day back.

The air in my office was stale, the wastepaper basket hadn't been emptied. Last term's apple cores were blue-green with mould.

I unblocked Nicholas's number. I sent a text. I told myself that it didn't matter how I felt about it; we were where we were, and it had to be dealt with. And if it meant pretending things were okay, that what had happened was okay, then that was what I would do, because that was what needed to be done.

Hey there, I wrote. *Just back. U around?*

I was reconciled to it. Close it down and draw a line—because son, and husband, and job, and the need to get on with things.

And then I lifted the wastepaper basket and took it down the corridor to the kitchen, and dumped last year's rubbish in the bin.

Chemistry

He knows her.

This is the difference no this is just one of the differences that marks him out from the others. He knows her he has read her book even none of the others bothered to read her book he knows her and he knows what she is like he knows what she is capable of, that darkness that sings out to his darkness in notes that no one else can hear. The snag of her chipped tooth is the edge she has to her, the rawness only he and she know

They walked in wet and dark and he could feel the dark song off her, the breath of her body beside his one arm through the other under the umbrella. He could talk to her. He knew that she understood him in a way that nobody understood him and it meant so much at last to be known. They walked together press of arm against arm and nothing needed to be said about what they meant to each other, they knew it in their bones in their flesh

He had to wait and not be seen. He waited in the side shadows watched the girl skip to her car and consider herself in the rear-view mirror the sheen of lipgloss and the shine of seventeen and the world golden, not a hint not an edge not a glimpse of darkness under that shine and that good to watch good to touch good to your fingerprints all over dull that shine a bit but it is not a way to be known.

She opened the door for him a door onto darkness and knowing.

Be quiet, she said.

And he came into the little house, and she gestured him through to the sitting room and she moved in towards him and she said, Be quiet.

All these weeks and months there has been a ticker-tape

feed, tapping away, reeling out of his unconscious to pile up all around him tangling his feet tangling his thoughts with darkness and the body that she keeps beneath those buttoned to the chin clothes, and he has never slept with a woman who has had a child and can you know by the body, by the skin, the breasts, the feel of her inside her. He knows the reluctance she must signal this cant happen this cant happen because husband child career but under that is the truth of bodies and desire and she knows that its inevitable that it was bound to happen. She says this cant happen. But it can it does.

His hands cold on her hot skin and then she was underneath him on the sofa her skirt rucked up, there were silvery lines tracing her belly and her thighs. She turned her face aside, and she closed her eyes. He watched her being fucked, her breath shallow and her eyelashes dark against her skin and underneath her eyes the skin purplish and bruised and she didn't say a word and her breath came faster and he was coming he came and he was there, present in that moment for just that moment when he came maybe that was all but it was a moment in which he was in himself and he felt more and other than he had thought that he would feel.

Afterwards he touched her face kissed her and she was quiet.

And that was the thing that needed to be done and he had done it and nothing needed to be said and for a moment just this brief moment he was glad and he was there.

Back to the village through the dark and rain, the houses dark only the street lamps lit and here and there Christmas lights tangled through the trees, and then up the drive. He disturbed the dogs and set them barking.

The problem with them all is how they make themselves

available so open so dismissible. Meryl grubby-tired and tugging-at-his-sleeve, Karen half-sober half-hungover couldn't-give-a-fuck. Tim just a tagalong bubble of stink and need and self-disgust. He sent them on their way took himself to the billiards room and watched himself drink rum and knock the balls around till he heard Margie bustling round the kitchen, and then he took himself up to bed and lay down and didn't sleep. He can't think of anything but her about how she made him feel. He wants her to read what he has written. He wants to watch her face as the words slip inside her head and wash his colours through it he wants to make her see make her taste and make her feel make her feel.

I slammed out of my office and ran to the loo. I managed to lock myself in before being sick. I heaved and heaved till nothing more came up.

Fuck.

I wiped my mouth. I looked at my watch. The MA class started in twenty minutes.

The piece had come in as an email attachment—would he have shared it with anybody else? Christ, had he submitted to the MA group folder on the website? Twenty minutes and we'd be, what, all in that room together, discussing the literary merits of that piece, whether he'd captured the reality of that night, whether he'd really nailed the experience of nailing me?

Leaning on the cubicle wall, I spun back through what I'd just read. The verifiable facts down to the chip in my front tooth, which my tongue now ran over involuntarily, back and forth. I thought how what he'd written would fit so snugly with his classmates' memories of that night. And that the headline fact about him as a writer, the one rule of his work, was that he was the guy who Only Wrote The Truth.

I crept back to my office. I clicked the document shut and peered at the email itself. He'd written no subject line, and there was no one cc'd in. I clicked my way through to the MA group page on Moodle. Posted there was the cluster of files I'd already looked at—the new work from the other students—and that was it. Nothing from Nicholas.

I let a breath go; I hadn't realised I'd been holding it.

I glanced at my watch. Ten minutes.

As far as I could *tell*, it was just me and him. But he could have bcc'd many others in and I wouldn't know yet. And he could have just emailed it separately to who knows how many people. And he could still post it somewhere online, and start flinging out links like handfuls of gravel.

He wants her to read what he has written. He wants to watch her face as the words slip inside her head and wash his colours through it he wants to make her see make her taste and make her feel make her feel.

I am not her, I wanted to tell someone, but there was no one I could tell. *I am not his idea of me.* I found gum in my drawer. I unpeeled a pellet, crunched it. Mint to wash away the bile.

I hated myself for having texted him. I hated myself for not fighting harder. If I'd struggled till he'd given up, or hit me, I wouldn't be dealing with this now.

I glanced at my watch. Five minutes.

As I got my teaching materials together, I had this vision of myself just running away—thundering down the stairs and racing along the walkways dodging students and colleagues and Scaife's noodly hands and sprinting out across the grass and then into the woods and just keeping on running, sliding down the embankment of the M6 and dodging the cars and scrambling up the other side, and just running—but instead I was walking down the corridor, and then I'd reached the seminar room door, and this was it. I could hear them in there, not the words so much as the fact of communication, the phatic start-of-term easy back-and-forth of it, how was your Christmas, New Year, all that stuff.

I turned the handle, leaned on the door and went in.

Faces turned to look at me. *Hello, hello, hi there, hi, how are we all, yes thank you very nice.*

No Nicholas.

An empty chair where he usually sat. Though he could breeze in at any moment.

Meryl ducked to rummage in her bag. Steven and Richard were leaning back side by side, blue chambray and green-and-red plaid shirts respectively, chairs balanced on back legs. I resisted the urge to tell them to stop tipping their chairs. Karen was wearing an apple-green jersey dress, and her hair had been recently hennaed. I noticed her pendant—was it a Christmas present? She held it up for me to look at a piece of thistledown captured in a sphere of resin. I turned it between my fingertips, and considered the delicate pale fronds caught there; something between a spider and a snowflake, but uneasily beautiful. "Lovely."

I arranged my notes and the students' work on the table. My hands were steady. I took a breath. I appeared to be coping.

"Anyone seen Nicholas?"

A conventional, quiet murmur: not lately, no. In fact, not since the end of last term. Tim volunteered that they'd had plans to meet up, hang out, over the vacation, but that it hadn't happened, didn't quite know why. I was relieved by the normality of it all. And I felt a pang for Tim too, after what Nicholas had written about him. *A bubble of stink and need and self-disgust.*

"We'll just give him a few more minutes, shall we?"

I asked Tim if we could see some of the work he'd been telling me about at his tutorial. He'd get it to me next week no bother, he said, but without the earlier ebullience. He seemed a bit deflated.

I thumbed through my notes. We waited till five past the hour. It was an act of extreme endurance on my part.

"Well, maybe we should just get started."

I looked up and over my glasses, and caught Meryl's eye: she was staring right at me. Her jaw worked; she looked away.

"He'll turn up," Steven said.

"I daresay," I said. "He can't have disappeared off the face of the earth."

Meryl, eyes now fixed on the printouts on the tabletop, said something.

"What's that, Meryl?"

She shook her head.

"Sorry, what did you say?"

"I wouldn't be so sure."

"Don't follow you." I could feel my cheeks getting hot.

"You remember his story, last term?" she asked. "What he wrote about wanting to fall up into the sky?"

All her rising inflections, all those upward tilts of words, like pins, needles, poking in.

"Well, yes," I said. "But I don't think that's to be taken literally."

"You don't?" She stared back at me.

"It's not physically possible, for one thing."

She just stared at me. "Yeah, but where is he? You know he only writes what happens. If he writes it, then it's true."

My skin crept up into gooseflesh. I said, "That's what he *says*. But that doesn't mean we have to believe him."

She shrugged: "He wrote that he wanted to disappear, and now he's disappeared. So there's that."

I sent him an email.

> *Hi there*
>
> *Term started back this week—we just had our first class. I wondered if you had perhaps lost track? I received your work. We need to have a separate discussion about this, alongside submission guidelines and content. So please do make an appointment to come and see me.*
>
> *I can be reached at this email, or drop in to my office hours.*
>
> *I look forward to hearing from you.*

Every time my phone pinged I scrambled to check, but it was never Nicholas. I had to make myself take breaks from refreshing my email. Wait ten minutes. Wait half an hour. Give him a chance. I'd gone from dreading a message from him to being desperate for one. Days passed. Weeks.

". . . And I haven't heard a peep."

"You shouldn't let it worry you," Patrick said. "He is a grown-up."

We were waiting for the kettle to boil. I was aware of the line of my waistband, my toes inside my boots, the brush of hair against the back of my neck, the press of bra clasp into my spine. I felt irredeemably unkempt, shabby and disgusting. I was even wearing lipstick today and I still felt grubby and gross. I hated the feel of myself, my presentness, the way I had to keep dragging myself along with me.

"I am worried though."

"I get that. You're nice. You *care*. But you can't make yourself personally responsible for every single student. There are too many of them. If you get this involved every time, you'll end up sectioned yourself."

"I know, I know."

"You did the right thing contacting Student Services last term; send them an update about this absence, and then leave them to it. They're the experts."

Except I hadn't called Student Services. He hadn't wanted to talk. He'd wanted to write: he said writing helped. I'd accepted that; I'd empathised, I thought I fucking *understood*.

"I suppose so."

"So he'll either intercalate—" Off my baffled look: "That's suspend his studies for a while—or he'll drop out completely, or—and this is what my money's on—he'll turn up next week with a skier's tan and a half-arsed apology."

"I hope so." But I didn't know that I really did.

"Look. Here's the thing."

The kettle clicked off, and he busied himself with making coffee.

"The thing is, the way you're being pushed," he said, "the rate you're having to go at, if you're not careful you're going to burn out." He flared his fingers, electricity shorting: "Fsst."

"There is no other rate," I said. "This is where I'm at, this is what I'm stuck with."

"You can take a break, surely. You could take a day. An evening. Relax."

I shrugged.

"I know, babysitter, all that stuff," he said. "I get it, honestly. But I really think you have to make an effort."

"Make an effort to relax?"

"Yep. I'm afraid you really do have to work much harder at not working quite so hard."

"You're right. I'm dreadfully lazy about being lazy."

"Time to turn over a new leaf. A few of us are headed out on Sunday for a drink. You should come."

"Ah no," I said. "It's half-term, so Mark's coming up, my husband and I . . ."

"Even better. Bring him along."

That actually sounded good. That sounded like the kind of thing that people do.

"The Sun, on Church Street. Six. It won't go late; work in the morning and all that."

"Good."

"And stop fretting over this kid. Leave it to the professionals."

I smiled, I lied: "You're right, of course. I will."

I sent Nicholas a further email:

> *I just wanted to check in with you as you have missed a third MA session.*
>
> *I'll be in my office at the usual Office Hours sessions (4–6 on a Wednesday); please do call to see me. If you can't make it then, drop me a line and we'll make an appointment for you at a more convenient time. As things stand, you do risk falling behind; I don't want this to become an issue for you.*

OFFICE HOURS. 4–6. WEDNESDAYS.

The idea is that this is the designated period in which students can pop in and see you. The reality is that they knock on your door whenever it suits them, office hour or no, so that normal working hours can be shattered into pieces and whole office hours sail by without a single visitor.

I tackled Admissions to keep myself occupied. Or at least I tried to. The software kept glitching, refusing to open documents and deleting my notes and occasionally just freezing solid. I winced at extracts from a novel about body modification; got wrapped up in an awkward romance set during the Mass Observation project in which it seemed that a character out of a Richard Curtis romcom had landed right in the middle of *Saturday Night and Sunday Morning;* there was an outline of a five-part fantasy epic which promised quests for lost talismans (talismen?) and some excellent and specifically Irish dragons. There was a prodigious writing sample of that one. I don't know if it was the making-difficult by the gnarly software, or the fact that they were just different from the stories that I was currently dealing with, or the fact that they were taking me away from the present moment in which Nicholas might, indeed I had to hope *would*, appear; but these stories were just so wantable; I was fascinated by the transformation of the young person's body, wanted to know whether it would turn out to be caterpillar to butterfly or something more ambiguous, whether they lost or found themself along the way; I wanted Angry Young Men and Issues and nostalgia and yearning. I wanted Irish dragons, for Christ's sake; I wanted swarms of them. I was done with the truth and all its lies; I wanted fiction, I wanted to be beguiled, to be transported.

A knock on the door. A young woman, one of my undergraduates. "Sorry, sorry," she said. "I made you jump."

I waved her in.

Her eyes were red and she clutched a balled-up tissue. The family dog had just died—they'd had her all the time she'd been growing up—and she wanted to go home for the funeral. I gave her my sympathies and permission, and she nodded and mumbled her thanks, and left.

I checked my emails. Round robins and diktats from Faculty and minutes of meetings and a thing forwarded by Michael Lynch via Toronto suggesting that it would be really great if a Creative Writing staff member could join the Summer Programme teaching team: *passing this on to my new colleague (Hi there! Hope it's all going brilliantly!) as I'm out of the country. Take care. X*

A soft tap. I swung round.

Another young woman, this one ghostly and shattered. She sank into the seat and told me about the deadlines that were rushing at her like a herd of bulls. I sat on my hands, nodded. She asked for an essay extension. I sanctioned the extension, told her to get a couple of early nights. She nodded. She'd try. But she had an extra shift at Oscar's that night.

She trudged off, and I went back to work. And the motion-sensor lights, in the corridor, went out. I sat there in my own solitary pool of light from the computer as the world grew dark around me.

And then the lights blinked on again out there, the quiet series of clinks they make, and then a hum. And then a shape obscured the light, and the door opened.

"Tim!"

"Hey."

"Come in. How are you?"

Not great, by the looks of it. Pasty, heavy, his hair lank and hanging down over his eyes.

"Yeah," he said. "Hi."

He brought the rest of his ungainly self into the office, slumped into a chair. He had finally got a diagnosis, he told me, and that was something of a relief. He hadn't seen it coming, but then he never did. He'd been good up to the start of the academic year, and then he'd been too good; he could feel it happening but the fact is he liked that bit, the high. When you feel like you can do anything, be anything, when anything seems possible. Then these last few weeks he'd started to slide, started feeling it all slipping, started feeling really bad. He could hardly drag himself out of bed, couldn't face eating for days and then for days eating nothing but junk. His mum had figured something was wrong and come up and dragged him to the doctor.

Bipolar, he said, with a *who'd've thought it* shrug. He was now on medication, and it was weird and he didn't like it. He felt fuzzy and flat. Ironed out. Couldn't write. And if he couldn't write what was the point of the MA. He'd come to tell me he was going to drop out.

But. He wanted to apologise for the way he'd been when he was on a high; for not submitting work, the MA was one of his crazy plans—he often had crazy plans on a high—and now he was being realistic. He wasn't ready for it.

"But you can't leave!"

He sat back, looked surprised and pleased. I'd meant it, but not the way he took it: I had no idea at all if he was even any good. But I did know that I couldn't lose him as well as Nicholas; I couldn't let the whole damn thing collapse around me.

"You just have to push on through," I continued. "With a long project, everyone has a moment, or a week, or a month, where they feel like this. If you push on through, you'll have a novel at the end of it, but if you give up now, you won't."

This clearly made sense to him; he looked lighter for it. But I felt a twinge of guilt. I'd told him to do what was best for me, not necessarily for him.

"You know," he said, "One thing I've found really hard this term is the way that Nicholas has just dropped off grid. I think that was part of what tipped me over. I'd thought we were friends. I thought he'd have messaged me, or something."

"He's not in touch at all?"

He shook his head. "Meryl hasn't heard from him either. And they were *close*."

I became very conscious of my own gaze. I glanced at my boots, swung a foot back and forth.

"Look, the main thing right now is you take care of yourself," I said. "I'm sure Nicholas will turn up next week with a dodgy excuse and a skier's tan . . ."

"Do you think?"

"I'll chase him up again anyway. Don't you worry about it. And keep writing your novel. If you don't do it, no one else will do it for you. Stick with it. And submit something to class, eh?"

He thanked me and took himself off.

Half an hour till I had to pick up Sammy.

I got out my mobile, then I put it down again.

I wrote down a sentence on scrap paper. Then another one. And then an alternative, just in case. And a fourth. I filled a side of A4 with phrases and boxes and arrows. A whole potential conversation flow-charted, in which I would be pleasant and careful and clear. I would apologise for being out of touch for a while over the Christmas vacation. I would ask that we would draw a line under what had happened between us that night—without seeking further to define what had happened between us that night—and we would agree a way forward from here. He'd come back to class, and we'd say and do no more about it. On the understanding that he didn't write about it again. He couldn't write the whole truth anyway: nobody could. This would be one of the things he'd have to leave out.

Twenty minutes till I had to pick up Sammy. I rang Nicholas's mobile. It rang and rang, and went to answering service. I cut the call, set my mobile down.

I lifted my chunky office telephone and dialled the landline number listed on our student contact form. I could see the big house, the cold rooms, the phone buzzing away on the baroque console in the hall. It rang and rang and rang and I held on, teeth gritted, well beyond the point where an answer could be reasonably expected; then, at the far end, the receiver was lifted.

"Palmer residence, Andrew speaking." The voice was old, and rich, and brusque.

I said, "Hi. Um. Is Nicholas there?"

"He's out. Who's calling?"

"Uh, do you know where he is?"

"He's at the university. He had a class this afternoon. Who is this?"

"Never mind," I said. "I'll try again another time."

"Who is this? What do you want?"

I dropped the handset back into the cradle.

If I was on the other end of that call, I'd dial 1471. I'd want to know who I'd been talking to. But there was the main switchboard between that phone and mine—you had to dial 9 for an outside line—so Mr. Palmer might find out that it was someone from the university, but my extension shouldn't come up. I swept up my stuff and ran to pick up Sammy.

But if Nicholas was not at home, and not in class, where was he?

. . .

Mark was due that Saturday, around lunchtime, for half-term.

It would be the first time we'd seen him since Christmas. He'd warned me that he'd have to bring some work up with him.

Sammy was bright awake at six, giddy with excitement, Daddy coming, and no settling him to anything. By late morning he was climbing the walls; I suggested we go for a walk, take a little picnic. He didn't want to leave in case Daddy came while we were gone.

"How 'bout we head up the hill? We can look out for him from there. Like pirates."

And that did the trick.

I pocketed a couple of juice cartons and a snack pack of Bourbons and threw the breakfast crumbs out for the birds and we set off for a walk. That big blue-and-pink beauty was swaying on her branch—a jay, I'd learned a little from Sammy's *Pop-Up Book of British Birds*. She watched us, head tilted, as we left, and the smaller birds swarmed and fluttered and squabbled behind us.

We headed up, hand in hand. We'd never been that way before; weekdays we just raced for the bus; if we went for a walk at weekends we ambled down towards the village. After a hundred yards or so of road, the tarmac crumbled and fell apart and became a white limestone track. A wooden sign pointed the way through a gate, and up towards open moor. We followed the line worn into the grass, climbing through the buffetting air. The world around us became alien: bleached grass, coiled nubs of ferns, scabs of grey stone. Clouds tumbled overhead and their shadows dashed across the hillside. I felt like I had dreamed this place. Sammy and I chatted and huffed and puffed, but I looked around me and I was haunted by the sense that this unknown place was already familiar.

The brow of the hill was like the surface of the moon; the bare grey limestone was riddled with cracks and gullies, blotched with emerald-green moss and patches of grey or mustard-coloured lichen. Here and there stood twisted starveling trees. From where I stood I could see as far as the Lake District hills, blue and purple in the distance. Sammy clambered up onto the outcrop. I gazed round me. I felt like I'd failed to pay proper attention, had missed something, was now straining to catch an echo, to catch up.

"Careful."

I sat down as Sammy tottered and poked around. The wind dropped and for a moment it was calm. I held out a steadying hand to Sam and he leaned to peer into a hollow, then squatted to get a better look, then finally plonked himself down.

"Picnic," he announced.

"Picnic."

We could see the roof of our own little house, and below it the rag-taggle cluster of the farm buildings and the folds and dips that hid the village and the river below. Over to the right there was the town, the glimmer of the sea. You could see the university from here, perched on its own answering hilltop. The motorway a grey river. Everything echoed, but I couldn't catch it.

Sam lay back and stared up into the sky. Mirrored clouds tumbled across his dark irises. He blinked, and I caught the echo. Nicholas. He had written this place; he'd written this stone, these hills, this sky. This was his territory.

"Get up."

Sam lifted his head to look at me.

"Get *up*."

I scrambled off the stone outcrop, turned to scoop up Sam and swing him down onto the grass. Downhill the path was slithery and difficult.

"Come *on*."

He pulled against my hand. "But, picnic."

I rifled out the packet of Bourbons, opened them and thrust them at him, but he needed both hands to take one out and he squirmed his hand out of mine and stopped to give his whole attention to the biscuits.

"Give." I snatched the packet off him, took one out, handed the biscuit back to him. "There. Happy now?"

He burst into tears, and I saw myself as he was seeing me. Angry for no reason. Unpredictable. And therefore scary.

"Sorry. Sorry. Sorry, love." I scooped him up, onto my hip, hugged him close as I strode along. "It's okay."

His face was pressed wetly into my shoulder. I carried him down the hillside, aching with remorse. Also just aching: he was getting big.

"Hey," I said. "I'm sorry. It's okay. It's okay. I didn't mean to spoil it. I was just worried we'd be late."

He went quieter at this, muddy wellies dangling at my thighs, breathing soft on my throat. I rested my cheek against his head as we bumped along. And then, like a wish fulfilled, a little red car came scooting along the distant lane like a beetle, then slowed and took the sharp left at the crossroads.

"Cos, look," I said. "Daddy's here!"

Sam dragged Mark from the car up to the house, jabbering non-stop, all sunshine now. He skipped oblivious through the drift of feathers on the front path, but I stooped to pick one up. It was soft, and tiny, and pinkish grey. I glanced around the trees and bushes, looking for the jay, but the branches were bare, just a lace of twigs against the sky. I let the feather go and followed the boys indoors.

Mark was tired and stiff from the drive. We hugged in the hallway. He let me go and said, "You okay?"

And I told my easy lie—*just tired*—and he accepted it.

I made soup and crumpets for lunch. Mark lingered in the kitchen, shifting round while I opened cupboards and drawers. We talked about Sam, and about Mark's work; what had been going on with me, I told him, was too boring and annoying to even begin to describe.

"D'you know, the way things are at work," Mark said, "I'm so busy I don't know I'd see any more of you if you were in London."

"Is it that bad?"

"It's not bad," he said. "It's just busy."

"Well, thanks for making it up here."

"Well yeah, of course. That's not what I mean."

I suggested we go somewhere, while the weather held. The seaside, town, a playground, anything anywhere but here. Nicholas wasn't at home and he wasn't going to uni; we were on his turf, caught in the landscape of his imagination. He could turn up at any moment.

Mark said he couldn't face getting back in the car again; couldn't we just have a quiet time today . . . So I put a DVD on for Sam, and after lunch Mark fell asleep on the sofa, his weight dragging the throw down off the back of it, so that the worn blue fabric was exposed.

I went upstairs and I found my notebook. I could hear the rumble and jingle of the film below, and the rush of the wind in the trees, and I wrote about the fear that hit me on the hillside, and how fresh and cold a fear it was, nothing to do with what had happened to me on the street in Anerley, or on the blue sofa in my own front room; to do instead with the prospect of being caught up in someone else's story, of being written by someone else; the fear of having no say in who I was at all. After a while the sounds changed from below—I heard the title music to the film, and Sammy beginning to pootle around again, which might wake Mark, so I put my notebook away, went downstairs and we got out his Lego, and together we built a castle.

Then I had Sammy help me make the dinner. We peeled vegetables and smashed garlic; I let him tumble it all together in a bowl with salt and pepper and olive oil. We picked rosemary and sage in the garden, washed them in a mug and tweaked the leaves off the stems. Sammy chewed a sage leaf and pulled a face and shuddered. He stuck out his tongue and wiped it with his hand. I took the mangled leaf off him and dropped it in with the peelings.

"It's much nicer when it's cooked."

At dinner he picked his way carefully around the herbs, forked in couscous and mouthed a bit of parsnip and that was that. He seemed distracted, happy, turning from one of us to the other, watching, smiling to himself, trailing couscous down his front.

Later, when I was putting him to bed, he kicked his feet around under the duvet and grinned and wriggled. I asked why he was so excited, and he said it was because we were all together here at once in the same place.

"Ah, that's lovely," I said. "Bless you, sweetheart."

I wanted to say sorry for earlier, for being grumpy on the hill, but I didn't want to remind him. I brushed the hair off his forehead and kissed him. I knew we couldn't go on like this. It wasn't sustainable. It wasn't doing any of us any good.

"Okay?" Mark asked as I came back downstairs. He had opened a bottle of wine; he handed a glass to me. I took it, held it for a bit, then set it down on the mantelpiece. Even the smell of wine now.

"I've been thinking," I said.

"Steady on."

"I know. I'll get all giddy."

"But what were you thinking?" he said, glancing at his phone, pocketing it. No signal here of course.

"That this isn't fair on you," I said. "All the travelling. Living alone down there. You look exhausted."

"That's life."

"But maybe it shouldn't be."

"I don't follow." He sounded impatient, weary.

"I was just wondering. Should we tweak things? Could we try doing things a little differently?"

"What do you mean?"

"I realised—" I said. "Well, the thing is, I was desperate. Because of the—that man. The man in the blue anorak. I just wanted to get away. That was all I could think about, just getting away. I didn't think through all the implications. Not for you. Or for me either, or for Sammy. But maybe we could take the time now to think of something else. Together."

"You were desperate."

I nodded.

"For three years you were desperate."

"I suppose the point is, the point I'm trying to make, is that whatever we do it shouldn't just be me who wants it. It should suit us both. Suit us all. Not this, or just back to where we were, but some third thing we haven't thought of yet. So what if—what if you look for a deputy headship somewhere? We could move wherever. I'd get a job, any kind of job, take care of Sammy and fit in around you. And then if you wanted, we could maybe have another . . . A little sister or brother for Sammy. How would that be?"

"Don't you like your job?"

"Yes, but—"

"Aren't you happy here?"

"I should have realised. It's not just me, is it? There's us."

He shook his head.

"What?"

"After all this, all these years, all this—upheaval. Now is when you start thinking about us?"

He doesn't get angry often. I'm not used to it. It scares me. He stood in silence for a moment, and then he said: "You made him your priority. That asshole."

"No—"

"You made him the priority when there were better things, more important things, you could have been thinking about: your family, us, our little boy."

"No."

He shrugged. "It's true."

"I wish I'd dealt with it better," I said. "I wish I was better at dealing with that kind of thing. But I was just trying to—cope. And it was never just about me. I wanted Sam to have a nice place to grow up. Somewhere safe."

"That doesn't include me."

"I hoped it would."

He shook his head. "It doesn't matter."

"It matters. *You* matter. You've always mattered. I never meant for things to end up like this. And I think that's half the problem, thinking like that. We haven't ended up; this isn't an end. We're still in the middle; we just have to figure out what comes next."

"I've been very lonely," he said.

The cow's lick up in his fringe, highlighted now with grey. The freckles on the cusp of his forehead. I noticed it all now again in a way I hadn't for years—the way the lines formed at the corners of his eyes, the way his lips twisted—because I knew. You can know that stuff before you hear it. He said: "I'd been lonely for years." The slip in tense. Not lonely any more. He looked up at me, those blue eyes. "Will you have a drink?"

I shook my head.

"It's so quiet here," he said. "It's so empty. It'd drive me to drink."

I could hear the wind in the trees and the hum of the pylons and the cows down in the Metcalfes' farm. I could hear a curlew call. I knew it wasn't empty. Every inch of it was occupied; Nicholas permeated the whole landscape, his words wove through it, his breath touched everything. He had disappeared into this place.

Mark refilled his glass, gestured to mine with the bottle.

I shook my head.

His lips were stained with wine. "Look, the thing is, it's not easy. But I have to. We agreed we would, this weekend. We'd start the process."

"We?"

"Me and Amy—"

"You and Amy?"

"—we were both lonely. In our marriages."

"Amy from work?"

"And it's reached a point where we have to acknowledge that

we have needs, where we have to put those needs, if not first, then at least on the list."

"Amy from work?"

He nodded.

"Your boss."

"She's senior management, but that doesn't mean that she's my boss. I'm not finding any of this easy, you know." He was blushing.

"Okay, yes, but can we just pause all that, please. Rewind."

He and Amy were not "we." *We* were "we." Him and me and Sammy were "we."

"We're both telling our partners this weekend," he said again. "Clean sheet, everything out in the open, no more lies."

"No more lies?"

"I owe it to you to be open with you, to tell you the truth."

I turned my face away. "Please don't."

"I feel dreadful," he said. "I really do. But I can't go on like this forever, in limbo, in transit. Nowhere's home."

"I didn't leave *you*."

"But you're gone."

"Come to bed," I said. "Just come to bed, Mark; we'll sleep on it, we can talk in the morning. We can work something out. Come to bed."

"I'll sleep down here." Those sweet blue eyes. The day's haze of stubble.

So I went upstairs and took a pillow and a blanket off my bed. He was sitting there on the blue sofa, the throw crumpled underneath him, when I came back down and handed the bedding to him.

"For what it's worth," he said. "I am sorry."

I nodded. A grey hollow space swelled in my chest. I couldn't swallow and I could hardly breathe. Sammy would be . . . God, it didn't bear thinking about, how Sammy would be. "You'll—what, go back to London in the morning?"

"I told Mum I'd bring Sam down to see her." He dropped the pillow down at the end of the sofa. "Well," he said. "Good night."

"Yeah," I said. "Good night."

I didn't sleep.

In the morning he asked where the towels were kept and I walked away. His bag was already by the door. When he broke the news about a trip to Grandma's, Sammy nearly burst with excitement. Grandma's house was Liberty Hall. Things on ration at home—sweets, telly, junk food—were always in glorious over-abundance at Grandma's. But oh God I didn't want to let go of Sammy. I couldn't bear for him to be away from me. And there would be so much more of this, over the years to come. Hand-overs in train stations and pickups and drop-offs at front doors and sometimes she'd be there; him and her together; the new "we."

"Make sure he gets to bed at a decent time."

"I will."

"He has his routine, so you have to stick to the routine, other-wise it'll take me ages to get him back into anything like a sensible bedtime."

"Okay. I do know."

"And make sure he eats something green."

"Of course."

"Every day, I mean."

"I *know.*"

"And give my love to your mum."

"I will."

"Okay, bye." And the words came out by reflex: "Love you."

It hurt. Mark reached out a hand to me.

"Look," he said. "I didn't want, I don't want to— Can we just— get along?"

"Give it a while, yeah?"

"Okay. Yeah."

"It's hard."

He nodded. I could see that he felt bad.

I waved to the departing car, holding it together for Sam's sake, but as soon as it was round the bend, my face broke, and I ran inside. I slumped to the floor and covered my face with my hands, and cried.

When I had cried myself out, I washed my face and put on makeup. Things were no worse than they had been, after all; I'd just not known how bad they were. This was, at least, information. I knew where I stood now.

I couldn't stay alone in that place. I gathered up my stuff, locked up, and made my way to the bus stop. My hands felt empty. I felt like I'd forgotten something. That I'd left something behind.

Chemistry

The American girl used to send book reviews and accounts of her day and questions about his and observations of the quirks of English English, the oddities of English people and of England in general. She'd send emojis of sunshine and ice cream and animals, photographs of where she was or things that took her fancy. She'd text quotes from Plath and de Beauvoir and Camus. She became teasing, passive-aggressive, then transparent, pleading, and then faded out altogether into silence as she finally got the message in that she wasn't going to get a message, not from him.

And now he waits, watching his phone. Wanting an emoji, a message, a few words. Anything.

Thinking of that night is like the crash of a wave over him he stands shocked and sharp-awake and breathless. He wants to see her, he wants to be near her. What he feels now is different from what he has felt before. After the dark waters he has struggled through alone for so long, all this time this feels different again not the cleanness of his lost girl but something else again, something astringent, salt.

He tries something uncomplicated and noncommittal; that is how to start. Hey there you.

He watches his phone and she does not reply.

She has work, she has the boy, people always say that they are busy especially at Christmas, they go on and on about how busy they are, family, shopping, all that stuff. He catches the bus into town. He wanders round the shopping centre, past the queue at Greggs, past Poundland and in through Boots and out again. He scans Neros and Costa and Starbucks since people shop and drink coffee and shop, and she is in none of these places when he goes into them.

He walks into The Hall and stands there, just on the scuffed wooden floor like a school gym scanning the echoing space and noisy with talk and coffee-grinding and steam and vintage pop and the boys with beards and the girls with pixie cuts and the customers with their MacBooks or babies and the twinkling prettiness of Christmas lights. He wants her to be there, wants the joy and miracle of it in the last place that he'd looked, anticipates the thrill and has the thrill wash from him, because she is flatly not there. He could talk to the pretty girl behind the counter who has tattoos like the flourishes of Uncle Toby's walking stick, he knows he could catch her interest but doesn't want to. Now that the anticipation has washed away what's left behind is anger. Anger that he has been hijacked like this.

You busy? *he texts.* Thought we could meet up in town. Go for coffee. Bring the boy.

He keeps it light, keeps it friendly, keeps it easy-going. Like he's okay with fitting in around her life.

And he watches his phone and she does not reply.

And he watches his phone and still she does not reply.

That's it. He's done. Won't text her again. He doesn't have to take this.

Christmas Day is wet. After church his parents get quickly drunk. Gideon has not come home for Christmas this year; he says he has to go to Hannah's; he says it is an obligation, one year he has to be there, one year he can be here, but the truth is there will always be a good reason to be elsewhere and who's to blame him. Nick feels the absence of his own girl; this is when he misses her most, in the long hours trapped with his own family. Time passed differently with her, together they could swallow hours whole, drink down days and still not have had enough. There was never quite enough time.

Taking the dog out, he says.

Up the village street and up the hill, along the lane and through the farmyard and up to the very edge of the moors. Where the little house stands with the faint glow of one light left on in the hall, announcing its emptiness. No Christmas tree, no decorations. The dog snuffs around then stares up at him and then sits down then lies down at his feet on the damp tarmac.

She has gone back to London, of course she has taken the boy and gone to be with him with that man. Husband. And it comes to him that this is why she has had to absent herself so entirely from him. The man, the necessity of covering and appeasing and behaving as normal. When she gets back, though. Leaving the husband behind. But the jealousy the anger. That she does as she pleases and does what she needs as though it doesn't concern him.

He fumbles with umbrella lighter cigarettes. He smokes looks out across the fields to where the city casts an orange glow up into the sky, and the old hay barn stands a black block in front of it. Metcalfe has let the building fall into ruin, wraps up his silage now in black plastic and leaves it standing in the fields. Can't even see the worth of things themselves, the old man, of stone and slate and timber. Can't see what matters when it's right in front of him.

He drops his cigarette butt it fizzles out in the rain. The dog is shivering. He jerks her to her feet and they head off home.

Days pass. When he writes he imagines her reading his words, imagines her reading this, the words that he is writing for her. He never thought that he cared about being read; the point was to write, but now the idea of her reading is everything, he imagines the words entering her mind and shaping her thoughts and making images swell and he knows

*himself to be in charge of that and it makes him feel better.
His writing will get inside her and change her leave her
different.*

*New Year's Eve and he has not slept a whole night in he
can't think how long. Head falls, swings up again, he writes
and he walks and then there is a party in town and there is
a girl there, and he gives her some of the stuff he's got and
then they are kissing chewing the faces of each other and
then they are in one of the bedrooms, and they are fucking,
and she is arching her back and gasping and he knows, cold,
watching her and watching himself watch her, in his gut he
knows that she doesn't feel it, couldn't feel that, high or not
she just knows what she is expected to feel and so she does
what she is expected to do. He is watching himself watching
her and it is not at all real or true and doesn't mean a thing.
He pulls out of her and gets back into his clothes and she is
what the fuck and then she is shouting crying too so much
feeling here but he doesn't believe a word of it not a tear of
it it's just market-stall fakery he gets away from her down
the stairs and out the front door and out into the street and
up the hill out of town and along the dark lanes, and it is
silent, since everyone has got where they are going to tonight
and is with the people that they want to be with. He goes by
the moonlight and the shadows and it occurs to him that if
he had stayed there in that upstairs room at the party and
finished in her, if he had given her his number, then in time
he would get a text, he would get an emoji, he would get a
little waving ghost, a glass of wine, a cup of coffee. He would
get a ream, a raft, a bundle. His phone would be bursting
with balloons and chicks peeping out of eggs and glasses of
fizz and party-streamers. He hears the bells peal out from
the town hall clock; fireworks streak into the sky and burst. It
is New Year's Day.*

He texts her. Because he misses her. He is such a fucking pussy. He is such a girl.

Happy New Year.

He stuffs his hands into his pockets. He stumbles on along the dark lane, and the fireworks break overhead and burst into stars, and fall, and die.

He is forgetting about his lost girl. The only reason he ever had for writing. The only reason he ever wrote at all.

He hates her for making him forget. The anger and the jealousy and the making him forget.

You know this now. You cant not know it. You cant pretend that it isn't true.

A tap on the door. I yelped.

Mina was frowning in through the glass panel. I closed the document and waved her in, then slid my hands under my thighs, and sat on them, because they were shaking.

"It's Sunday?" She stood there on the threshold, looking beautiful, in a soft dress printed with leaves and birds of paradise. Today her nails and lips were Morello cherry.

"Um. Yeah."

She made a baffled expression, gesturing round the office: "Should you really be here?"

"Mark's got Sam. So I'm—you know—catching up."

"Yeah, but Day of Rest and all that?"

"You're here too."

"Needed a book."

"Would that be a work-type book, I wonder? Or are you reading for pleasure?"

She smiled, caught out. "Reading for pleasure? What's that? It rings a vague bell . . ."

"There you go then, you haven't got a leg to stand on."

I put the computer to sleep. Didn't know what to do next. I had nowhere else to go. I'd been half-considering crawling in under my desk to sleep there.

"We have this age-old tradition round here," Mina was saying. "I don't know if this is something you southerners will have ever heard of."

"What's that?"

"It's called Going to the Pub."

"Northerners don't have a monopoly on that."

"Prove it."

"Alright."

The lights blinked out behind us down the corridor. I wondered if I could miss the last bus home. I wondered if I could crash that night on Mina's sofa. But that still left tomorrow, and I had no idea how to deal with it.

The pub is instinct made solid. Faces to the fire, backs turned to the weather, chugging calories and dis-inhibitors—that's human survival right there in a nutshell, through ancient migrations, through the ice ages and bad winters: that's keeping on going to another spring, to better times, and better places. It was the fellowship I needed, not the drink. I bought myself a lime and soda, bought Mina a glass of pinot grigio, and we went to find the rest of them.

They were collapsed in two sofas near a wood-burning stove, just half a dozen from the department; some of the younger teaching assistants, as well as Patrick, Kate, and Lisa. There was shuffling and the dragging up of extra stools.

I ended up being talked to by Kate Speirs, who I hadn't seen in a good while despite us having next-door offices: our timetables just didn't overlap. She had just got funding for research leave and had this joyous post-coital flush about her. She never managed to get any research done while she was teaching, she told me: "Because it's all drawn from the same well, isn't it? The teaching and the writing, and if you keep on drawing from the well for other people then there's nothing left for you."

I said, "But also maybe teaching renews the water, keeps it fresh?"

She gave me a look. "You're new," she said. "You'll see."

"Ooh, there's Laura." Mina was on her feet and squeezing out past people's knees. "Scuse me."

She headed across to join a group of women standing by the bar, slipped an arm around one of the women's waists, and kissed her. I got a glimpse of blond hair and cheekbone and a soft green sweater. Me and my knee-jerk heteronormative assumptions. I felt a bit stupid.

"They got married last summer," Patrick said.

He and I were sitting side by side on a sagging sofa, too close to actually look at each other without it being awkward.

"Ah, that's lovely."

"Never seen so many flowers."

He smelt Christmassy, of oranges and spice. I remembered how'd looked at me, that time I'd met him in Greggs. How he'd seen me shattered, threadbare and panda-eyed and said that I looked lovely. And now it turned out that he wasn't Mina's. I wondered if he was anybody's.

"Mark couldn't come then?"

"He's, um—No. He's taken Sammy to visit his grandma."

"That's a shame."

"Family." I shrugged.

"Yeah, but how are we supposed to judge him if he doesn't show up?"

I laughed; and it continued from there, the two of us talking, gazes parallel at the fire, as the logs collapsed into bright coals, people gathered and drifted away, and the music changed, and then went off. Last orders.

"You want another drink?"

I glanced at my watch and then around the almost-empty bar. My heart kicked into panic: "Did Mina go already?"

He peered across the room with me. "Looks like it. Was she giving you a lift? Shall we ring her?"

"Uh no, don't bother."

"You want to go get a cab?"

I bit at a thumb. "I guess so."

"I'll walk you down to the rank."

He grabbed his jacket, and we pushed out of the pub doors. Outside the air was speckled with rain; the streetlamps looked like dandelion clocks. It was peaceful, quiet. Fear twisted up inside me.

"You don't miss it? London?"

I just said, "It got difficult." I let him imagine house prices, schools, commutes, all of which was also true. "My—Mark loves it though. London. He says it's too quiet for him here."

And then I thought of Amy, and felt sick.

Then Patrick said: "I read an article recently about Antarctica."

"Antarctica?"

He touched my arm to direct me down a side street. The wet cobbles gleamed in the lamplight like tiger's eye.

"Yeah. There's this tiny human population there. Four thousand people in the summer, and maybe just a thousand or so in the winter; there's one cinema on the whole continent; seats sixty people, and it only shows South American films. And beyond that, there's just hundreds of thousands of miles of wilderness. Snow and ice, and penguins."

"Okay."

"So what I'm thinking, to some people, that might sound like a cold version of Hell. But to someone else, if you were really into ice sculpture or penguins or Latin American cinema, you'd be happy as Larry."

We came to a junction, and there was the taxi rank. The fear twisted tighter.

We crossed the road together. "Or as someone already put it, and rather better than I did: *There's nothing either good or bad, but thinking makes it so."*

We'd reached the pavement. The cabs were lined up beside us.

"Well here we are. See you tomorrow."

"Yeah," I said. "Goodnight." I should have headed up to the top of the rank and got in a cab, but I was stuck fast.

"Okay?"

I nodded.

"You know what . . ." Patrick said. There was rain on his glasses; the droplets caught the light. He dug into his pockets.

"What?"

"Never mind. Forget it."

"Forget what?"

"Forget I said anything."

"You didn't say anything."

"Yeah, that's becoming a habit."

A crowd came past us. Loudly cheerful kids, staggering and embracing. They clambered into cabs and were gone. The remaining cabs nudged forward.

"I had some news today," I said. "I've not told anyone yet."

"Oh?"

"Mark left me."

"No."

"Yep."

"Oh God. I'm so sorry."

"It happens every day," I said. "People leave people. Marriages break up."

"Yeah but. It doesn't happen to *you* every day."

"No," I said. "That's true."

"What about the wee lad?"

A young woman swung into the back seat of a cab, bum first, legs tucked after, calling something to her friend. The roof light blinked out, the taxi pulled away, and no new cars joined the rank.

"Sammy doesn't know yet."

"Couldn't you get counselling, go to Relate, or something?"

"Mark's gone; I mean emotionally, he's gone. He's committed to this other woman now. I know him. He's fiercely loyal."

"D'you think that might be a tad over-generous, in the circumstances?"

I closed my eyes. The blood pulsed in my eyelids; the rain fell on my face.

I thought of Sammy down at his grandma's asleep in the icy old spare bed, and Mark hunched over a pint in what used be be his local. I thought of Amy in some dank flat in Penge telling her husband she was leaving him and then being stuck in the same two rooms as him all weekend. Or, the heartsinker of it, tripping over to Anerley to our flat, with her own set of keys, letting herself in. I thought of the dark house out there, and Nicholas haunting the place, his presence seeping through the woods and lanes and moor. I thought how I had caused it all, had *chosen* it; not always the freest choice maybe, but still these were all my decisions. None of it would have happened if I had handled things better. If I had known the right way to deal with the man in the blue anorak.

"I don't know what to do." I hadn't meant to say it out loud.

"You could come back to mine," Patrick said.

I looked at him.

"Just for a bit. I'll make you a cup of tea. We can talk. And I'll call you a cab in a bit."

"Please," I said.

We walked on, down through the town centre, past women in huge heels and tiny clothes and men with short sleeves and chunky jewellery, through bouts of loud lad-singing and huddled earnest conversations and clouds of cigarette smoke and vape and alcohol. In Wilko's doorway, a girl dressed in tiny lacy black was scrummed with mates, sobbing, and her friend was saying, *He isn't worth it, Izzy, he really isn't worth it.*

We climbed out of the town centre, over the dark glittering canal, and into quietness. We passed a shuttered corner shop, a pub, and turned down a street of solid-stone-built terraces. *Three bedrooms and a garden*, I remembered; a tree house big as our flat. The kind of place where we would have been living, if Mark had only wanted it too.

A flat-fronted terraced house; three stone steps and Patrick fumbling open the door. He flipped on a light and we were in his front room, which was warm and smelt of woodsmoke. Books, lamps, pot plants, books. Books everywhere. He toed off his shoes, and so I unzipped my boots, and we left them side by side there on the mat. He held out a hand for my coat, and I took it off and passed it to him.

I followed him through into a back sitting room, with a TV and newspapers and magazines and abandoned coffee cups and a cold log-burning stove, and from there down bare stone steps into a little cellar kitchen; I felt the need to touch, fingertips on plaster, on chipped paintwork, on the cup-ringed wooden countertop. The layeredness of this place, the sense of time passed and passing here.

"Have a seat," he said, and drew out a stool for me. "Are you hungry?"

I shook my head. It hadn't occurred to me to be hungry, though now I came to think of it . . . I lifted it and turned my hand; the tendons were standing proud; the skin was pale, almost transparent; it was trembling: "Maybe."

"Toast?"

"Please."

"And tea."

"Tea."

He filled the kettle, then rummaged for bread, then spooned loose tea into a matte-white bamboo-handled teapot.

"I like your teapot," I said.

"Thanks."

"I also like your socks."

Attention drawn to them, his toes ran a little Mexican wave.

"I like the stripes, the way the colours are all—complementary."

He stood there with his hand on the belly of the pot, studying me, cheek bunched in a half-smile.

"I've been wanting to—" he said. "I've thought that you— For a while I've been thinking. You seem so—" He flapped a hand around, frustrated. "Jesus, Patrick, finish a sentence here, would you?"

"Tricky things, sentences."

"Aren't they. What I'm trying to say is, do you remember that kids' show, *Crackerjack!*, or are you too young?"

"I'm not sure . . ."

The kettle began to rumble and steam.

"They had this quiz; kid would answer all these questions and each time they'd get handed a prize. Footballs, skateboards, Kerplunk, Operation, all that kind of stuff. But if they got the question wrong they'd get given a cabbage. They'd keep getting questions and they'd keep getting prizes and cabbages. They had to hold everything they'd won, cabbages and board games and SodaStreams or whatever, right up until the end of the game, and if you lost hold of it, everything would go tumbling, all the stuff you'd won, and all the cabbages too, all of it tumbling on the floor and you lost everything."

"I don't think I ever saw it."

The toast popped up; he fished it out of the toaster.

"Well, that's what I think of. When I think of you. That's not *all* I think of." He flicked a glance at me. "But it's like you've got the prizes and you've got all the cabbages too, and people keep handing you more and more cabbages to hold, and you're desperately trying to cling to everything, cabbages and prizes, so as not to lose it all. And I just wanted to—I dunno, take some of the cabbages off you. Stop people handing you any more."

I watched as he poured water into the pot, and stirred it, and clunked the lid into place.

"Butter? Jam?"

I cleared my throat. "Just jam, please."

He busied himself with a jar and knife.

"And now here's Mark," he said, "who by rights should be helping you handle the cabbages, and the prizes, but instead he's gone and lobbed a giant mammoth cabbage for you to catch. And meanwhile here's me, and I want to help, but I don't really have—permission." He put the plate of toast beside me. He set down a cup of tea. "Do you take milk?"

I shook my head. He touched the backs of his fingers against the back of my hand. I bit my lip. Then he slipped his hand under mine, and lifted it, so that it lay in his warm palm.

"And I just wanted to say that. Sorry. I hope that's okay."

I bit harder on my lip.

"That's got to hurt," he said. "Can you say something, please? Maybe before you actually draw blood?"

I slid off the stool, and put my arms around him and rested my head against his chest. On the rise and fall of it, the thud of his heart. He let his arms come around me; his hand cupped the back of my head. I let a long breath go.

And we just stood there, just breathing, till he squinted down at me and said, "Still awake?"

I nodded. I'd left a smudge of mascara on his T-shirt. I touched it. "Sorry."

"Doesn't matter."

"I really should go home."

"Or—not? If you don't fancy going back to an empty house, you could stay here?"

I hesitated.

"Too much?" he asked.

"I don't want things to be awkward."

"No, that's okay. I get that. And you know what, these past few months it's been a treat, just bumping into you at work and trying to make you laugh. And I'm okay if we go back to that. I didn't imagine that it'd ever be anything more than bumping into you and making you laugh."

"I don't want to—have sex. Tonight."

He went sweetly red. "Well, I'm glad we've cleared that up, thank you very much."

"But I don't want to mess you around either."

"That's not something to worry about. There's a spare room, if you want. Or you can come in with me, if you want. Just for sleep, and company."

"That's what I want," I said. "That is what really I need. Sleep and company."

"No ghost stories, now."

"I promise."

He pushed the teacup closer to me. I lifted it, and drank. I felt the warmth in my hands, and felt the warmth spreading through me.

Chemistry

The little boy's a scribble and she's an upward brushstroke
their voices sing. Crouched on the old floorboards, scuff the
scabs of fallen mortar and the birdshit and birdbones
underfoot and roll the matted spiderswebs between fingertips
and watch the two of them climb into the wind. Voices come
in bits and drabs, broken scattered. Sheep's calls, curlews,
oystercatchers. The cold of fingertips and nose and shivering.

He rests his head against the wall, it sticks to cobwebs
and damp lime.

He is so tired but he doesn't sleep he has given up trying
to sleep. He is keeping watch, but from the distance that he
has to keep, he cant see what his words are doing to her, cant
see how they colour the world for her.

Later he hears a car and he creaks up onto his knees,
looks out sidelong towards the cottage, his body jagged and
crooked with stillness. A man climbs out of the car. That's
him. Another upward stroke, darker than hers. And she is
swinging back down the lane towards him, swept with the
wind, the kid in her arms and held to her, clinging like a
tick and

If he could be closer what would he see.

The child's hand resting on her collar bone, at the open
throat of her shirt. Sweat beading there, the warmth of blood
under the skin. The man's easy smile and the easy kiss. From
where he is just the two lines of them coming together and
then parting, and then the scribble swung across from one to
the other and stuck now to the man. They go inside.

He sinks back down below the windowsill, only the
rubble wall cobwebs and fallen lime, his own head his whole
body full of her of them.

He could just go down the creaking ladder and across the

lane and in through their front door like Banquo's ghost all
the lies that they were telling themselves and each other they
would all fall away; she will have to say what she is what she
has done to him and all that she has made him feel.

But he does not go. And does not go. And does not go.

Because his thoughts are pulling together and making a
story that begins to work. Here it is. If he tells the man then
the man will see the truth will see her for what she is will go
he will take the boy and the boy will stop being there sitting
on her hip hand on her collar bone blood and sweat. He
tells the man and the man is angry is done with her and he
takes the boy and she is free she is free to be with him. It is
colder and he shivers and his nose drips and he. Won't be her
student anymore and she won't be his tutor and they can be
together and

He creaks to his feet, stands to the side of the window.
Lights blink off and on the little boy is being put to bed. His
joints ache. He breathes on his fingers, and then stuffs his
hands into his pockets, and he watches the lights and the
movement of shadows. He could go over there now. He could
go over there.

A light in her bedroom window. He can see flickering
movement, just here and there, as though a bed is being
made or clothes picked off the floor. His stomach drops like
a stone. The two of them in bed together the two of them
together he will be sick at it.

But the lamp is still lit downstairs. And she comes to the
bedroom window and is silhouette and alone

He watches longer and she is alone

He imagines himself in that room, the yellow wallpaper,
moving in behind her, his hands slipped onto her hips, her
straightening up to press back against him, and smile at him
in the mirrored window. He shouldn't be angry it is difficult

*for her she is drained she is leeched all over by the man and
the boy and the work and if she were free*

*She stares out at the night. He stands foursquare in the
window and stares back at her. She is looking at him she is
wanting she doesn't see how easy it would be to have if she
would just be brave enough. He hurts with wanting, hurts
with her pain. He scrambles down the ladder, leaves the
darkness of the barn for the moonlit field. He walks towards
the cottage. She will see him she has seen him she knows that
he is there and*

*He comes to the field gate, stares across at the lit window
at her silhouette. He wants to break something, wants to
smash something, shatter the windscreen and kick in the
headlights of the little red car. He grips the cold metal top bar
of the gate and he stares up at the top window. The light on
her skin she raises her hands to cover her face. He glances,
quick, at the downstairs window, and there is a low lamp
lit there too; he looks up again and she is there still and still
alone. She doesn't look at him but he knows that it is meant
for him that she is telling him. Signalling.*

*She will be brave. But she must take her time. He must
be patient.*

Then she tugs the curtains closed.

*Aching sick wanting and the damp and cold and alone
he turns down the lane, and quietly through the farm, the
dog teeth and eye in the kennel and a flick of torchlight and a
snarl and he goes on quietly through the wet night*

Monday morning. I woke at six with my head pillowed on Patrick's
chest, my knee over his thigh. I'd slept all night without surfacing
once. I don't know when I had last slept like that.

He got up to make coffee and we drank it in bed. There was

a new toothbrush in the bathroom cabinet, a fresh towel on the rack. When I came downstairs in yesterday's clothes, there was toast and more coffee waiting for me in the kitchen.

I slipped out of Patrick's car on the perimeter road of the university, leaving him to park. We walked into the department separately. It was early; raindrops glittered the grass; a groundsman was picking litter from the roadside shrubs. It felt all bright and wholesome. Good things could still happen.

I turned the corner in the corridor and there was Scaife. "Ah yes, hello there; there you are. Do you have a moment?"

"Not right now, sorry; really busy." I went to go past him, but he shifted into my way; I stepped back.

"Something's come up," he said. His eyes travelled down, as if he were considering the way I was dressed. No worse or better than usual; I ran my fingers over my shirt buttons to check they were fastened. At a glance he couldn't possibly know I was in yesterday's clothes.

"Is it urgent?"

"You're busy?"

I nodded, impatient; he grimaced.

"Come to my office, tomorrow morning first thing, eh. We'll have a proper chat then."

He stepped aside; I slipped past him and dodged into my office, and was just booting up my computer when Patrick dropped by, bringing coffee. He stood in the doorway and asked distinctly, so that anyone could overhear, if I got home safe last night, how Monday morning was treating me, which made me smile. I had this strange split vision, of this lovely glow of this new thing with Patrick, and beyond him, looming like a storm, was a snarl of darkness.

When Patrick had gone off to his own office, I checked my email, and there it was, this charming new piece of work from Nicholas. My world had been falling apart around me, and Nicholas had watched it crumble, and made every moment, every gesture be about him. As far as he was concerned, I didn't exist beyond the meaning that he gave me.

And the way that he wrote about Sammy. My stomach curdled.

I skipped out of work, going the long way around to avoid passing Patrick's door. I caught the bus.

I hadn't really thought about the barn beyond the first day's noticing of it. It hadn't seemed significant. Swallows had swooped in and out of it late summer, when we'd moved into the house. Of an evening, it cast a long shadow across the grass.

I wrestled with the twine that held the gate shut, and then I gave up and climbed. My hands gripped the cold top bar, where his had grasped. I stumbled over the rough ground towards the barn. Sheep lifted their heads and stared at me. Rabbits fled. It was quiet. Just the sheep calling, and birdsong, and the sound of a distant car grinding along the country lanes.

The barn doorway was high and arched, big enough to let a hay cart through. I stepped from daylight into shadow. I breathed in the smell of sheep and hay and creosote and damp. There was a shaft of cold light from a low window, and another from a trap-door, a ladder leading up. I picked my way towards it, past rusted bits of farm machinery, feeding troughs and plastic sheeting. The centre of the ladder treads had been scuffed clear of dust, where he had climbed. I climbed too.

Bare boards, rubbed-flat cigarette ends, crushed cans, food wrappers. The stink of urine. But he wasn't there. I moved across the timbers, gingerly; the floor was uneasy underfoot; the whole place felt soiled and sordid. I went to the window, looked out at the front of our house.

I heard that car again, closer now. And then I saw it swing around the bend. Our little red C3. Cogs spun in my head and wouldn't mesh: it shouldn't be here; Mark wasn't back, Sammy wasn't back. They were due on Wednesday. It wasn't Wednesday. But the little red car pulled up outside the cottage and the engine died.

"Hey . . ." Breathless, swinging my leg over the top bar of the gate. Agony and confusion and pleasure to see him.

"Hey."

"What's up?"

"Yeah, change of plan." Mark was getting out of the driver's seat; he squinted up at me, ready to be irritated. "What are you up to?"

I slid down from the top bar of the gate, brushed my hands together, ignoring the question. "I thought you said you'd be back on Wednesday."

He turned to open the back door. "That *was* the plan."

But the look of him, shattered, harried. The habits of love are so hard to break. "Are you okay?"

"Fine."

He hoisted Sam out and passed him to me. Sam was dopy from the drive; he slumped into my neck. The weight of him back in my arms was a relief.

"What's going on?"

"Mum. Mum's going on."

"What happened?"

"She wasn't exactly chuffed."

"Oh . . . ?"

"About any of it." Mark ducked back in to unshackle Sammy's car seat. He set it down on the tarmac, dumped Sammy's bag inside it. "In fact it's fair to say that she went ballistic."

Mark's mum was a receptionist at a medical centre down in Shrewsbury. She was indulgent, comfortable and warm. She liked food and liked to feed people and she liked a glass of wine; she was an easy kind of mum to have; she was certainly an easy kind of mother-in-law. I couldn't imagine her ballistic.

"What did she say?"

"Quite a lot, actually. She had some very strong opinions. She wanted me to know what she thought about compromise, and about relationships requiring work, and not just being all sunshine and flowers, and about some things being completely off the table once you have children. She wanted to remind me that you are lovely and have had a very hard time these past few years. And that I, perhaps, should start behaving like a grown-up rather than a child."

I held my sleeping boy tight. "What did you say?"

"That she should realise I'd been through all of that myself already."

My eyes were suddenly full.

"She's right. She's just—right. I couldn't argue with her. But I couldn't stick around for the disapproval either."

She had fought my corner, and I was grateful. I kept my eyes fixed on Mark, kept them steady and wide. If I looked away for just a moment they'd spill over, and there'd be no coming back from that.

"So what are we going to do?"

He shrugged. "We are where we are."

"But, I mean, do we have to be? If you've changed your mind, at all. We could go somewhere else, like I said. Try something else."

I trailed off, my cheeks burning. Remembering Patrick, remembering this morning, my cheek on his chest, the warmth of him.

"I didn't mean geographically," Mark said.

"I'm just saying. We could try. If you wanted to."

"That's not practical now. Look," he said, "this'll all become normal soon enough. We'll all get used to it. Even Mum. Can you call me, maybe next week, so's we can sort out access. Maintenance. All that stuff. Start proceedings."

I blanched. "Is that it?"

"Okay then. Take care of yourself, yeah?"

"Is that all you have to say to me?"

He got back in the car, started it up, then wound the window down.

"Can we be civilized about this, please?" he asked. "I understand that it isn't easy, but for Sammy's sake can we at least be nice?"

He shifted the car into gear and I stepped back, still holding Sammy, onto the path to get out of the way. He did an ugly three-pointer in the road, bumping up onto the verges, crushing the grass, then pulled away.

Dick, I thought. *Nice.*

I went indoors and laid Sammy down on the sofa; he rolled round onto his side and mumbled. I'd cancelled nursery till Wednesday. I had to work. Alongside everything else I was due in for that meeting with Scaife tomorrow morning. I could hardly bring my toddler son in to that. I sank down beside him, and bit the skin around my fingernails, and, as Mr. Metcalfe had once suggested, I thought on.

I thought on Blue Anorak Man. On what his life had been like, that had brought him to that moment, that he could pass a stranger in the street and decide that he hated her enough to go back and hurt her.

I thought on Mark. How he had been lonely all these years. *Lonely in our marriages,* he'd said. Lonelier married to me than he would have been alone.

I thought on Patrick. How kind he had been. How I knew that if I asked him, he would help. But I hadn't, in the course of things, actually thought to get his phone number. And even if I had his number, I didn't have a signal unless I went outside, and stood there in the field gate by the barn to make a call.

I thought on Nicholas. How his style and subject matter gave the impression of a complete breakdown; how he was, nonetheless, composing extended passages, and then capably emailing them off to me. And if he was doing that, he can't have been hanging round the barn twenty-four-seven: he'd need to charge his laptop and jump onto someone's Wi-Fi. He was probably going home to sleep and eat. Certainly his parents didn't consider him to be completely AWOL. They thought he was going in to class. He was clearly behaving normally enough for them. I considered it all, and the conclusion I arrived at was that he was not as disturbed as he made out. That he didn't necessarily believe that what he was writing was the truth. And that therefore talking to him would make no difference. He was set on his path intentionally, not because he was deluded. It was a deliberate fiction.

I stroked my boy's arm. I touched his pink cheek. He slept on.

I thought on calling the police. That it would mean detailing the events of that night in Michaelmas. It would mean people at work finding out. Scaife would have to be told.

I got as far as the front door. I even had the phone in my hand. Sammy slept on, curled on the sofa. I looked through the stained-glass panel, through the patches of purple and tobacco and green glass. Out there, everything was seething, whispering, just waiting for me step through the door, and into Nicholas's world.

I couldn't do it.

I went back to the sitting room and sat down again beside my sleeping boy. I glanced at my watch. I was missing a third-year undergraduate class. They'd be wondering where I was. But we were tucked up tight, and that was all I could do for now. Tomorrow. Tomorrow. Tomorrow. I'd pull myself together. I didn't see I had a choice now. I had to go to the police.

Sammy woke, flushed and disoriented, around four that afternoon. We made our tea together. I put on bread to toast and I put soup in a pan to heat. Outside the weather worsened, tumbling up into a spring storm, all squalls and blusters. Sammy rode on my hip and we made a game of it as I walked round the house checking the window fixings and drawing the curtains, even though it wasn't yet properly dark.

"Cos it's a horrid old night, isn't it? Got to keep that nasty weather out."

We huddled in the sitting room in front of the fire with the curtains drawn. We played with his Duplo. We fed the fire. I chewed at my thumbnail, glanced round at every noise.

"It's like we're camping out indoors," I told him.

He went along with it, but kept looking at me, checking on me, uncertain. They are canny little creatures, toddlers; they'll suss you out quicker than any grown-up. He decided—I could see him making that decision—that he'd play along for now.

I listened hard. To the wind in trees and the creak of branches and the rattling loose slate on the roof and the drip-drip-drips from the eaves and the water pounding down the guttering, and the soft huff and suck of Sammy's breath. He was watching me listen.

"The wind makes all those funny noises," I said as I picked through the books on the little shelf by the telly. "What story would you like?"

He chose books and I read them. The words came out of my mouth and I turned the pages and all the time I was running a separate system scan—ticking off the sounds of the night and of the house and the weather.

The story finished, I set the book aside and asked him what next.

He got up and trotted over and pulled out another. *There's a Dragon at My School.* We settled down to read.

And it went on like that, books and more books, while Sammy's head grew heavy and he blinked slow blinks. He wasn't even in his pyjamas yet, and his teeth were still unbrushed. He leaned into me. His breathing slowed and softened. He fell asleep.

I set *Mog the Forgetful Cat* aside. The door creaked in the wind. A slate rattled. Water dripped. I carried my little boy upstairs, and laid him down on my own bed. I turned the key in my bedroom door and locked us in. I lay beside him, drew the duvet over both of us, and flicked off the light. I listened to the trees thrashing in the wind. A *ter-wit, ter-wit* from an owl. After a while, I got up and went to the window and lifted the edge of the curtain. I watched the wet, tangled, tossing darkness. I could make out the outline of the barn, against the muddled sky. No light from its window. No one watching from the gate. But then he'd always been a step ahead of me: he'd only ever written what he wanted me to know.

It was maybe after three a.m. when I dozed off, and I woke again just before six, curled round Sammy like a comma. He was still sleeping, his eyelashes long and dark on his cheeks. The wind had stopped and the day was calm; the sheep were calling to each other across the fields. I got up carefully. I stretched myself out and eased the crick in my neck. The first bus was at seven fifteen. We'd leave at the last minute. Run for it.

Patrick's house; we were in the kitchen, and it was still weirdly early to be anywhere but home. Patrick had received us with a kind of bemused calm, brought us in for second breakfast. Sammy was now ambling up and down the stone steps from the room above. Whenever he got to the foot of the steps, he'd peer through the doorway into the kitchen, and then he'd turn and start climbing the steps again.

"Some of your third-years turned up, looking lost. Lisa fobbed them off. She said you'd called in sick, promised to reschedule. So you'll have to remember to thank her."

"I will. She's a star."

"So what exactly happened?"

"Mark dumped Sam and ran; I had to drop everything."

"What an ass."

"I wanted to let you know, but there wasn't time; I don't have your number so I couldn't call. I'd already cancelled his nursery too. I'll have to see if they can squeeze him back in. He's really dropped me in it, Mark has."

All of this was true, and it felt like enough, for now.

Sammy peeked around the corner at us. He smiled, and then ducked away again and began again to climb.

"The little guy doesn't know? He hasn't worked it out yet?"

"Not yet."

"You'll tell him though?"

"I guess I'll have to."

He topped up my coffee cup. "Are you teaching today?"

"And I was due to have a meeting with Professor Scaife."

"Okay," Patrick said. "Well, here's a thought. You phone Lisa, tell her you would have called yesterday. You explain how you have no signal at home and you were too sick to go outside. Say you're sorry about the third-years but you were in an awful state, you were throwing up all day. But you'll pop in and see her this afternoon."

"Okay . . ."

"She'll tell you to stay home. After you have a sickness bug, you have to stay away from work for a further twenty-four hours."

"Oh."

"Policy. This way you get a bit of breathing space. You'll have to reschedule teaching but that was going to happen anyway after yesterday. You can call nursery from here. And, if you'd like to, we can hang out today. I'll work through the weekend instead."

Sammy was coming back down the stairs.

"You can both stay over tonight, in the spare bedroom, if you'd like."

"God," I said. "That would be amazing."

"I don't know about that."

But it was a day's grace, and that alone seemed wonderful. I pushed everything to arm's length: tomorrow was soon enough.

He drove us up to Gill House to collect our things, with Sam on my lap and my seat belt round both of us, and my arms wrapped round his little body. I called nursery from the car: they conceded, with considerable tooth-sucking and muttering, that they could fit Sammy back in tomorrow. I felt wrapped up and cocooned in the car, just letting us be driven, and it was only when we climbed the rise out of the farmyard, rounded the bend, and the barn loomed into view, its narrow eyes slitted at us, its dark mouth trailing worn mud and stones like vomit, that it dawned on me that by letting him bring us out here, I'd gone and dragged Patrick into Nicholas's sights.

I scrabbled overnight stuff together, but Sammy insisted on packing a bag too, because if you're going anywhere, and you are three years old, then you will need to bring a backpack full of toys and books. Patrick was patient with him, chatting as they filled a bag and I ran around scooping up toothbrushes and pyjamas and underpants, glancing through the windows, and at my watch.

I locked up, and we drove away.

Sammy burbled in the back of the car, kept handing toys forward, between the seats, for Patrick to inspect. I intercepted them, held them awhile, handed them back, kept saying *Not now, love, Patrick's driving.*

We pulled up on the prom; the tide was out, leaving behind an expanse of rippled silver silt; beyond, the Lake District hills were layered blue and purple, still veined with snow. The air was brisk and made my eyes water; Patrick was already hoisting Sam out of the back seat of the car; he swung him round then set him down on his feet on the pavement. The wind made Sammy skittish: he did a little frolicky dance there, his parka rippling and ballooning; I caught Patrick's eye, and we shared a smile.

Patrick hustled us across the road, through an arched iron gateway, to a little park, where a brass band was parping out that particularly northern brand of nostalgia between borders planted with primulas and daffodils and hyacinths. Kids darted round on scooters, wobbled on small bikes. Dogs dragged old ladies after them.

"Is the little guy allowed an ice cream?"

"I should say so."

Patrick bought Sam a 99 with raspberry sauce, and coffee for us. Sam's eyes went wide when the ice cream was handed down to him. We walked with paper cups and dripping cone, past crazy golf and damp children, swing-boats hitched like horses and a merry-go-round under a tarpaulin, a splash park closed out of season, and a miniature railway chugging round its miniature track. Sammy walked in wonder, and munched at his soggy cone.

"This is a really lovely place," I said.

Further along was a timber-built adventure-playground. Sammy shoved the last of the cone into his face and belted off at high speed then clambered up and over and scrambled and slid down, until he was spent, and flumped in the damp sand and dug it with his hands, and shook his head at the invitation to do anything more at all. Patrick shook out the last drops of his coffee then handed the paper cup down to Sammy as a makeshift bucket. I hunkered with Sammy and we made elaborate sandcastles with the paper cups.

Later, on the prom, we ate chips and watched the tide race in. Sammy huddled between us on the bench, zipped up to his chin in his parka, posting chips in through the porch of his hood with quiet concentration. The sun was setting, coral pink and golden, and the lights of little towns across the bay began to prickle out and trace the lower contours of the land. And I felt—I remember the quiet revelation of it—I felt happy. And I just wanted things to stay like this.

"How can I have not done this before?"

On the far side of Sam, over his hooded head, Patrick's glasses were sheened with silver and pink.

"Busy life," Patrick said.

I asked Sammy if he was done with his chips yet, and he shook his hooded head and rummaged in the paper wrapping, totally focussed; Patrick chuckled quietly. It was perfect, and it was a bubble. It was a moment suspended out of time. It couldn't last, but I wasn't going to burst it deliberately myself.

"You're enjoying those," Patrick said.

Sammy turned his hooded head to stare up at Patrick. He said, "They are *nice*," with great seriousness.

I put Sammy to bed in Patrick's attic spare bedroom. The room had the kind of stark tidiness you only get in a childless household: storage boxes in the corner, a clothes rail with a couple of suits still cellophaned from the cleaners, a double futon that Patrick had made up for Sam and me in austere charcoal grey. We tipped Sammy's bag out onto the floor and I realised he had been absolutely right to pack all these gaudy bits of junk, the spacemen and the racing cars and jingly Blue Hippo who he'd had since he was born. The room had been in need of them.

"Did you have a good day?" I asked him.

"Best day *ever*," he replied, rosy cheeked and fighting sleep, not wanting it to end.

I lay with him till he drifted off. My head on the pillow beside his, my brain flushed with love for him, watching his face as his brain processed memories of the best day ever.

Patrick was in the back sitting room, lighting the wood-burner, when I came down.

"Thank you for today," I said.

"I was going to say the same to you."

"Sammy's spark out. He had a great time."

"I had a great time too. I loved how he ate his chips." He got to his feet and dusted his palms. He handed me a glass of wine.

"Thank you." I glanced round for somewhere to set it down. "But—uh—I don't, so . . ." I handed it back to him. He took it off me with a puzzled frown.

"I just—don't. Any more. No biggie."

"I guess you've got enough to do without having to do it all hung-over."

"Yeah, there is that. And I wanted to ask you, because work. We'll be, you know. Discreet?"

He tilted his head, equivocal.

"What?"

"Might be a wee bit late for discretion. 'Shameless flirting.' That's what I was told."

I put my hands to my face. "Oh God. Who said that?"

"Mina."

"Oh *God*. God."

"Me, not you."

"That was flirting?"

"That's how good I am at it. You don't even notice when it's happening . . ." He reached an arm out along the back of the sofa, with a quizzical expression, offering a hug.

I sank in against him, and breathed his scent of oranges and malt. His chin grazed my hair. His arm was warm around me. I found myself thinking of that bit of thistledown preserved in Karen's pendant. That you couldn't properly look at a thing like that until it was captured in resin. That in its natural state it would collapse between your fingertips or blow away, or be glimpsed on a summer's day, drifting against a blue sky.

I slipped in beside Sammy a little after midnight, and slept until my alarm woke us both. He snuggled up to me and smiled against my skin. We pottered downstairs, to the kitchen, where Patrick was making breakfast.

With that new shared consciousness of each other's bodies, Patrick and I brushed by each other, caught smiles off each other. He drove us to work; he dropped me and Sam at nursery. Sam skipped in, chatting to Jenni first then bolting off to join his friends.

Then I had to go straight into that rescheduled third-year class, and from that to my usual Wednesday mid-morning sessions. I had the MA in the afternoon but between one and the other, I'd look up the local police station's number and I'd call them. Once that was done I'd go straight and tell Patrick, before he heard it anywhere else.

I was just on my way to my office to make the call. I wanted coffee and a bun, but would leave that till afterwards, as a small reward for doing what I had to do. But as I was passing his office, Professor Scaife lunged out and stopped me dead.

"Uh, that meeting?"

"Hi, yeah, sorry—I was ill; didn't Lisa let you know? Can we reschedule? I'm running to catch up with myself at the moment." I gestured as though going to slip past him but he lifted a hand to fill the gap.

"I'd rather we do this now."

"I've got so much on."

"Nonetheless." He gestured back into his office.

Just get it over with. Then there might still be time for me to make the call before afternoon teaching began. He still held his office door open, waiting for me to slide past.

"After you," I said.

"No, after you," he insisted.

I smiled fixedly, stood my ground. He blinked and went in. I followed him. I perched on the edge of his green Parker Knoll. It was a sinking kind of seat.

"I suppose you already know what this is about?"

I shook my head.

"Not even a guess?"

"Does Professor Lynch want me to write up all of last year's student feedback for him?"

He looked baffled. "I don't think so . . ."

"You want someone to redesign the entire creative writing programme from scratch and I'm the woman for the job?"

He narrowed his already narrow eyes, puzzled. "Not immediately, no."

"Maybe the windows need cleaning?"

"I see. You're being facetious."

"Not really," I said. "They're looking rather grubby."

"I've received a complaint about your conduct," he said.

"No."

"Well I have, so, yes."

I thought of Steven, aggrieved by my mishandling of the conflict between him and Nicholas. I thought of Richard, offended because I'd laughed at that quip about pies. I thought of Tim, who I'd allowed to tank completely, and whose request to read extra work out of term-time I'd refused. And now I was reading Nicholas's extra work at all hours; though presumably Tim didn't know about that. I said, "Complaint?"

"I received this from one of your students," Scaife said.

He reached for a folder on his desk, and selected a document carefully from its contents.

"It makes for interesting reading, even if she does go on a bit."

MERYL SHARRATT

Complaint Cont.

But I wouldn't have said a thing. I wouldn't have breathed a word. I wouldn't be considering this action at all if Nicholas had been happy, and the rest of the class had been taken care of.

I knew relationships between faculty and students were frowned upon, but I also knew they happened; I'm not a total innocent. If Nicholas had been continuing with his classes and thriving and getting the work done, and particularly if he had been open with me about it—openness and honesty being so very important to me—I would've left them to it: let him sleep his way to the middle if that was what he wanted. After all, I had bigger plans, and I'd revert to their original version: I could still be Simone de Beauvoir; I didn't need a Jean-Paul Sartre. Or I could always find myself another one.

But Nicholas wasn't happy. He went quiet. He shut down. All that vacation he didn't answer any of my texts or phone calls, and then the next term he didn't show up for class.

And then I thought, maybe it wasn't cynical on his part. Maybe he really liked her, loved her even, and things went wrong between them. Maybe she'd used him and cast him aside. Maybe that's the kind of person she was. It happens.

Then her teaching dropped off too. I knew from the get-go that second term that she was keeping something from us. You could see it in her, the twitchy self-consciousness; the distractedness. He might have been absent, but she was barely there herself. You'd think with him gone we'd all get more individual attention, but no.

You pay nine thousand "quid" and come halfway around the world to present your work only to be asked *Well, what do you think?* Well, what I think is that it just isn't good enough.

And also, you see: Nicholas was vulnerable. Anyone who'd been in that classroom knew this. *She* knew this. So when he disappeared I was worried about him. I didn't expect or by then even want us to get back together, but I was worried about him. He wasn't replying to texts, and phone calls went straight to voicemail, so I had no choice but to go to his home. I took the bus out there. I wasn't going to ask Karen to drive; it would be just too awkward. And I knew there was a good chance of this being a wild-goose chase—that I'd get there and there'd be no one around or he wouldn't answer the door or they would've moved out or left the country or something crazy like that. But what else could I do?

The house, in spring daylight, looked unpromising and gloomy. I stood on the street awhile, nervous, not knowing now how to proceed. The front door hadn't been opened last time, and going around the side of the house to the kitchen door seemed presumptuous. I looked up at the top window, to what I guessed was his bedroom. The curtains were closed as if someone was asleep in there. Was he sick, I wondered, with a little leap of hope; was he in fact desperately ill? My mind spun a little fantasy, in which I was allowed, first as a visitor, and then soon there-after as a nurse, into the intimacy of his bedroom, and the rift between us was healed as he got better and grew strong again. I think I'd probably read that somewhere . . . maybe *Shirley*. Anyway, it didn't happen. Someone came out of the front door and across the gravel towards me; it wasn't Nicholas. It was a heavy-set man in a sweater and shirt and chinos. He moved like he had a bad hip, stiff and wincing. He had those same silver-blue eyes, but his were dim and bloodshot. He looked like a coarsened, fattened version of his son.

"Hallo there. Hallo. Can I help you?"

He came up to the gate. He was red and he smelled like liquor.

"I'm here to see Nicholas."

I offered a hand to be shaken. He looked at me narrowly. I lowered my hand.

"I'm Meryl. I'm from his class. Is he home?"

The man—Mr. Palmer senior, I presumed—spoke briskly. "You've missed him, I'm afraid. He's just gone in to class."

"We don't have class today. He hasn't been coming to class all term."

His jaw worked. He cast around him, then he said, "You'd better come in."

We crunched over the gravel and I followed him into the hall. He bawled out his wife's name up the stairs. "Jan-ET!"

She came in a fluster of draped clothes and long limbs. "Don't shout at me, Andrew." Seeing me there, she adjusted her expression. She had the hyper-carefulness of a daytime drinker. I've seen it before.

"Who's this?"

"You need to hear it from the horse's mouth," he said. "Go on, tell her."

I told her about Nicholas's absence from class, that I was worried about him. She seemed as surprised as her husband had been, and seemed to eye me with equal suspicion. I felt very uncomfortable. This was not what I'd intended. I'd come to support Nicholas, to offer an honest hand of friendship. And here I was, snitching on him to his parents.

"Not again," she said.

"Just pissing it away," he said. "Just *pissing it away*."

"What'll we do now," she said. "What on earth are we going to do now . . . ?"

He gave her a look; she went quiet.

"First things first, eh. I'll drive you back to the university," and he gave me a smile. It was a strange smile, fixed and uneasy. He got his keys out of a side-table drawer and jingled them.

"I have a round-trip ticket, so I'm good, thanks."

"What time's your bus?"

I glanced at my watch, puzzled. "A while yet."

"Well, you'd better go and wait at the stop," he said.

"Okay."

"You can find your way back there, can you? Or shall I walk you?"

"That's fine," I said. "I'll manage."

"Well then," he said. "Safe home."

Outside again, the cool spring day was just as it had been, a blackbird hopping across the border and the breeze in my face and a little shrub all in frilly yellow flowers already, and I thought, I've opened a can of worms, and I didn't even know there was a can of worms, and now it's split and the contents wriggling all over the floor. I could hear their voices still behind me; they were loud, disinhibited by alcohol: they couldn't see me so they assumed I couldn't hear them. To tell the truth, I couldn't hear individual words, but I could hear perfectly well the way that they were spoken. It was ugly.

I was worried for him; things were bad for him already, and now I'd alerted his drunk and potentially abusive parents to behavior which they clearly disapproved of. I walked away, my cheeks burning, ashamed and afraid of what I'd done. At the gate I paused and glanced back at that high bedroom window. The curtains had been drawn back, and I glimpsed movement, and it might have been him, hidden away up there, alone and maybe needing me. But what could I do? I felt like I'd just rushed in where angels fear to tread and started rearranging the furniture.

I didn't have any options left, but this. I decided to write up everything that had happened, beat by beat. I'd name names. I'd tell the story straight. I'd make an official complaint. Because it's important to me that the right people are held to account.

Everyone's free to make their own decisions. I acknowledge that. We're all adults here. But when the effects of these decisions ripple out and put at risk everything a young person has worked for all her life, all the sacrifices she has made, all expenses she has gone to, then that must be recognized; that requires redress.

"Let me see that." I lunged forwards, jangling the chair springs. He handed Meryl's statement to me and my eyes dashed over it.

"A tad histrionic, and like I said, it does go on a bit. But that's Creative Writers for you, eh?"

I snapped it out straight, tried to focus.

"You can keep that copy."

"But she's got it all wrong."

"You mean you didn't sleep with this student, or that you haven't shown him any favouritism, or that your teaching hasn't been below par?"

I just looked at him.

"These things do happen," he said. "These . . . entanglements. That's precisely why we have protocols, so that nobody gets their nose put out of joint."

My mouth was dry. "I know the protocols."

He leaned in confidentially, rubbing his palms together, then meshing his long fingers and sliding them back and forth. "Look, we'll make some redress to the young woman, show good-will, offer her some extra tuition perhaps. People rarely object to favouritism if they're the object of it."

"You want me to give her catch-up classes?"

"That's just one idea. But before we start soft-soaping her, the bigger issue here is the boy. You'd better let me know exactly what happened with him, so we're all on the same page." He slid his hands apart, rested them on his own knees. "Then I'll pop a note on his file—we can backdate it actually, to avoid any awkwardness; no one need know—and then I'll make all the necessary adjustments. If you could just tell me what really happened."

I suppose he was being kind; he was certainly offering me a way out.

"And of course I'll have to write it up for your file too."

"My permanent record?"

"I'm afraid that's how it works. You tell me, as your Head of Department, I write it up; it goes on your record. Job done."

I swallowed.

"It's best we get this sorted now, quash it all for good. Otherwise it all gets rather complicated and official and, well, noticeable. I'd be obliged to pass Ms. Sharratt's complaint on to the Faculty Disciplinary Committee. You'll have to submit a statement and go before the panel to answer questions. Her account is pretty persuasive, and in the current climate I don't fancy your chances much with the panel. So I strongly advise we sort this out between us now, rather than risk a much more . . . exposing . . . situation."

"And it has to be you?" I asked.

"Hey?"

"It has to be you?"

"Well, yes it does, actually."

"It can't be Mina or Kate that I talk to?"

He gave me a look then, and there was an edge there of real hostility. It was as though he was seeing me for the first time as a person, and not just a convenience.

"I think we're past that," he said. "Past the time for you to pick and choose a confidante. The Palmer boy is in a secure psychiatric unit. He's been sectioned. You do know he's had a complete breakdown?"

"Since when?"

"His attendance has been patchy, his behaviour erratic, for some time, hasn't it? But you didn't report that, or refer him. Which matches what Ms. Sharratt says. And is a potential whole other kettle of fish; should *he* choose to make a complaint, or his family . . ."

I nodded. I rubbed my arms. Scaife talked on; I barely heard him.

"I don't think he's had a breakdown," I said across him.

"Are you his psychiatrist?"

"No."

"Well then." He sat back, and crossed his legs, and folded his arms, bundling himself up like a pile of sticks. It made me feel less ill-at-ease, knowing that I was disliked by him.

"Who's on the panel?" I asked.

He reeled off a list of half a dozen names. I recognised one or two, but didn't know any of them personally.

"Okay."

"You won't resolve this now?"

I shook my head.

He tucked himself up still tighter, legs hooked under his chair. "I don't understand you. I really don't. What *is* your problem?"

That he had never had my best interests at heart. That he felt entitled to put his hands on me. That if I told him the story of that night, I wasn't certain that he wouldn't enjoy it.

I shrugged.

"Well then, I'm sorry to say that you're suspended, effective immediately. You're not to contact your students. Stay away from the department. The dean will be in touch, as will your union rep."

"That's it then? Can I go?"

He nodded, and I left.

This, I think, is a major flaw in my character. I don't complain, I don't explain. I just strike a match, and torch the bridge, and walk away, my back warmed by the flames. I am too much like my mother.

I glimpsed Patrick through his office door before I knocked. He was reading student work; there was a chunk of computer print-out face down on his desk, an open Jiffy bag lying on the floor. I tapped. He looked up from the sheaf of paper. I went in. And everything was different.

"What is it?" I asked, but I already knew.

He lifted the pages from the desk, to show me the title page. I went to take it off him, as though gaining possession of it could change anything. He moved it out of reach, put the whole thing back down on his desk.

"It's not true," I said.

He busied himself with tamping down the edges, getting the pages into alignment, not looking at me. "It was in my pigeon-hole," he said.

"You should have come to me."

"You mean, I shouldn't have read it—"

"—It's not true—"

"The thing is, though, you see"—he still didn't look at me—"he's really got you."

"What?"

"The way you are."

"Don't."

"It's you." And then he looked at me. The light reflected in his glasses and I couldn't see his eyes. "I mean." he said. "It's you. It's. Convincing."

I felt sick. I reached for a chair, sat down, put my face in my hands.

"Since Beth left—" Patrick went on, "I'd not really wanted to, not get close to anyone. But I've been, for ages I've been—daydreaming about you . . . I really liked you."

"Yes."

"But it was all—rather—easy. The two of us, you and me."

I looked up. "Easy?"

"I mean, Mark was barely out of the door when you and I—got together. So. What I'm wondering now is if maybe you're just like that. Maybe that's just what you do." He took off his glasses, pinched the bridge of his nose.

"You know what?"

He gave me a look, wrung out, exhausted. "What?"

"Even if it were true, you don't get to be like this about it."

"What. Given the circumstances, it's not unreasonable to be . . . upset."

"But the thing is, you see, whatever happened, this is before you, so it's nothing to do with you. Even if I'd fallen into bed with every single man I ever met, it would be none of your business. Everything I did before you, and everything I do after you, has got fuck all to do with you, Patrick. It's only *while* and *during* that's any business of yours whatsoever."

He chewed on this. "Okay, well, tell me this then." He touched the manuscript with tented fingertips. "Because this is the kid you were telling me about last term, isn't it? And here he is writing about an obsession with you, writing about you in an intimate way, and you can't deny that. This isn't a coincidence. I need to know what I'm missing here. What don't I understand?"

I took a breath, I let it go. "Late last term. He walked me home and . . ."

Patrick sat back. "So you did sleep with him."

I half shook my head.

"What then?"

"He put me in a situation where I—gave up saying no. I

decided to give up; it was a conscious decision not to fight. But that doesn't mean . . . And then he started writing this stuff, started acting like we'd been . . ."

Patrick came over, hunkered down beside my chair. He put his hand on my arm.

"All this time and you didn't say," he said.

I shook my head, wiped my hands down my jeans. "I don't understand."

"I don't either. It's completely incomprehensible to me, why someone would go and do a thing like that."

"No, I mean, I don't understand why it's better."

He squeezed my arm. He studied my face. "I don't follow you."

"That it's better, far as you're concerned, that this happened to me, rather than I had a nice time. Than I had consensual sex with someone that I liked, before you and I got together."

He buffered at this. "I—"

"But that's where we are. That's what this all means. This sympathy. You're happier with this, now, than you were with that."

He stood up.

"So," I said. "Okay."

He went back to his seat. "What do you want me to do with this document?" he asked.

"Best hang on to it for now," I said. "I suppose it's evidence."

I went straight to the ladies' loo and locked myself into a cubicle. I stood there breathing till I could breathe normally. Then I went to the mirror and tidied up my face.

I sprung Sammy from nursery. I bought him a new toothbrush in the Spar on the way past, because a new toothbrush always makes him happy. I found myself wondering what had made Nicholas happy, when he was three years old.

We caught the bus. I read Meryl's statement through as we jogged along, read it clearly, from start to finish, and I felt I began to get a fingernail at last into this. A bit of purchase. We got spat out at the crossroads in the drizzle.

The worst was happening—my marriage was over, my job probably was too; that fresh new thing with Patrick was certainly done for—but I felt somehow lighter for it. I'd manage. I'd get a new job; I had other skills. Well. I could acquire other skills. There'd been a little recruitment poster on the back of the bus driver's cab *Join our team!* They were promising 22K a year and that they'd put you through your PSV licence, so that was a possibility. Or maybe I'd be a postie. Sammy and I could buzz around the neighbourhood in a little red van. We'd get a fucking cat and call it fucking Jess. And when Sammy started school I'd deliver the post in the mornings and in the afternoons I'd write; we'd have time and sunshine and rain on the windows and crumpets over the fire and my novel would be good because I wouldn't be drawing water from the same well and dishing it out for other people all the time, and my agent who hadn't heard from me in years now would be thrilled with the new manuscript and we'd sell it for a six-figure sum, and I'd get on a couple of shortlists and the *Guardian Weekend* would profile me, the postie novelist of north Lancashire.

Nicholas was sectioned, Scaife had said. He was in a secure psychiatric unit, so that was something. I couldn't teach, I couldn't even go into the department, so all I had to worry about for the moment was looking after Sammy and exonerating myself. I had to get my story straight, and to do so I needed to fill in some of the gaps in Nicholas's, stat.

We rattled down to the village. Me and Sammy and the pushchair, heading for the Palmers' house. What had struck me from the final part of Meryl's statement—aside from its stinging hostility towards me—was that the Palmers had seemed mightily concerned that Meryl get straight back to campus, and not hang around the neighbourhood looking for Nicholas. Why the urgency? Were they worried that she'd stumble on something they didn't want her to know, or, I wondered, were they afraid that she was putting herself in harm's way?

There was an old Jag cooling on the drive. Sammy had fallen asleep in the pushchair; I'd rather been banking on that. I rang the doorbell. They didn't know me, I reminded myself, shoving shaking hands into my pockets. They didn't have clue one who I was. It wasn't that I expected them to offer up much; I was just going to have a scrape and poke around here, see what set the nerves jangling. I waited at the door through a long silence, and then clicking footsteps, and the door opened. A woman in her early fifties, saluki-built and dressed in cream and beige. Behind her, that familiar hallway. The smell of vacuuming and lilies, perfume and afternoon drink.

"Ah, hello. Mrs. Palmer?"

She glanced me up and down as though expecting a lanyard, an ID card or a parcel to be proffered. But there was just me, with my child in a pushchair.

"Yes, what is it?" She asked, speaking quietly, because of the sleeping child.

I wafted my staff card at her, a finger over my name. She barely glanced at it, but she stared long and hard at Sammy.

"It's about Nicholas."

She looked at me now. "He's not here."

"No, I know. I know. I'm from the university."

"I'm sorry—who are you?"

I pocketed my card. "I just have a few questions."

She went to close the door. I put a foot across the threshold, a hand on the glossy wood, smiled brightly.

"It really won't take a moment."

She called over her shoulder:

"Andrew—could you come here, please?"

There was a shifting and lumbering and a figure creaked down the corridor; she stepped back so that he could move in front of her. He filled the doorway. A bulky, bloodshot, liverish man; a hard, distended belly under a shirt and sweater.

"What's the problem?" he asked.

"I need to talk to you about Nicholas."

"I don't think so." He applied his considerable weight to the door. My foot was getting crushed.

"I'm here from the university. I was just telling Mrs. Palmer. We have some questions about your son's file; we're missing information, you see; I thought maybe you could help us. Just bureaucracy, you understand. In the circumstances. Keeping our records up to date."

A glance between husband and wife. Mr. Palmer lessened the pressure on the door.

"Okay great, well maybe if you could just tell me what he was up to in his gap years?"

"Gap years?"

"Yes, all those years out. Did he travel, or do voluntary work, perhaps?"

"I don't see what that's got to do with his current situation."

"Or did he have any . . . previous problems of the kind he's now experiencing?"

"What do you know about his problems?"

Mrs. Palmer called from behind her husband, "We want to talk to Michael Lynch."

Mr. Palmer leaned in close to me; his breath smelt of wine. "You know what, we don't have to answer anything. You tell me. You tell me why our son, with so great an investment on our part, should be allowed to drop out of his course like a stone, without so much—"

"Why would you talk to Professor Lynch, though? What's he got to do with it?"

Mrs. Palmer spoke round her husband's shoulder. "He over-saw the whole thing. He was so helpful. If there's anything to be said, we'll say it to Michael."

"In what way helpful?"

She moved in beside her husband, wrapped her cardie tighter round herself.

"Nicholas's results don't reflect his abilities; Michael could see that. He knew Nick deserved a second chance."

"How did Professor Lynch come to know Nicholas?"

"He's always known him."

"How's that?"

"Michael and I were at school together," Mr. Palmer said. "He's an old friend."

"Okay, I see."

"Who exactly are you anyway?" Mr. Palmer asked. "Who sent you here?"

"I'm just doing my job," I said.

"And what is your job?"

"Filling in the gaps, like I said. Trying to understand."

Mr. Palmer seemed to consider all that had been said and weigh up the different elements; he offered up a concluding thought: "Look, just fuck off, would you?"

He shoved against the door, and my foot began to crumple, and I yelped and yanked it out. The door slammed shut.

Sammy jerked awake, and looked around him, startled.

"Hello there, lovie," I said. "Sorry about that."

We rattled back up the road to Gill House. I might not have filled in any gaps, but I had a better sense of the background fabric now.

"It's just you and me, Sammy-boy." He peered round at me, forehead bunched. "You and me against the world."

He considered this, still frowning, then he lifted his toothbrush and turned back to face the world as it rushed towards him. A little Don Quixote in his pushchair, tilting at the rain with his toothbrush.

As we crossed the farmyard, Mr. Metcalfe was coming out of the tractor shed. He raised a hand to us. I wiped my face and summoned up a smile.

"You're home early," he said. He looked small and wiry and windblown in his blue overalls and cut-down wellies.

"They sent me home." And I laughed again, because it sounded like I'd got caught smoking behind the bike sheds.

He frowned, rubbed the rain from his nose with the back of a hand. This was a man for whom work was grained into every object that he touched, every moment of his day. "Why'd they do that then?"

"Spot of bother with a couple of my students."

"You'll need a brew."

Mostly it's just the slogging on, head down against the weather; that's how stuff can slip you by: the grizzled old farmer, the rundown farm, the elderly woman out wandering, looking for her daughter, Sarah. It never occurred to me that their troubles were in any way entangled with my own.

I unbuckled Sam. We left the pushchair in the farmhouse's stone porch; Moss the dog followed us in. The kitchen was unlovely and hard-worn, the air warm and stale. Mr. Metcalfe called up the stairs: "Gracie! Fancy a brew?" and there was a reply though I couldn't hear the words.

He put the kettle on, shifting it from the enamelled side of the Rayburn onto a hotplate. The dog curled up with the cat in front of the stove, and Grace came slowly down the stairs and into the kitchen, housecoat on over her skirt and sweater, feet in zipped-up slippers.

"It's that nice lass from Gill House, Grace, remember."

"Where's James?" That anxious edge to her voice, as though panic were only ever held at arm's length.

"James is out int top field, fence needed mending, remember."

She gripped her housecoat closed at the neck, spotted Sammy. "Is that our Sarah's child?"

"No," said Mr. Metcalfe. "This'un here belongs to yon lass, remember."

She nodded uncertainly. I rested a hand on Sammy's head to confirm our connection. Sammy shuffled back in towards me.

"I'll be . . ." she said, and she turned away and went off up the hall.

"She has the dementia," he told me. "What she does is, she tries to fit people in with what she can remember. Have a seat."

He rummaged in a cupboard and lifted out a melamine cup; he slugged in milk and twisted on the lid and handed it to me with a nod to Sammy. The cup was decorated with a bunny and a ladybird and a few blades of grass; its spout was worn rough by other children's teeth. The kettle whistled; he made the tea and took a cup through to his wife; when he came back he said, "You'll be wondering about Sarah."

I wasn't really. I'd figured her a bustling grown-up daughter, rushed off her feet with work and kids and popping in and out of the farmhouse to check on her parents when she got a moment in her busy day. I realised now I'd only heard her mentioned by Grace, and when Grace spoke of her, Sarah was present tense. But now John talked about his daughter, and it was in the past perfect.

She had been a happy girl, full of sunshine, loads of friends. She had planned to go to Agricultural College. She had always said that she couldn't wait for him to retire so she could be in charge of the farm. Once she got her hands on it he wouldn't recognise the place.

Sammy handed the empty cup to me, and I set it on the table. He leaned in against me.

"What happened?" I asked.

"We're all Chapel, up here; Methodist; drink is, well—we don't hold with drink. That summer between school and college, she'd got new friends, she'd get back late, crashing around the place. We'd try and get her to stay home, or see her old friends, but. That Palmer kid would turn up in that eyesore of a car of his, and she'd dash out to it, and that was that. Short of locking her up, what could we do."

"The Palmer kid?"

"Aye. The younger'un. Nicholas."

The three syllables of his name, and I realised: I knew this story. The lost girl now had a name. It was Sarah.

Mr. Metcalfe told me about nights that she didn't come home, how he'd go out looking for her, driving round the lanes and pubs and the streets in town, peering at women and girls, making a fool of himself. One night he had to knock on the Palmers' door at two in the morning and was sent away with a flea in his ear, and had to be up for milking at half five. And the next day she fell out of that little yellow Audi that swung round and was gone in a spray of muck before he could get his hands on the little . . .

Then her brother, James. He'd stood there in his school uniform, told them that the crowd his sister was hanging round with had a reputation, and Sarah had that reputation too now, and the reputation was for drugs.

"It might not seem like such a big thing to you, perhaps, coming from London where I s'pose everybody and their auntie's on the drugs, but the strongest thing we have in the house is Benylin."

"It's not my thing either," I said. "And when it's your own child . . ." I stroked Sammy's head.

They drew a line. She wouldn't be seeing any of that crowd again. She'd be starting at college and knuckling down and no more nonsense. And if there were more nonsense, they'd be calling the police. And she, well, she just shrugged. It was like it didn't matter, like nothing mattered. All the sunshine was gone out of her.

He went quiet. Remembering.

"The Palmer get went back to university, and Sarah started her course, and I thought it were over and she'd settle back down and be alright. But she were pregnant."

They had to drag themselves down to the big house again, cap in hand, talk to the Palmers, thinking the kids could maybe make it work; maybe it would be the making of them, bit of responsibility. But the Palmers were having none of it.

"He said my Sarah was a . . . I'm not going to say the word. He said she were trying to get her claws into their son. That's what Andy Palmer said. Like that boy were such a prize."

"That's awful."

"We did what we had to. We put up and shut up. We'd raise the baby, me and Grace. A late one of our own, like; very late. But there's always room for another child, on a farm. Sarah could still have had her life. She seemed resolved to it. Happy even, getting back on track. It certainly weren't end of the world."

In my lap, Sammy curled round on his side; his thumb slid into his mouth.

"Those are the last memories Gracie has. She weren't poorly back then, or we didn't know yet, if she were. She got properly poorly after Sarah died."

"How did it happen?"

"Sarah? She took an overdose. This stuff called ketamine. Have you heard of it?"

I nodded.

"They say it gives you hallucinations; too much and it messes up your lungs, and then it stops your heart. She'd taken off her clothes; she were out in the snow, but it were like she were too hot. And all the time we thought she were tucked up safe at her friend Judith's. So the last thing she said to us were a lie."

He cleared his throat. The collie got up from the rug and came over and lay her chin on his lap, and he stroked her forehead with a calloused thumb. "She were a good lass and expected that of other people; it weren't her fault if he took advantage."

"I'm so sorry."

He raised a shoulder. "It were term-time so he were at college, he said, like that meant owt; like he couldn't get up here in a few hours in his car. They checked her phone records but, nothing."

"You suspect . . . ?"

"I reckon. I believe. They arranged it in advance. The place they used to go to in the woods, middle of the night, middle of his term, meeting up together like they did before the summer ended. He brought the stuff. Persuaded her to take it."

"Was there no evidence?"

"His dad's a lawyer, so. Nicholas played it all so well. Stuffed his car on the bypass not long after, dropped out of college. Like he were all messed up. But also the car went in the crusher and that's that. He got himself admitted to some nuthouse, breakdown they said, heartbroken. And it were never considered a crime. Misadventure, they said. Like I said, she had a reputation."

"But you don't believe that?"

"She'd promised us she wouldn't take anything. Once she knew about the baby."

I rubbed my arms. I remembered a class, early in the MA, how I'd talked about story structure, about pebbles dropped into a pool, and charting the ripples that they made. What pebbles had Nicholas dropped, I wondered; what ripples had he watched run . . . ?

"He's back now, swanning around without so much as a by-your-leave," Mr. Metcalfe said. "And I tell you what, I ever see him up this way, I'll shoot the little get right in the face. And I'll call that misadventure."

"You'd go to prison. And then what would Grace do?"

He tilted his head at this, mouth hard.

Then I said, "I've had dealings. With Nicholas."

He gave me an appraising look. "Are you alright, love?"

I cleared my throat. "He's out of the picture for a bit, you'll be glad to hear. He's in a psychiatric unit."

"First sign of trouble, and old man Palmer fixes him up in some comfy ward. The sly get."

"Anyway, I feel better, knowing he's locked up. Thought maybe you would too."

"Aye well, that's not where he belongs." He moved the dog's head aside, then pressed his hands down on his blue-overalled knees and groaned up to his feet. "You need owt, you knock for us, eh. I'd best be getting on."

I walked the three hundred yards home in a swarm. I thought how Nicholas only wrote the truth and how I'd seen him twist it. How his truth wrapped around and slotted into John Metcalfe's like the black and white curls of yin and yang. What he'd said in class about death and telling lies and trigger warnings. If he had indeed been there the night she died. If he had given her the ketamine. If he had known that it was too much. If he had watched her take it, watched her sweat and struggle and peel off her clothes, watched her sink down in the snow to die. If he had considered it all with a cool appraising eye . . . That was a lot of "if"s. That was five "if"s in a row. And at any one of them, my line of thinking could stumble and fall. Except that there was this: Sarah had been John Metcalfe's sunshine, a young woman with an inner life and friends and interests and a future; and all of it was so ordinary and beautiful and full. But when Nicholas wrote about her, the lost girl's only meaning was what she meant to him.

A raw dripping cold. Snow sliding from bare branches, landing with a hush. The beck whispering to itself again, burbling over stones. Sun shafting through low cloud and the temperature creeping up, and the snow creeping away.

A black-and-white springer thunders through the woods, nose to the ground, tail thwacking; she circles away and back, away and back, from the straight dotted line the man walks. A heavy man, heading for his work. Pheasants need feeding, or they roam looking for food, and aren't there when they're wanted for the shoot. From time to time he brings a whistle to his lips; only the dog can hear, and she comes galloping; sits, has her head ruffled. G'lass.

He trudges along through crusted mud. High up on the bank above him, among the beeches, the dog barks. He whistles but she doesn't come. Whistles again. She doesn't come. She whines now, yowls; he's never heard sounds like this from her before. Dreading the hurt she'll have done herself, the blood and pain and vet's bills, he's scrambling up the bank till he is under the tall beeches, and he is stopped dead, in his footprints.

The body is blue-white against the rotting beech-mast. The dog is snuffling round it, wagging anxiously, whimpering. He pushes the dog aside.

He sinks to his knees, presses his fingers into her throat. He knows her.

There is no pulse. No warmth. His thoughts stumble through a web of connection, her mother father brother friends, and out along a life that should have spun ahead of this girl, lying here, cold as the earth. Sarah.

TRINITY

The meeting of the Disciplinary Committee was set for the last week of term; I was to submit a statement a fortnight in advance. I'd planned to tell it straight and simple, just refute the accusation of favouritism. But somehow it just wouldn't let itself be told that way.

Huddled up in isolation, the words came; they filled pages. The document swelled and grew; other voices nudged themselves in. I barely spoke a word to anyone apart from Sammy. I'd nod to John Metcalfe maybe, wave across a field to their son James, or say thank you to the grocery delivery driver. Sammy and I were curled up together in a mammalian ball, backs turned towards the world, communicating in murmurs and nudges and squeezes.

It stopped raining. A whole week went by and the sun shone. I'd glance up and there'd be blue.

I saw the jay again, swinging on a lilac branch; maybe it was a narrow escape the day it left feathers on the path. Or maybe it was a different jay.

I noticed small things, though. Details. The heather in bloom. Two humps of it, one on either side of the concrete front path, smelling sweet as honey, tiny bees picking their way through it. I noticed the different birds' song, though I couldn't name them all yet. I watched the blackbirds in the lilac, and the scythe-billed curlews as they peeped and flapped over the moor. There were crowds of black and white oystercatchers in the back field, that rose shrilling into the air as we approached the garden fence; their flight was rendered as an intricate paper web in Sammy's *Pop-Up Book of British Birds*. The trees were suddenly gorgeous, green and burgundy, the chestnuts spread their hands like magicians, and the hawthorns frothed with milky blossom. I really fell in love with the place then, that late spring, early summer, Trinity, when it was already too late for me to fall in love.

I did tell John Metcalfe about Nicholas's eyrie, though, and he came and took the ladder away and nailed boards across the trapdoor, making it inaccessible, but keeping it all locked away up there, preserved as evidence.

"Been thinking we could sell the old place," he said.

"The barn?"

"The whole lot. Get ourselves a nice little bungalow somewhere, maybe Silverdale."

"Won't James take the farm on when you retire?"

"It was always going to be Sarah's. James does his best, but his heart's not in it. There's nothing for him round here, a lad like him."

One Tuesday afternoon, the postman's van pulled up at the verge and a letter flumped through the front door and landed on my mat. It was from Hartwells, my lettings agency. A change in circumstances, the letter said: the proprietors suddenly found themselves obliged to put the house on the market, and I was hereby given notice. Until that particular moment, when I stood in the hallway with the unfolded letter in one hand, and the torn envelope in the other, birdsong coming through the open door and Sammy pootling up the hallway trailing a purple lilac bloom from his fist, I hadn't made the connection between this house and that family. Everything had gone through the agency; I hadn't met the owners; or at least I thought I hadn't. When I signed the lease the name had meant nothing to me. *Mr. and Mrs. A. J. Palmer.*

We were leaving anyway; this was just them handing me my hat and showing me the door. But house-hunting would have to wait; everything else would have to wait until I'd got this written.

It was like that for weeks, quiet, work-filled, inward; and then it wasn't.

It was late; I was in my favourite white cotton pyjamas, and had my blue and white scarf wrapped round my shoulders and thick socks to keep out the night-time chill. Beyond the faint hum of the laptop and the tap of my fingers on the keys, other noises came to me like echoes: the ghost of an owl's cry, the after-shock of a fox's yelp, and the sheep calls across the fields like memories.

But when Nicholas wrote about her, the lost girl's only meaning was what she meant to him.

I clicked *Save* and closed the laptop, and stretched out the ache in my shoulders, and ambled through to the kitchen to put the kettle on. It was late; it was nearly midnight. I felt exhausted, but also satisfied. I felt that I had told my truth.

I opened the back door and leaned there, looking up at the full, bone-white moon, breathing in the scent of lilac and of cow dung and catnip. The kettle came to a boil, and clicked off; I turned to make the tea and caught a glimpse of my own reflection in the window, hair a scrubbed-up mess, white PJs, pale scarf around my shoulders. I set the kettle down. I was back in that rainy evening, months ago: Sammy standing in the sink, staring out the window, fists on the glass.

Man, he'd said.

Man.

At the time I'd thought that it was John Metcalfe out in the fields, or that Sammy had imagined it. But when he'd helped me get a babysitter, Nicholas already knew where we lived. I'd assumed it was from the bus; but it could equally have been from a letter left lying open months before, from the copy of the lease that I'd signed and carefully returned in August. He could have been expecting us. He could have been out there, even then, watching. It could have been Nicholas that Sam had seen.

And. I rubbed at the back of my neck, where a shiver grew.

And.

My photo was on the departmental website. My photo was also on the back flap of my book. But when we met, that first time, on the square, no hint of recognition, just the sly flattery of taking me for a student. Nudging me along, nudging me with glimpses of vulnerability and talent and trust. Nudging me into being what he wanted, into doing what he wanted. And when I didn't want to do it, he went on with his narrative anyway. Making me a character in his story. Writing his version of me.

A flare of professional irritation now, as well as fear: Why couldn't he do what the rest of us did and just *make something up*?

I closed the door now, and locked it, then went to check the front door was properly locked too. I climbed the stairs in moonlight, the curtains undrawn. Upstairs, I looked in on Sammy, who was sleeping, then I went to the bathroom. I'd spooked myself; I knew he was in a secure unit, but still . . . I had to share this with the police. This was not just about that night now. It was not just about me.

The moonlight was strong through the bathroom window so I didn't bother switching on the light. I scrubbed at my teeth. I was thinking about the happenstance of all of it, how someone could just crash into your life and send you sprawling, and you just have to stagger on in your new trajectory and adjust to it, or fight your way back to the old course and try to hold it steady though you're still reeling and can't catch your balance. I bent to spit, scooped a handful of water from the tap, and as I straightened up I caught my own dark gaze in the mirror. Behind me the landing was now washed in yellow light: the outdoor security lamp had come on. I set my toothbrush down, wiped my mouth with the back of a hand.

Sammy turned in his bed. No other sounds. It was a perfectly still night, bright and clear. No wind to stir the branches and set the sensor off; a fox maybe, maybe a cat. That prickling of fear was just the ordinary everyday fear I carried with me; Nicholas was in the unit; all was well. Calm yourself. I picked my way downstairs.

The light shone through the stained-glass panel of the door, making coloured patterns on the tiles. Patches of purple, tobacco, bottle green. I hadn't thought to draw the bolts earlier; I stood on tiptoe now and pushed the top bolt into place. I dropped to my heels, and at the same moment my focus shifted, from the surface of the patch of tobacco-coloured glass, to the other side of it.

He was there. Standing on my path, one hand in his jeans pocket, head bowed as though lost in thought. Just a panel of old glass between me and him. I watched as he drew his hand out of his pocket, and picked something from his palm, then lifted his face towards me.

I dropped to my hunkers. Inward cogs spun and crunched and wouldn't synch: he couldn't be there; he was in a secure unit; he was right outside my door; this could not be happening; it was happening. It was happening *now*.

His shape against the light; I heard the scratch of metal against metal; and then I heard the tumblers turn inside the lock.

They owned the place. No great wonder that he had managed to get his hands on a key.

I shoved at the lower bolt, shunting it into place. At that same moment, right in front of my eyes, the latch slid back with a click, and the handle levered down. The door flexed inward; he leant his weight against it, but the bolts held.

The bolts were as old as the door; and the door was as old as the house. The wood was parched and brittle, and coming apart at the seams. I couldn't move: I was caught in the trap of myself, of body, toothpaste perfume pyjamas flesh and fear, and love; because Sammy, upstairs, still asleep.

Nicholas muttered something. I could hear the frustration, but I couldn't hear the words.

His footsteps scuffed away on the concrete. I creaked up to my feet. He was leaving. We'd stay locked up tight for the night and in the morning, we'd go straight to Mr. Metcalfe and then to the police . . .

. . . *back door.*

Shit.

I slid along against the hallway wall. The back outside light came on; his shape loomed. This door was new, sturdy, UPVC, locked and the key left in so it wouldn't open from outside. He tried his key, levered the handle up and down, pushed against the resistance. Then his shadow took a step back. Maybe he'd just give up and go. Decide the place was empty. Decide if he couldn't sneak in quietly and catch me sleeping, it wasn't worth his while.

Then a fist slammed into the door. I yelped. He leaned in close against the textured glass. He'd heard me.

He said, "There you are."

I held my breath.

"Come on now," he said, "let me in."

I didn't speak.

"You know you have to," he said. "You know this is what was always going to happen."

I bit my lip.

"Stupid bitch," he said. Then he was gone.

The rear security lamp blinked out.

I was stalled there, in the dark hallway, no idea what to do next.

But then front security light flicked on again. His darkness formed beyond the glass. And then it all crashed into utter chaos.

He threw himself at the door. The whole house thudded with the impact. I just stood, watching, as he flung himself into it again; the doorjamb splintered, the bolts jolted. I skidded over, put my shoulder against the door. He slammed himself against it; it whacked into me. And I remember the clear cold thought, that this was where any excuse or explanation must fail, and that he must know that, and that he must no longer care.

"Nicholas, please."

A pause, but there was now steady insistent pressure on the door; it creaked under the weight of him; I could hear the breath of him, just beyond the panel. I glanced up at the top bolt: the screws were loosening from the wood.

"Go home," I tried. "Go back to the unit. Get well, Nicholas. We'll talk another time. When you're better."

Just his breath and the press of his weight against the door. My stockinged feet slid on the tiles.

"Nicholas. D'you hear me? You go on like this, it can't end well for you."

He spoke then. He said, "It was never going to be a happy ending."

Then the pressure went from the door, and a second later he slammed into it again. I could get no purchase on the tiles, so I slid to the ground, set my back against the door. It was giving way. The reality of this was forming in ice crystals inside me. I couldn't stop him. I wasn't strong enough to stop him. And he was right; this was always going to happen.

"Mummy?"

He stood at the top of the stairs in his blue pyjamas with the green monster on the chest, his hair stuck up in tufts. A rush of love for him. It hurt. I raised a finger to my lips, then waved him away.

Go hide, I mouthed, *go hide.*

But he padded down the stairs towards me.

I frantically waved him back, but he kept coming. Nicholas crashed into the door, and the door slammed into my back, and Sammy slid down and put his back against the door too.

"Sweetheart," I whispered. "Darling. Please. Run away and hide."

He shook his head.

"Mummy says go and hide, so *go and hide.*"

His wide eyes caught the light. "I helping."

The door whacked into us, and we flinched together. I took his hand and squeezed it. It couldn't last much longer.

"We have to go."

Sam nodded.

"We'll get out of the back door, yes? We'll go to the farm, okay? Go see Gracie and Mr. M. and the doggie? Away from this silly man."

He nodded again. I'd carry him; we'd be faster that way. Nicholas would break the front door down and search the house and we'd be long gone out the back. I went to get up, to shift Sam onto my hip, but then there was a crash, and a shower of glass sprayed out overhead. I swung Sammy onto my lap, huddled over him. Shards rained down; a rock spun and slid to a halt on the hall tiles.

I could see the back door—down the hallway, through the kitchen—but between us and it, the cold hall tiles glittered with broken bits of old stained glass. Sammy's soft bare feet dangled. My feet were in my bedtime socks. I knew we had to go. I knew that this was the last moment of not hurting.

Nicholas's hand—grubby, broken-nailed—came in between the broken leads and reached round for the top bolt.

I heaved myself to my feet, still planted in my own footprints. I lifted Sammy with me. "Hold on tight, my love."

I told myself: *Worse things happen than this; worse things than this happen all the time.*

You hear stories of incredible feats. Of gunshots and broken bones and dislocations barely noticed. Of the surge of adrenaline and dopamine that sees you through it all and out the other side, until you're safe enough to be in pain. But I felt each scrap of glass that cut me. At the back door, I stood on one foot to pick out a piece, still clutching Sammy. We went out quietly and locked the door behind us, left the key in the lock there so that Nicholas wouldn't be able to open it from inside.

We stumbled off across the garden as I helped Sammy round from my hip and onto my back.

"Hold on tight."

He wrapped his arms across my collarbones; I tied him on there with my scarf; we swung over the wire fence and I caught my hand on a barb, winced and eased it off. I sucked the blood from my palm and we jogged out across the field. The wide space of it, alien, the grass silver and the trees casting shadows you could fall down; all lit by the huge bone-moon; and me in my white pyjamas, with my blue and white scarf, so painfully visible, and so sore and heavy and slow.

We came to the cusp of the hill, and then staggered down towards the hedge, and dropped into the darkness underneath it. The ground was hard and stony underfoot. I wished there was something I could do to cover up our whiteness. I hunkered down and loosened the scarf and Sammy slid off my back and shuffled round to me. I put an arm around him, my breath raw.

"Are sore, Mummy?"

"Little bit."

The second storey of the cottage peeked up over the rise of the hill. We watched the landing light came on, then Sam's bedroom light. Nicholas was searching the house. If we had left bloody footprints, he hadn't noticed them. I slid my phone out of my pocket, cupped my hand round it to cover up the light. Blood dripped from my cut onto the screen: no signal here either. I wiped it on my pyjamas, pocketed it.

The Metcalfes' farm was two fields over to the left. We'd go in shadow, round the edges of the fields. I took Sam back in my arms, winced to my feet.

"Tell you what, Sam," I said. "When this is over, Mummy's gonna get herself a good pair of trainers and go running every day and get properly fit. You wanna do that too? I'll get you a three-wheeler if you like, for when you get tired."

He nodded and said, "Silly man."

"Yes," I said. "I know. Silly, silly man."

I knotted him tight, and we headed on. The soreness of my feet now hit me fully; each step burned. My socks were soaked with blood. We crept gingerly along the line of shadow, clambered over a patch of wooden fencing; we picked our way along the edges of the next white-lit field, and it was like the ground was made of knives. My head see-sawed. My ears buzzed. I blinked and shook my head to try to clear it, but that made me feel sick. I bit my lip. I could not pass out, not now, not yet.

"Keep a look out, lovey, for the silly man?"

I felt Sammy half turn; I hitched him higher, and the ground yawed beneath me. We staggered out across the field. There was the side wall of the Metcalfes' farm; the broad back gate, the con-creted yard, the cluster of barns and sheds. Here there'd be peo-ple, help, a working telephone. Just a couple of hundred yards. I thought, we'll be okay; we'll make it.

"Mummy! Look!"

I glanced back; saw a flashlight's beam bouncing across the field towards us. I thought, why bother with that big heavy Maglite of his, with the moonlight soaking everything, and clear enough to read by?

"Hold on, sweetheart."

We ran.

The buildings danced before me; the moon streaked like a sparkler's burn. The world went past like a zoetrope, frame after frame after frame. The stink of cattle and the sound now of his heavy footfalls and the grass swishing and my heart thudding and Sammy breathing. We reached the gate; I let go of Sammy, rattled at the latch; the world spun. Nicholas was close, the yellow of his flashlight flicking around us now. I had the latch open and the gate swinging back: I glanced over my shoulder and he was there, slowing to a lope; we were cornered.

"Change of plan," I told Sam.

I unhitched the scarf, set him down on his little bare feet round the end of the gate; he stumbled on to the concrete beyond, looking back at me. I shut the gate behind him; the torchlight cast my shadow over him. I could feel the thud of Nicholas's approaching footfalls. The beam of light danced over us. If this was the last time Sammy ever saw his mum . . . I reached through the bars of the gate and touched his cheek; I smiled.

"You remember the farmhouse?"

He nodded.

"Go there. Now, sweetheart, go find our friends."

He frowned up at me. It's the loveliest thing I've ever known, his little face.

"Fast as you can. Go find them. Go. Do what Mummy says now, please."

He nodded. He turned and stumbled away, barefoot on the mucky concrete.

I turned to face Nicholas; he came to a halt, the Maglite's beam trained on me. I held up a hand to screen the glare.

"Nicholas," I said. "Please."

I still thought that there were words that could be said that would make things different. I still thought there was a way of dealing with it somehow better.

"If you stop now, if you end it here . . ." I tried.

He changed his stance, as if considering this; as if there was a part of him that still entertained the possibility of things ending differently for him and me. I held on to the top bar of the gate to steady myself. My thoughts were wrapped up in a bundle and gone with Sammy, stumbling away towards the farmhouse. All alone. Too small to even reach the doorbell.

But if I could just hold it together. If I could just get Nicholas to talk.

"There's still hope for you," I said. "Things can be better. I'll say you're not well. If you stop. Here, now, please."

I didn't even see it coming. The light slammed itself inside my skull. Brilliant and blinding.

For a moment there was nothing. My hearing flattened out to a hum. I remember my hands on my head, the heat and wet I felt there, I remember curling up on the ground, feeling like I was going to throw up. I'd thought the worst had happened already but the worst had not happened yet: I still didn't even know how bad the worst could be. And I understood why he'd brought that heavy Maglite when there was moonlight enough to see by.

Then I remember his breath on my face, level and steady. I remember him hauling at me, I remember grabbing at the gate and getting hold of something and not letting go. He levered at my fingers, then gave up and smashed his Maglite down on my hand. I let go.

He heaved me up, his arms under my arms, my feet scrabbling for purchase on the stony dirt. He hauled me away. Away from the gate, and from the farm, and from Sammy. I dug at his hands with my good hand, I tried to pull away, but it was like struggling in a dream, where the bedclothes are tangled round you, and you're slow and feeble and nothing works as it should. Sometimes when I dream that kind of dream, I stop trying to fight or run or struggle, and instead I swim; I swim up and out and up, slipping through the air, away from everything, and it's so much easier than struggling; I keep swimming up, higher and higher, and am skimming through the sky with the birds, and wondering why I didn't do this sooner, why I didn't do this all the time.

So maybe this was where I could just swim away up into the air and join the birds, and have done with struggling. I felt so tired. So sick. So sore. I'd done what I could; I thought. I had nothing left.

I remember noticing the torch lying abandoned on the ground, the wedge of yellow light laced through with grass stems; I remember it getting smaller as we left it behind. I remember the way my feet bumped over the ruts and stones as he dragged me away. I remember the way my hand was a throb of pain, the way his breath came and went above me; the way the warmth of his body bled into my back.

I remember that he was speaking as he heaved me along, and it took me a while to connect what he was saying with what was happening to me. But he was telling me something. He was offering me an explanation. He hadn't wanted to have to do this. It shouldn't have been necessary. But I just wouldn't do what I was supposed to do; he couldn't understand why I just wouldn't do what I was supposed to do, but instead was so unreasonable, so difficult, so very fucking crazy indeed.

Fear is disabling, and I'd been afraid for so long. But anger— anger's helpful. It clears the mind. It's energising.

I lifted my feet; he had my whole weight now. He fumbled, swore, half-dropped me, but clung on. I lunged away; his fingers sank into my arms. I heaved against his grip; he cursed and yanked me back, hard. And I went with the pull, added what force I could to his, and smashed the back of my head into his face.

My own pain was bad. But a crack like that to the nose is blinding. He let go, and I ran.

See-sawing, sick, blood in my eyes, I ran; the night tumbled and boiled around me. I could hear him yelling, cursing as he came after me. Crazy bitch stupid cunt fucking whore. I had no breath. Stupid crazy cunt bitch fucking whore for not just doing what he wanted me to do. I staggered on towards the fallen Maglite, the gate, the farm.

Then the night burst apart. I dropped to my knees, my hurt hand cradled to me. A thin whine of white noise, then the night meshed itself back together again, its fingers intertwining. *Here's the church, here's the steeple, look inside and . . .* There was John Metcalfe, shotgun at his shoulder. A blur as Moss skimmed past me; teeth and hackles. And then other shapes swam into clarity, became James Metcalfe in wax jacket over pyjamas, who was pounding up towards me; became Grace baffled in her blue dressing gown, became little Sammy, hand in hand with her. I tried to call out to him, but there was no breath left in me.

I glanced back; Nicholas still stood there, brought up short by the gunshot and by Moss, who had planted herself between him and the rest of us, lip curled, snarling. There was blood trickling from his bust nose, but that was my doing; he hadn't been shot. James came thudding to a halt beside me, squared up to Nicholas. Nicholas took it all in with those strange pale eyes: the young man standing over me, and the old man with the gun, the slavering dog, the old woman and the little boy, and me, getting unsteadily back to my feet. A long, still moment as he and I looked at each other. Then his face somehow cleared. He turned, and sprinted off into the dark. Moss made a lunge after him, but John Metcalfe called her back. I swayed; James wrapped an arm around my waist. John Metcalfe broke his gun and strode towards us; Sam wriggled out of Grace's grip and belted over to me. I went to scoop him up, but my head swam, and I was almost gone; Grace picked him up and leaned in to me, and she wrapped her arms around both of us.

"You said you'd kill him, if you ever saw him," I said to John Metcalfe, a little later, as we waited in the farmhouse kitchen. "But you only fired one barrel, and you missed." My voice sounded strange, hoarse and ragged.

"Aye well," he said, "you were in the way."

I laughed, and the laugh collapsed into coughing, and John Metcalfe said, "Darned inconvenient of you."

Because when it came to it, we both knew that he wasn't up to it. John Metcalfe couldn't do a thing like that. To look a person in the eye and pull a trigger and watch the blood bloom on their chest; to place ketamine in a trusting palm, and watch the sweats and horrors come upon the taker; to weigh your will against another's life and decide that your desire is what matters most; that's an astonishing degree of self-importance right there, and Mr. Metcalfe just didn't have it. He just didn't feel entitled.

Beyond the kitchen window, blue and white lights skimmed through the distance; I heard the sound of sirens.

A triage nurse peered at my head wound, checked my pupils for concussion, took a look at my hand, winced; winced again at the state of my feet:

"Now they are a proper, proper mess," she said.

She gave me two Paracetamol and a plastic cup of water, and sent me for x-rays.

After the x-rays, a second nurse, who was plump and Scottish, cleaned my head wound, stuck it together with glue, and pressed a dressing over it. He gave me a local anaesthetic, picked out bits of glass from my feet—he kept flicking back and forth between the x-ray on the computer screen and my fleshy mess—then washed and stitched the wounds. He cleaned, glued and dressed the barbed-wire cut on my palm, and strapped up my hand with a splint. I was lucky, he said, that nothing was broken, but the bruising was going to take a while to go down. He gave me a dose of antibiotics, then washed the blood off my face with cotton wool. His hands were careful and gentle and by the time he had finished I just loved him. I wanted to take him home with me.

Sammy had fallen asleep on the police officer's lap. Her name was Tracey. She just sat there, on the hard chair, letting him sleep. She was lean and freckly, with brownish-ginger frizz escaping from her ponytail. Whenever I caught her eye, she smiled, and she had dimples; the smile and the dimples and my boy sleeping on her made me choke with love. It might have had something to do with being doped up on painkillers, that I kept falling in love with people that night, but it was mostly to do with their kindness.

"You're going to have a fair few scars," the Scottish nurse said. "But because of where they are, no one will know unless you want them to."

It was nearly daylight by the time we were done at the hospital. We were driven in an unmarked car to a redbrick semi on the edge of town. The sound of the motorway was like waves on a beach; I could hear birds singing too. Across the road, a horse stood in a scrubby field, cropping the grass. Sam and I had passed this place a hundred times or more on the bus. It was a nothing place, not town nor country nor even suburbia, but an old dead shoot of a development that never grew into anything, the kind of place where, in the normal run of things, you would never have a reason to go. I guess that's why they had the refuge there.

Tracey carried Sammy from the car for me; I followed along in washed-out trackies and disposable slippers. A woman was at the door; I said hello and she took my good hand in hers, and showed us in. Her name was Pamela and she said she was duty staff here. She was lean and rangy and wore a purple fleece.

Our room had two single beds and a chest of drawers. Tracey laid sleeping Sammy down, and he rolled over and snuggled in, and I whispered my thanks.

"Shouldn't have to keep you here so very long," she said.

Before she left, she hugged me, and rubbed my back. Then she let me go and said she'd be back to check on us, and let us know if there was any news, and she left with a glimpse of cool outdoors, the birdsong, traffic. I pressed my tired eyes.

Pamela showed me around the place while Sammy slept. There was a communal sitting room with sofas and a basket of grubby toys and shelf full of fat broken-spined paperbacks, there was a quiet room with a table and chairs; there was a kitchen with a jar of Nescafe and milk in the fridge and bread and jam, to which I could help myself, and a steam sterilizer on the countertop and the cupboards with a clatter of baby bottles and sippy cups and weaning spoons and toddler cutlery in the drawers. Out the back, a few outdoor toys, and the view was a high clapboard fence, and beyond that scrubby fields and milky sky and a distant wind turbine turning.

Pamela left me to rest and settle in.

The stair treads creaked, and then a woman came into the kitchen; a girl really, thin as string, with a scrappy ponytail and a skinny baby, nightwaking shadows underneath her eyes. She introduced herself as Bethany, then held up the dozy little bundle and kissed a flaky cheek, "and this is Sienna." She told me to put my feet up and she'd make me a coffee, and she handed me her baby, and sent me to the seating area, and I sat back on a charity sofa and let the baby sleep on my chest. When the baby woke, her mum laid her down on a blanket on the floor and we both watched her spread and curl her tiny fingers and kick her legs around while we drank the instant coffee and it was the best coffee I had ever drunk. Then the girl made up a bottle and chugged it into the baby, and then the baby fell asleep again, and then I fell asleep.

When I woke up there were two matching teenage girls sitting in the armchairs, staring at their phones, and another woman moving around in the kitchen area. The woman asked me if I'd like a cuppa and called me love; she had a soft lined face and mousy curls, two black eyes, and Steri-Strips on a cut across the bridge of her nose. She and Pamela shuffled round each other in the kitchen like old friends. I was getting up to answer her when Sammy called for me from the safety gate at the top of the stairs. One of the twins waved at me to stay put, and went herself to fetch him down. He came with her softly, hand in hand.

"You want some breakfast, little lad?" the woman called from the kitchen, and Sammy nodded and ambled through to her. He looked at her fascinated, but didn't ask if she was sore. When he had spooned in his Rice Krispies, he came and sat on my lap, and then laid his head down on me, and we just lay there and cuddled and dozed.

Later, the telly was on, the sound turned down, and Sammy was crouched at the coffee table tucking into a flaccid cheese sandwich and a packet of Skips and there was a plate beside him with another sandwich on it, and a mug of tea.

I levered myself up and round and reached for the mug, and drank. The twins' mum was standing in the kitchen door.

"He told me he was hungry, but I didn't want to wake you. Hope that's okay."

"That's great. Thank you."

Sammy nodded enthusiastically, mouth full. And then the local news came on, and I dragged the plate over to me and lifted a sandwich, and then my attention was caught by the TV. Because the first item was me. Or rather it was Nicholas.

The twins' mum noticed my shift in attention and came over and sat in on the arm of the chair.

I had never seen that particular photograph before, but I knew the room and the night that it was taken. I knew the faces surrounding his, though they were blurred out now: Meryl, Karen, Tim. He was in sharp focus. I saw again that broad, strong face; that dark hair in an artful mess, those pale silvery eyes. The way

that he was almost ugly, but wasn't, and that it didn't matter anyway if he was. I saw too the way that he remained at one remove,
a step away from the people clustering around him.

I wondered who'd provided the photograph—perhaps Richard
had taken it, or Steven, that night. The night that he had walked
me home. I wondered what they were making of things now.

I heaved myself up, reaching for the remote. The image
shifted and now showed the lane outside Gill House, twined
across with wind-tugged police tape. I pegged away at the volume
and it was suddenly loud, blaring into the room, making the twins
raise their perfect sculpted eyebrows.

*. . . members of the public are advised not to approach the suspect;
anyone with information should call the police hotline . . .*

I fumbled to lower the volume again, and the twins' mum
took the remote off me and sorted it out, and then it was *in other
news,* and the twins' mum said "Okay?" and I nodded and she
switched the telly off. She rubbed my arm, and put her arm round
my shoulder, and I leaned against her.

That night I lay in my jangling single bed across from
Sammy's and I watched him sleep, and then I stared at the ceiling.
I got up and took a blanket and went and made a cup of tea, and
lay on the sofa and tried to read one of the wrinkled paperbacks.
I blinked my way through a hallucinatory half chapter, set it aside
and closed my eyes. I woke and it was six fifty, and I winced my
way upstairs and lay down in my bed, to be there when Sammy
woke up again.

Mark arrived that afternoon, straight off the motorway, all
frazzled concern. He went to take my hand but then saw that it
was splinted and let his own hand fall. He studied my face, peered
at the dressing on my head. He looked around the place. The
institutional carpet, the donated furniture, and the net curtains
and the aspidistra on the windowsill. I saw it all through his eyes
now. How very vulnerable I must seem; how prone to harm. I

could not be left alone. I needed someone to look after me. He had decided that that someone would have to be him.

"Come home with me," he said. "We'll work it out. We'll get things sorted."

"What about Amy? Aren't you living together now?"

"Yes."

"And she's uprooted herself, ended her marriage, done all that to be with you?"

"Well, yes."

"So no, we can't get that sorted. We can't work that out. That's just too messy."

His face twisted; I was making him fight for something he didn't want.

"But this is your *life*. This is about your safety."

"Yeah but," I shrugged, "this isn't how to fix it. So."

"We could," he said, but his voice had gone thin. "We can."

"Not on those terms, honey, no. I can't."

Tracey brought some of our things from the cottage. A bag of clothes, some books that I'd asked for, my laptop, some toys and books of Sammy's. Out across the valley, a helicopter hung like a wasp; the buzz of it skimmed back and forth through those quiet days. They were using a heat sensor, Tracey told me, but all that showed up so far were sheep, and cars, and cows. They had boots and paws on the ground too, but they'd turned up nothing yet. They had the PCSOs on the beat in town, checking out the derelict buildings, bridges and ginnels, talking to homeless people and street pastors and hostel workers, but had turned up nothing there either.

It seemed that he had, after all, done what he intended to do; he had disappeared.

"I was told he was in a secure unit; I was told that he was sectioned. How did he even get out?"

"He was never sectioned, he wasn't in a secure unit," Tracey said. "You were misinformed."

"Where was he then, all that time?"

"A private clinic down near Clitheroe; more like a retreat, or a spa, really; he could leave whenever he liked. His parents said . . ."

"What did they say?"

"That he was depressed. That it was brought on by the end of a relationship. And that the relationship was with his tutor. Meaning you."

"That's not true."

"You weren't in a relationship, or it hadn't ended?"

"No. The first thing. Weren't ever in."

"Then why would they think you were?"

"Maybe they prefer to think that. If I consented . . ."

She just waited. But my voice was parched and the words wouldn't come. "Consented . . . ?" she asked. "You did have sex with him, then?"

I cleared my throat. Nodded. "I didn't want to."

"Did you say? Did you make it clear?"

"Yes. But then I gave up."

A moment's pause. Then she said, "When was this?"

"November. We'd been drinking. It was after a party. I was drunk. And I've wondered since, I didn't drink that much in fact; I wonder if he spiked me."

She sat back. "You didn't report it at the time?"

I shook my head. I was expecting to be asked why.

"Giving up is not consent," is all she said.

Her freckly face, her calmness.

"No," I said. "It's not."

"Would you be able to make a statement now about what happened that night, do you think?"

I said, "Yes."

·   ·   ·

Late that night with Sammy spark out and the twins upstairs in
their room and Bethany making up a bottle in the kitchen, Nicholas was on the news again, the same photo, same news, warnings not to approach. BBC One at ten o'clock and there was the
same shot of the lane to my house twisted with police tape. The
same information distilled down for the national broadcast, and
then a piece to camera from someone I didn't recognise, a grey
fluffy man from the village, and he was saying that it was not
the kind of thing they expected to happen in a place like that; he
seemed at once outraged and rather thrilled that his peace had
been so rudely shattered, and to find himself on camera. But his
point was a familiar one: Why would a boy like that, with everything going for him, why would he go and do a thing like that?
That's what this fellow didn't understand.

I scowled at the telly, chewed my lip.

And then they moved on to a piece about the badger cull. Mel,
the twins' mum, leaned in a shoulder against mine as we watched
the badgers' stumpy-legged frolics in green night vision. "Stupid
question."

"Sorry?"

"Or, um, stupid *rhetorical* question."

"What is?"

"'Why would he go and do a thing like that.'"

"What do you mean?"

"What I mean is, you don't have to understand."

"You don't think it helps, to understand?"

"It won't help *you*. I spent fifteen years trying to understand,
and you know where it got me?"

I shook my head.

She touched the scabbed bridge of her nose: "A&E."

"I'm sorry."

"Three times. First he broke two ribs; then he broke my wrist,
and then he broke my nose."

"God bless the NHS, eh."

"God bless the NHS. Cos the NHS is what made it better. Not knowing why he did it."

I looked down at my stockinged feet, elevated on a flattened cushion on the rickety old table. I felt a nostalgia-in-advance for this place, for this companionship; I knew that it was all, of necessity, transitional; that even if Sam and I could stay here, the other residents would change around us week by week, and it would never quite be the same again.

"I wish they'd stop killing badgers," I said.

"I know."

"It's not like the badgers have anything to do with anything."

"I know."

"I wonder, though," I said.

"What do you wonder, hon?"

"If I was wrong to say I wouldn't go to London, back with Mark."

"Because of Sammy?"

"Mark's his dad, after all. And he was going to give it another chance."

"Because of what happened."

"Well, yes."

"And he wouldn't have, otherwise?"

"His mind was made up. His heart was."

"And he'd sacrifice that for you two. So you'd be safe."

"Looks like it. Yes."

"He sounds like he's a decent man."

"He is."

"Thing is with kids . . ." Mel said.

I spread my toes tentatively. My scabs snagged and eased. "What's the thing?"

"Kids actually need you to be happy. Well, happy enough."

"Happy *enough*?"

She nodded.

"Happy enough but not too happy?"

"Who's too happy? Nobody, that's who. Happy enough is all anybody's ever going to get. But what I'm saying is, you have to take your own happiness into account. The kid can't really be happy if you're miserable."

"You are very wise."

Mel's snort seemed to signify all the years, the broken ribs and wrist and nose that it had taken her to arrive at this understanding:

"Yeah," she said, "right."

I had stopped expecting anything to happen, and I was quite content with things not happening, with the slow knitting back of flesh and the itchy peel of replaced dressings and the quiet roll-around of bland meals and the cyclical kindness of coffee and tea. So when the unmarked car pulled up in front of the house one morning, it took me a moment to register that it might have anything to do with me.

It was a cool but cheerful summer day. Sammy was playing out in the back yard—there was one of those red-and-yellow kiddie pedal cars that look like they've been stretched upwards; he'd been beetling around on the paved area for ages, perfectly content. The twins were out there too, involving themselves with him in a low-key way; keeping an eye out. I could hear their voices from time to time, and his higher-pitched patter as he gave them lengthy replies. I heard a car coming up the road; it pulled over; the engine died. I didn't think anything of it. Then there were voices, footsteps and a knock on the door.

"How are you doing? Okay?"

Prickly with apprehension, actually; swallowing with a dry throat, shoulders up and knotted. But: "Okay."

I had to excuse the abruptness of this, but they could only

hang on to this for so long because the news were on to it already and they wanted me to hear it from them, and not through any other channel.

They had found him.

A rush of adrenaline.

Or rather: They had found his body.

What.

Yes, I'm afraid so.

Are you sure that . . .

Father has identified.

And so . . .

Tracey spoke so evenly, was so functional and steady, and I took it in but I took it in at a shallow level, a thin wash of understanding. He was found, and he was dead. And it was like someone had thrown a board game up into the air and sent all the pieces flying.

How?

They couldn't talk about that yet, not in any detail. For operational and legal reasons. But they could tell me that he had been dead for some time. They think he probably died later that same night. The night that he came for me. That would explain why the heat-detecting helicopter had had no success in finding him: by the time it was up and searching, he was already cold.

Where?

They'd found him in the beech woods, not far from the river.

I felt the aching ghost of his grip round my ribs; I could feel his breath on my neck, and at the same time I could hear the sound of Sammy and the twins drifting through from out back, feel the warmth bleed from my coffee cup into my palm. One moment overlaid the other like tracing paper; the shapes and colours of that night, along with the lines and patterns of his writing, leached through into the bright day and threw it into shadow.

"Was there a suicide there, some years back?" I asked.

Tracey sat back, remembering. "God. Yeah. The Metcalfe girl. God . . ."

"I think that might need looking into again," I said.

"Why do you think that?"

"I think Nicholas might have had a hand in it."

Tracey slowly nodded.

His suicide was confirmed at the inquest. He'd taken a load of ket-amine; he'd vomited, sweated, died there, his heart had given up. He was found splayed half-naked on the woodland floor. That was where I was being dragged to, that night; to the spot in the woods where Sarah had died all those years before. He was going back to where he started. That's how stories work: there's something instinctively satisfying about circularity.

He'd cached a waterproof rucksack there, containing his lap-top, along with a bundle of zip ties and a roll of duct tape, and a shedload of ketamine. All that time in the clinic—or retreat, or spa—he'd still been writing; I know that Forensics had a mass of stuff to look at, but I never saw any more of it, and I was glad to be spared that. The nylon ties and duct tape were of course super-fluous to suicide. They were meant for me; that ketamine was originally intended for me too: he had meant for me to die that night, and then, I guess, he was going to write about it. Make my death part of his art.

But I'd been one of those awkward characters, that swerves off and goes its own way, that won't do what the author wants. Because all I'd wanted, all along, was not to be a part of his story. To be left alone to get on with mine.

I'm still wary. That doesn't go away. I make sure the bin goes out in daylight. I don't answer the door after dark. It's not the dark I particularly mind; it's thresholds, the crossings-over, the transitions between spaces. There's always a chance that something will follow you across. I'm still a bit OCD about checking locks and bolts.

But there are tally marks on the cream gloss frame of my new front door; the pencil is tucked neatly on the windowsill beside it. Every time I come home and lock the door behind me, I notch up another day that I've got through without being hurt. Line after line mark these small victories, the growing sense that the world is somewhere I can mostly safely live. On my thirty-fourth birthday—a cupcake with a candle, a crayon drawing of Sam and Mummy—I worked out that I had lived twelve thousand four hundred and eighteen days—including leap years—on which I was not assaulted, and three on which I was. I'm no statistician, but it struck me that those weren't bad odds: it looked to me like I'd only a one-in-over-four-thousand chance of getting attacked on any given day, and I'm quite comfortable with that. So the maths helps. But still those three excepted days loom bigger and weigh more heavily than any of the others.

We're living in town now. In one of the new houses by the canal. This is where I keep my tally by the door. In the day, swans go sailing past the back fences, and people belt along the towpath on bikes, or they jog by in all weathers. Kids feed ducks with grandparents and the swans get uppity and hiss. At night the rats slip into the water and steam across, leaving the moonlight broken in their wake. On the far bank are old terrace houses and people living out their lives, watching TV, eating dinner, drawing their curtains, stopping to stare at smartphones, and once I saw a couple silhouetted, caught in the moment of a kiss.

Sammy and I go swimming out at the Leisure Centre on Saturday mornings. He thrashes across the pool and comes out sleek and pink-eyed and weak with hunger, and I feed him Bourbons and put him on the back of my bike and we cycle home along the towpath. He will start school next year, at the little local primary up the hill. I admire him, honestly, I do. His resilience, his kindness, his pleasure in small things. I know that till he's old and failing, he'll remember that night; the din that started him from sleep, the sight of his mother pressed against the door as the silly man tried to break it down. He'll remember the rock landing with a spray of bitter glass along the hallway tiles, the race across the night-time meadow; he'll remember having to go off all alone to find Grace, and he'll remember Mr. Metcalfe's gun. He'll remember the blood and pain and fear and the getting through it anyway. It'll be the archaeology of the man that he'll become; he'll always know what it is not to be safe. I hope that hasn't done him harm, but helps him understand the world, and how some people have to live in it.

He doesn't have nightmares, and he is certainly not afraid in a day-to-day way. Sometimes I watch him play, circling round the courtyard on his scooter or chalking on the paving slabs with the girls from two doors down, and I try to reel the image forward, try to grow him up into a man, imagine him with crushes, girlfriends, boyfriends, a husband or a wife; I know that things won't always be easy for him, and he'll mess up and make mistakes, but I can't imagine him being anything other than himself, essentially kind.

And I try, despite what Mel said, to reel the others back, rewind, to understand what made Nicholas the man he was, and Blue Anorak Man too: the brokenness, the lack of love, the excess of cortisol or unlucky quirk of brain structure, or just the simple sense of entitlement to a woman's attention, and her body, that brought them to act the way they did. I've come even to feel sorry for them, both of them, for the lives they must have lived, but that doesn't mean that I forgive them. They could always have just decided not to. It's always a choice. It's always possible to simply leave someone alone.

Mum and Dad come up to see us from time to time. It seems I've suffered just enough for Mum to forgive me just enough to resume contact, and get to know her grandchild. Sam was wary of her at first, this new stranger, but they were soon firm friends. She makes a huge fuss of him; I think she does it to needle me. She seems to be endlessly astonished that such a disappointing creature as myself could come up with someone as utterly delightful as her grandson. I'm okay with that. I do tend to agree.

We squeeze the two of them into the house okay, but when Mark comes up to see us, he stays at the Premier Inn. There isn't enough room for him; I don't think there ever could be, even if we had a place twice the size. He just takes up too much psychological space. He is, I think, happy, but he wouldn't want to flaunt it in front of us, and I haven't specifically asked. I don't want to. I half expect a wedding, or a new baby, but neither's happened yet. I signed the divorce papers, though; I contested nothing. My behaviour had, indeed, been unreasonable.

His mum comes to see us, more often than my parents do; she catches two trains to get here, two trains back, all in the one day; she doesn't stay over; says doesn't want to be an imposition and she never is. She brings me expensive moisturisers, little perfumes, pretty expensive things; she brings clothes and toys for Sam. At first, I think, she was trying to apologise, though no apology was needed.

We ran into Patrick in Sainsbury's a while back, in the main aisle that runs down the middle of the store. He wheeled out of Jams and Marmalades, and Sam pointed and announced delightedly, *Look, Mummy, there's your friend!* Patrick and I locked eyes; I smiled. I was going to say hi, and sorry; I was going to try and make some kind of rapprochement. But his expression went blank and vague, as if he'd not seen us at all, and then he did that *Oh I suddenly remembered something* face, and swerved into Pickles and Condiments. Often in a supermarket you see the same people over and over again as you weave up and down the aisles, but we didn't see him again; we did pass an abandoned trolley, though. I don't know that it was his, but it had Parma ham and olives and cheese and salad things in it, and they looked like they could be his.

I felt bad. I still do; I feel guilty about him. I mean, he still has to face that place, and those people every working day. Whereas I just burned another bridge and walked away.

But I still see Mina and Laura quite often; Sam and I go walking with them and their cockapoo, Teddy. Sometimes we meet up for lunch or tea. Laura makes amazing cakes, and Mina keeps me up to date with all the departmental gossip. Simon Peters still has an on-off relationship with the university: he gets signed off for a term; returns with a great show of determination and positivity, which lasts exactly long enough for him to be entitled to another four months' leave. Michael Lynch returned from Toronto and found the Augean stables waiting for him; he's had to roll up his sleeves and start shovelling, and take a formal reprimand for his unorthodox approach to admissions. They've already reappointed to my post, as well as creating two new jobs in Creative Writing; she'd taken a look at the workload model for the previous year, Mina said, and it was, to quote, off its fucking trolley; I was carrying about three times as much as I should have been; hence the new roles. Patrick is getting married in the summer, to a former PhD student; quite the whirlwind romance. Christian Scaife left at the end of the year for a post at the University of Malta; Mina has taken over as Head of Department. A sudden, stratospheric promotion; also, no one else would take it on.

"Place won't be the same, with Scaife gone."

"We'll muddle through somehow."

I scan the review pages every week. I'm expecting *Halfway* to appear any time. I'm also expecting it to become a massive bestseller; I'm expecting to go and see the film adaptation at the local Vue, and to feel, well, the kinds of feelings that only German has the exact words for. It hasn't turned up yet, but it can take longer than you'd think to finish a novel. I spotted Steven Haygarth's *Winter's Blood* on a table in Waterstones. On the cover was a softened, silver-blue image of a beautiful naked dead woman. It also had a sticker on it, saying that it's being adapted for TV. I don't know if Karen already had a title for her short-story collection; if she did, she never told me. I keep an eye out for her, though; I really want to read her other stories, follow all the grotesque transformations that she can conjure up.

It was strange going back to the village, stepping off that bus again, making my way down the lane. The Palmers' house had been sold: there was now a swing set on the lawn, and the grass was worn away in patches by children playing. I walked up to Gill House too; there's a board up at the end of the lane, advertising a new development of "Homes of Distinction"—the farmyard was a clutter of men in high-vis jackets, diggers, stacks of timber, builders' bags of sand, churning cement mixers. John and Grace have a bungalow now, near the sea. Sam and I cycle out and see them from time to time. Gill House itself had a new, old-looking front door to replace the one that Nicholas smashed up, and a conservatory tacked onto the side, and a glossy Merc parked on the lane.

I met up with the gamekeeper, the old fellow who found Sarah. He showed me the patch of the beech wood. He touched his nose with the side of his thumb. I apologised for making him revisit such difficult memories. He shook his head and said there wasn't a day went by that he didn't think of her anyway; it was like she was always there, curled up there in a corner of his head, and he was glad to be able to talk about it. He'd never got used to the idea that a girl like that, whole life ahead of her, could go and do a thing like that, and then it turned out that she hadn't, that it had been done to her, and now he couldn't get his head around that at all.

"It doesn't bear thinking about," I said.

But that was a stupid thing to say. It bears thinking about. It *requires* thinking about. I pick my way through the local paper archives, study the statements presented at my disciplinary hearing, and the findings of the inquests into Sarah's and Nicholas's deaths. I lay out pages on my desk, and photographs; I shift and slide them, finding the links, the connections. I have a photograph of Sarah that Grace pressed urgently into my hands, one day when we were visiting. Sarah's friend Judith had printed it out and given it to her; it was taken just before it all started to go wrong. Sarah's half turned from her friend's snapping phone; she is wearing a striped sundress, her hair a wild tumble of curls; it's a village fair, or show, or something of the sort; there are stalls and bunting behind her. Low sun, freckled shoulders, her teeth slightly crooked as she smiles. There she is. That is her. She's not his lost girl yet: she is her own self there.

My tongue still snags from time to time on that chipped tooth of mine; but like the dentist said I would, I've got used to it; I mostly just don't notice. Now there's also a white line on my scalp where the hair doesn't grow, and the soles of my feet are a web of pale scars, but I don't mind so much; nobody sees them. Wrapped up in socks and walking boots, I get around my route with my post-trolley perfectly well. It's a hilly maze of Victorian stone terraces, and a pleasant villagey 1930s council estate with mature trees and plenty of green spaces, and a sprawl of ugly private new builds—including ours—along the canal where the old cotton mills used to be. My new job leaves me time to think; the rhythms of walking are sympathetic; they help form sentences and paragraphs. At night, while Sammy sleeps, and the rats slip in and out of the water, and next door's cat paces across the patio out back and stops in the spilled light to stare in at me, I sit in the glow of my laptop, at the kitchen table, and I write. I edit. I tamp the different sections into shape, then shift the shapes into place. This is how it fits together. This is how it happened. It may be messy and imperfect, but this is my truth.

Acknowledgements

I'm very well aware of how fortunate I am in the people that I get to work with. My editors, Jane Lawson and Diana Miller, are both brilliant: their patient, intelligent guidance has been enormously enabling in bringing this book to completion. I owe my agent, Clare Alexander, a huge debt of gratitude; her insight and steady patience, with this book and with all the others, have been utterly invaluable. I'm also immensely grateful to Anna Stein for her support, for the clarity of her eye and intellect. To Alison Barrow and Abigail Endler, for all the good things they make happen, heartfelt thanks. And as for my first reader, Daragh Carville: I don't know where I'd be without him.

Jo Baker is the acclaimed and bestselling author of *Longbourn* and *A Country Road, A Tree*. Her new work *The Body Lies* is a thrilling and layered novel that explores violence against women but is also a disarming story of gender politics in the modern world. She lives in Lancashire with her family.

LONGBOURN

Jo Baker

'If Elizabeth Bennet had the washing of her own petticoats,'
Sarah thought, 'she would be more careful not to
tramp through muddy fields.'

It is wash-day for the housemaids at Longbourn House,
and Sarah's hands are chapped and raw. Domestic life
below stairs, ruled with a tender heart and an iron will
by Mrs Hill the housekeeper, is about to be disturbed
by the arrival of a new footman, bearing secrets
and the scent of the sea.

'A reimagining of *Pride and Prejudice* from the point
of view of the servants . . . a joy'
Guardian

'A genuinely fresh perspective on the tale of
the Bennet household'
Sunday Times

A COUNTRY ROAD, A TREE

Jo Baker

Paris, 1939

The pavement rumbles with the footfall of Nazi soldiers marching along the Champs-Élysées. A young writer, recently arrived from Ireland to make his mark, smokes one last cigarette with his lover before the city they know is torn apart. Soon, he will put his own life and those of his loved ones in mortal danger by joining the Resistance . . .

Spies, artists, deprivation, danger and passion: this is a story of life at the edges of human experience, and of how one man came to translate it all into art.

'Skilful . . . daring . . . an extraordinary story'
Guardian

'Insightful . . . beautifully paced . . . authentic'
Irish Times